LAST HOUR TILL SUNRISE

CHEVALIER PROTECTION SERVICES – BOOK 2

LISA PHILLIPS

TWO DOGS PUBLISHING, LLC

Publisher Lisa Phillips

Cover design Ryan Schwarz

Edited by Christy Callahan, Professional Publishing Services

Published by Two Dogs Publishing, LLC. Idaho, USA

Paperback ISBN: 979-8-88552-011-9

1

———

"Target incoming." The voice of her team leader came through the phone in the cup holder.

DEA Special Agent Lucia DeSoto glanced at the passenger-side mirror of the BMW they'd been using for the duration of this undercover operation. Now it smelled like old cheese.

"Copy that." Simon, the ATF agent in the driver's seat, was a decent guy. She'd known him a few months, since she joined the multiagency task force. He had a wife, but in Lucia's experience marriage didn't always mean a guy knew how to treat other people with respect.

In the back seat sat Bill, older than her and Simon. One of those old school guys who thought every time a woman was part of a mission that she should use her "feminine wiles" to get the job done.

Lucia was pretty sure she had none of those, whatever they were. She'd be entirely more inclined to shoot someone to get the job done. Whether that was Bill, or the target.

This particular target? She would shoot him any day. Todd Lydell was wanted on suspicion of several counts of weapons possession, sexual assault, drunk and disorderly, and one case of elder abuse. So basically, he was a scumbag.

"There he is." Simon flashed the headlights.

A red truck angled toward them. Lucia strained to see inside. "Two guys, maybe more if the back seat is occupied. Lydell and a couple more."

"Keep it tight," the team leader said. "Once you get out of the car, we won't be able to hear you." Assistant Director Pierce Campbell liked to state the obvious, and give unnecessary instructions.

"Copy that." Simon glanced over at her.

She didn't meet his gaze, but felt the pull of her lips. Some semblance of a smile. Really all she was capable of, when she considered there wasn't much to smile about.

Lucia studied the warehouse district in this part of Wyoming. Pretty generic, with no surveillance cameras. Little police presence. It was the perfect deserted spot to have a Sunday night meeting.

"DeSoto?" Campbell barked her name.

"Yes, sir?" She had a feeling she wasn't going to like this.

"We already know he has a thing for you. It might not be your forte exactly, but if it comes down to a win on this op? Face the fact you might have to make *friends* with this guy. So maybe try and smile a little."

Someone snorted—whether in the car with her, or on the other end in the surveillance van, she didn't know.

They weren't close by, because Lydell was super uptight about his meetings, but they were near enough to help if things went wrong. She'd be uptight as well if she was the number two guy for a man who ran a compound the feds hadn't been able to breach in any of their attempts. Short of ramming the door down, there wasn't any hope of getting inside to see what was really going on in there.

Lydell's boss, Franklin Burgess, ran the compound like it was a cult. Recruiting locals—men and women. Advertising himself as an ecowarrior, he came across more like a religious leader. The men were trained in weapons as though there was a war to fight on American soil.

And the women…

Lucia didn't want to dwell on that too much. Not with a guy like Lydell as second-in-command.

The assistant director had set up a couple of hidden cameras around the parking lot. If things went sideways, the rest of the team would move in.

"Yes, sir."

What else was there for her to say?

Lucia reached up to touch the necklace she usually wore, but it wasn't there. She'd left it in her backpack.

The temporary tattoo on the inside of her forearm was her only attempt to blend in with guys who sold stolen weapons.

"Make the buy," Campbell said. "That's enough to get Lydell in custody. We'll get him talking."

Lucia wasn't sure of that, but he sounded confident enough, and it wouldn't be her problem.

"If you can find out what else they're up to at that compound, all the better."

"Nearly ten thousand acres?" Bill shifted on the back seat, and the car rocked. "He ain't up to nothin' good behind that fence."

Satellite footage hadn't shown much. A few buildings clustered at one end, lots of people moving around. Men, mostly. The bulk of the land was overgrown with trees and hills. This part of Wyoming wasn't super populated anyway, but with the reputation Burgess had established for himself, the feds needed to know what he was up to.

Simon cracked his door. "Let's go."

The two of them walked together to meet the occupants of Lydell's truck. Bill followed behind—the muscle who kept his head on a swivel. She and Simon were the brains of the operation they'd presented to Lydell. Out-of-towners big in Denver, ready to get a foothold in the local business here.

Lydell approached. He'd been in the passenger seat like her, so she kept to Simon's right so the number two guy wasn't in front of her.

The guys he'd brought with flanked him.

They all dressed the same. Jeans and boots, T-shirts worn like they were a uniform. One had a leather vest on. All three had a few days growth of facial hair, and Lydell was in serious need of a haircut.

"Hey." Simon lifted his chin.

Lucia said nothing. Guys like this didn't need her butting in. Feminists might want to assert their womanhood, but that only put you in the middle of all the attention. In Lucia's line of work, that wasn't a good thing. Not with guys who had rap sheets like these did.

Lydell motioned with his head at the back of the truck. "Get the case."

One of his guys broke off and grabbed a long storage case from the bed of the truck. He hefted it onto the hood of the truck, and Lydell flipped the latches.

Simon moved to look inside. He whistled. "AR-15s. ACOG rifle scopes. Couple of sniper rifles. M16-A4. This is prime stuff." He glanced at Lydell. "Do I have to worry about it being hot?"

"Military surplus."

Lucia said, "So you stole it from the army."

His lips twitched, and not in a good way. He looked at her. She wanted to look away, but that would be conceding defeat, and this guy wasn't going to best her. He had to see her as strong, despite the fact he thought he had power over her. He might be a predator, but she wasn't vulnerable prey.

"Where we got it from is our business." Lydell took a step toward her.

It had been so long since she'd had a romantic relationship, the dance was foreign to her. She knew enough to know this wasn't him attempting to woo her. Far from it. Attraction was just another way for him to assert his dominance.

Her boss had been right about one thing. Making it clear he had no shot wasn't going to win them any points. In fact, it could tank this whole operation.

Lucia shrugged one shoulder, drawing his attention to the fact the skin there was bare. Literally her entire plan to distract him involved wearing a tank top. Plus the fact doing that made it clear she wasn't wearing a wire was a double bonus.

At least he hadn't decided to pat her down.

She'd have pulled the knife in her boot. She said, "No skin off our nose if it's stolen. Military stuff isn't exactly top shelf, though."

"This is. Primo product."

"Yeah?" She lifted her chin. He was a lot closer now, but she didn't give away the knot in her stomach. "What if I was interested in other product as well?"

"Diversifying?"

"Just feeling out the local market. Who knows what sells?" She motioned to the crate. "This stuff is for protection. What have you got that's for fun?" She smiled and tipped her head to the side.

He erased another couple of inches between them. "Come back to the compound, and I'll show you."

She wouldn't have been surprised had he grabbed his crotch to emphasize the sentiment. She lifted her brows. "The last guy you did business with who made it to the compound didn't come out."

"You know about that?"

She wasn't going to tell him what she knew about the two Canadian men he'd transacted with a month ago. They hadn't been seen or heard from since they visited the compound. Lucia doubted they were still alive. Fifty square miles was a lot of space to bury a body or two.

"She's not going anywhere with you," Simon said.

Lydell didn't move his gaze from her. The skin on his forehead flexed. He didn't like that. He had every intention of taking her, somewhere. Somehow.

"We'll take the gear." Lucia folded her arms. "The invitation can wait for another time. We're still new here. You're an unknown."

Simon clicked shut the latches on the case and slid it off the hood.

Lucia turned back to the car and started walking.

A block away, right where the surveillance van was parked, an explosion rocketed into the sky.

"Andre?"

The asphalt on the highway, scorched by Texas heat even at night, streamed under Andre at eighty miles an hour. Tethered to the underside of the eighteen-wheeler, he held on with one hand. With the other he reached out and planted the small charge on one end of the axle.

When it blew, it would take out the front right tire.

"Hey, Andre?" The voice buzzed against his earpiece.

He adjusted his grip and took a second charge from his vest, reached out, and affixed it to the axle on the left side. "Kinda busy, Badge."

The voice came again through his earpiece. "What's brown and sticky?"

Andre let out a sigh. "A stick."

"Ah, man. You've heard that one." Badger paused for a second. "Judah, Google another one."

Their British teammate responded, "Google it yourself. I'm busy not crashing this SUV and leaving Andre to get run over."

"Guys." Zander, their team leader, only needed to say that

one word. The authority in his tone brought a silence Andre was grateful for.

Andre said, "Two minutes."

"You said that two minutes ago," Eas reminded him.

Badger erupted into laughter. "It's always the quiet ones."

Andre worked his way to the back tires and placed two more small charges of C4 on the underside of the semi.

"Half a mile and they'll be turning the corner," Zander said. "After that we'll be in view of the US–Mexico border. I don't want to end up on any traffic cameras or surveillance video."

Zander didn't tell him to hurry it up, he merely gave Andre the facts he needed. That level of respect from his boss was something Andre had earned over the last ten years of their friendship and working together. Now they were no longer Delta Force, but a private security firm, there were more than just army guys on their team.

Zander and Badger had served with Andre.

Judah was a former Marine in The Royal Navy, and Eas had a background no one knew—one that meant the Asian man always wore a mask. He couldn't show his face to anyone but them, and then only when they were tucked away in a safe house or on a mountain with no one else around.

Andre didn't envy Eas the trouble he would have when whoever was hunting him showed up at the door.

But the rest of the guys and Andre would be there when it happened.

Just not Isaac.

"Andre."

At Zander's prompting, he pushed away thoughts of the teammate who had betrayed them a month ago. He figured that might just be what happened when you trusted someone who was a former spy. They knew how to lie to everyone.

Andre unclipped himself from the underside of the truck. "I'm coming out."

Judah said, "Roger that."

Andre grasped the underside of the truck with his gloved hands, feeling the heat in the engine through the padded material. He lowered himself toward the ground and felt the second before he made contact with the road.

Strapped to his back was a reinforced sled, though Andre refused to call it that. This was anything but fun, considering he was about to shoot out from under the semi like a bullet. He also refused to call it a shield, but only because that had been Badger's suggestion. Too many Avengers movies and wanting to be Captain America.

Andre was going to buy him the costume for his birthday so he could dress up like the guy he idolized.

Andre thought he was more like the Winter Soldier than Cap, but what did he know?

The reinforced aluminum hit the ground for the second time, the first being when he'd moved from the SUV—at that time in front of the semi—underneath it. Now he shot out the back to where the SUV rumbled along behind.

Attached to the underside of the SUV was a mechanism based on the arresting gear from an aircraft carrier, the wire that caught a landing fighter jet. But the fact of the matter was that no matter how well the contraption Badger had rigged up worked, this was still going to hurt.

Andre saw a brief flash of the night sky, then he was under the engine of the SUV. The aluminum shield on his back screamed against the asphalt. That was something they had to know for next time, because the noise alone could give him away.

He went all the way under the SUV and out the back, thanks to Judah's driving skills and a desire to not run Andre over on the highway in Texas. He'd specifically used all those words.

Andre used both hands to grasp the cable. The SUV swerved a fraction, and the motion shot him sideways a few feet, toward the rumble strip. But he managed not to flip over onto his face. That would be a very bad idea. He'd crashed a motorcycle once and gained road rash all down one arm and one leg, despite the protective clothing he'd worn. Not a good day.

"Sorry, sorry," Judah said.

Despite the British accent, Andre didn't exactly feel reassured by the apology coming through his earpiece.

The back of the SUV opened, and Eas's masked face came into view. He hit a button, and the cable began to retract. At the same time Zander lowered a ramp onto the highway. When he was close enough, Zander and Eas hauled Andre off the ground, up the ramp, and into the SUV.

Eas hauled the ramp in and shut the door.

Andre said, "Someone hit the button."

"We can give you a minute." Zander glanced at him.

"If you give me a minute, I'm going to use it to barf. So let's just do this." Andre rolled over and pushed up to sitting. He grabbed his weapon and readied it.

Zander reached out and squeezed the back of Andre's neck. "We'll send Badger next time."

The idea of that made Andre grin, while in the front passenger seat Badger erupted into a series of arguments and Judah, in the driver's seat, started laughing.

Zander cut him off, a slight smile on his face. "Hit the button, Ry."

The team leader always used Badger's real name if he could. Andre knew it was so the kid felt more connected to who he was, rather than the person he became when he operated. The identity he'd chosen. A jokester, versus the kid they'd met the first day he graduated from Delta Force training.

Andre figured the guy could be whoever he wanted to be, for whatever reason. If he needed to hide behind a different personality the way Eas disguised his identity with a full face covering, that was entirely his prerogative.

"Three, two, one. Go." Badger hit the button on his iPad on the last word.

Just before the bend in the highway, a bang as loud as a small firework bumped the semi a few inches off the ground. All four charges detonated at the same time, disabling the truck but causing no damage to what was inside.

"Nice."

Judah hit the brakes as though he hadn't been aware the semi was about to stop. He pulled to the side of the highway behind the truck and stopped close. Just some ordinary citizens rendering assistance to a broken-down trucker.

Except that they all wore protective clothing and climbed out of the SUV carrying weapons.

Judah and Zander headed down the left side of the semi. Badger and Andre took the right, and they cleared the front seats.

The passenger immediately reached for a weapon to fight back, as he realized what was happening here. Zander's side erupted with gunfire at the same time Badger and Andre took out their guy.

They returned to the rear of the truck, where Eas stood guard. There was no other traffic on the road this time of night. But there could be, soon enough.

Zander said, "Let's get this done."

Eas used a bolt cutter to get through the padlock on the back of the truck and pushed up the door. It rolled up and back with a clatter, revealing a single crate strapped down in the middle.

Finally, the missing nuclear warhead they had been tracking for the last few weeks was in their grasp.

After they'd found radioisotopes in an Estonian warehouse, they'd been doing some digging. A scientist had been kidnapped and forced to write a computer program for a targeting system. Could he also have been required to build a bomb before he was murdered? Maybe there was another specialist in play.

Badger hopped up onto the back of the semi and strode to

the crate. He used a multitool from his pocket to pry open the corner of the lid. He threw it aside.

"There's nothing in here but bags of rice."

"The manifest said rice, but a whole lot more than one crate." Zander looked ticked.

"So the nuke isn't in here, and we were wrong about everything?" Andre didn't like the sound of that. Where on earth was the warhead?

Judah said, "Back to square one?"

Even Eas let out a noise of disappointment.

Andre gritted his teeth. Things hadn't been going all that well for the last month, despite Zander at least being happy with his life now.

After Isaac's betrayal, and the arrest of the former head of the Department of Clandestine Service, none of them had much motivation. A warhead was enough to get them all back on missions.

"Pack it up," Zander said. "Let's get going."

2

Wyoming

Everyone shifted to look at the source of the explosion. Except for Lydell, who kept his gaze on Lucia. She didn't take her attention from him either. Not when he would surely do something behind her back.

"What are you doing?"

This had to be him. Lydell was in no way surprised about an explosion in the vicinity of the surveillance van. It didn't indicate anything good. Even his two guys hadn't been all that surprised.

They knew what was going on here.

She was about to ask him again when Simon spun around. "Let's go," he demanded.

Thankfully in the confusion he didn't mistakenly use her real name. Lydell didn't need to know who they really were. If they managed to get out of this and figure out what was going on their cover stories with Burgess's people were intact.

Simon said, "We're out of here. This is crazy town."

Lydell pulled a gun from inside his jacket and shot Simon.

His body jerked, and he hit the ground.

Lucia couldn't hold back the flinch. She took a step back, ready to leave—whether Lydell thought he was going to allow this, or not.

She took another step back.

Bill swung around. He glanced at the three men surrounding them. "What the—"

Lydell shifted his gun to her other colleague and pulled the trigger again.

Lucia turned and made a run for it. She had her own weapon but doubted she could kill all three of them before they shot her. She had only one choice left.

Get to a defensible position, then take them out.

She ran as fast as she could toward the car they had shown up in. Simon had left the keys in the ignition. If she could get there, she could—

Arms banded around her, their legs tangled, and she started to trip. Lucia went down with two hundred pounds of redneck on her back. Her jaw slammed the concrete, and she cried out.

Her gun skittered across the ground.

He shifted and grabbed her hands, pulled both behind her back, and secured them with something that felt like a plastic tie. It cut into her skin.

She kicked out with her legs but couldn't make contact.

Her head swam and bile rose in her throat. She could smell gunpowder from the two shots. The blood that had spilled on the gravel. Tears filled her eyes.

He lifted his weight off her. Lucia shifted enough she could twist her shoulders and reach back, down to her boots. She pulled a knife free of its sheath and scrambled to her feet, holding the knife behind her back.

Lydell pointed his gun at her. But he wasn't going to kill her.

Lucia twisted the knife and cut her hands free. She held up the blade in front of her, ready to use it on anyone who thought they were going to touch her.

These men had killed her two colleagues and possibly the rest of the team as well. What she didn't know was why.

If Lucia was the only one left, then she had absolutely nothing to lose.

She ignored the niggling thought that she was in denial, lying to herself about having no connection to another living soul on this planet. If her colleagues were gone, there was one person who might shed a tear over her.

One.

Maybe for a second, before he went on with his life. Then again, probably not considering how things had ended a lifetime ago.

Life was about the here and now. The same way she had been living for fifteen years. Day to day, keeping her head down and doing the best she could to make up for everything she had done.

But now things were going bad. Both her colleagues were dead, and backup was possibly not coming at all. This might get a whole lot worse before it got better, but relying on herself and all that was in her was what Lucia did.

She didn't have backup in her life.

If anyone was going to get her out of the situation, then it was her.

"Like I said." She faced down Lydell. "What are you doing?"

He motioned with his gun and said to his men, "Take the knife and make sure she has no other weapons."

If there was a risk that any of her task force would come and fight for her, Lydell didn't seem exactly bothered by the threat. She wanted to ask if they were all dead, but his guys were coming toward her.

She stared them down. "You think you're gonna touch me?"

The first one grinned. The other one had an expression on his face that wasn't much better.

"Try." That one word was her invitation and a threat all

wrapped up in one. But they were going to find out what she was made of in a second if they kept coming.

Lydell chuckled. "As amusing as that would be to watch, we don't have time for it." He closed in on her until the barrel of the gun touched her temple.

Lucia hissed as the heat seared her skin. It was still hot from being fired twice.

She had no choice but to surrender the blade to these guys and stand still while they patted her down. Checking for weapons, and copping a feel at the same time.

She glanced at Lydell. He wasn't going to see her back down, or submit. It just wasn't in her nature.

He grinned at her.

"So all this is about me?"

"The minute I met you, I knew there was something between us." He closed in on her then, the gun still touching her head. "And when I want something, I get it."

"I hate to break it to you, but you'll be disappointed." She lifted both hands, her palms empty. "You see, I'm kind of a wet blanket. Everyone says so."

At least, she figured they did behind her back. She didn't exactly socialize with her colleagues, not beyond the odd birthday party or Christmas gathering. Even then she left early. Being around people was a recipe for disaster when she would rather be at home online, playing any one of a number of games she'd been leveling up on for the last ten years. New games just didn't hold the same appeal. Not when she would have to start all over from level one.

Lucia wasn't a level one kind of girl.

"You can be whatever you like. It doesn't matter." Lydell lifted his free hand and ran a finger down her cheek. "I'll get what I want anyway."

A shot was fired in the distance, probably from the rooftop where surveillance had been stationed.

One of Lydell's guys fell to the ground, a bullet in his chest.

He grabbed her wrist and pulled her unerringly toward his vehicle.

Another shot fired. The bullet pinged off the side of the truck.

He ducked his head and pulled open the front seat, shoving her in before he climbed in after her.

The other guy with him ran for the truck as well. Lydell hit the gas and pulled out before he could reach the passenger door.

Another shot missed the tire.

If this was one of her colleagues, they wouldn't shoot the man left behind. They would capture and question him.

She turned and looked out the back window. The second Lydell stopped, or even slowed the truck at all, she would shove the door open and get out.

He could shoot her. She wasn't going to go with him.

The reality that this could turn real bad, real quick stayed with her. Just like the idea that the one person who maybe cared about her might shed a tear.

She started to turn back to the front when Lydell swung out his arm and slammed his gun into the side of her head.

Any hope of making a run for it evaporated then and there. Pain ricocheted through Lucia's skull, and she heard herself cry out, unable to stop the sound from breaking free of her throat.

I'll never be able to get out of this.

That thought was like a mantra echoing in her head as he drove the highway for an hour.

After a bumpy thirty minutes along dirt roads, over a train track, and alongside a river Lucia could see glint in the moonlight.

Lydell took the winding roads like a madman, and with every mile she thanked God that he wasn't pulling over to a quiet inlet where he could get started on his plans.

And yet, the idea of where he was taking her—if she was right about it—meant she would be in far worse trouble when they crossed through those gates.

She and God weren't exactly on friendly terms. Her father had followed Him like a heavenly general, issuing commands to be obeyed. But whatever kind of God He was, Lucia knew she needed Him now more than she ever had.

The truck swayed around the bend. She slid across the seat and her head slammed the window.

She blinked. Tried to bring the world into focus.

Lydell drove under an arching gateway into the compound. The heavy gates closed behind them with a clang she could hear over the truck engine.

Just another woman who disappeared into this place and was never seen again.

Texas

"SOMEONE KNEW WE WERE COMING." Andre sat in the middle row behind the front passenger seat.

Eas was back in the third row, where there'd be no chance anyone would see him. Zander sat beside Andre. Judah drove while Badger stared out the side window and said nothing.

Andre glanced over. "That has to be why the warhead wasn't there, right?"

Zander nodded to concede the point. Judging by his expression—and the fact Andre had known the guy for ten years now—he wasn't happy. But he said nothing.

Zander's relationship with Nora Gladstone had mellowed him a lot. After prior failed missions, he'd have burned a house down because they didn't get what they wanted. Metaphorically, except for that one time. Andre had been on the receiving end of his uptick in training, so the mistake or misstep wouldn't happen again.

Now Zander was thoughtful, though he probably had a dozen scenarios spinning in his head.

Andre saw only one thing. Treachery. "Isaac."

The car erupted with noise. Agreements and disagreements. Only Badger remained quiet. Too quiet for a guy who wrapped humor around himself like a comfort blanket.

Andre poked him in the shoulder. "I'm sure Hannah will call you back."

Zander's head snapped up. He glanced between the two of them.

Before they could get off track, Andre said, "Maybe Isaac knows we're still looking for the warhead. Heaven knows it shouldn't fall into the wrong hands. What if he's tracking us, and he knew we were going to try for it? He could've intercepted."

"Ted confirmed that's not possible," Zander said. "We cut him off so he has no way to track us." The discordant clang of betrayal rang in his tone.

"And if he took the nuke for himself, they wouldn't have still been driving."

Judah hit his turn signal and rounded the corner. The guy needed more driving practice being on the correct side of the road—the right side—but in the meantime they all had to suffer.

Andre gripped the door handle. "Maybe. He could've paid them off to try and kill us." The passengers in the truck had intended to shoot them. That was why they'd taken the two men out.

"Phones?" Eas said from the back seat.

Zander answered, "We'll see what Ted can get from their cells. But if Isaac had anything to do with the warhead, then I doubt we'll find anything."

Andre banged his fist on his thigh a couple of times. He needed to take Eas's tactic and go for a run. Burn off some of his frustrated energy.

At this rate, Zander would have them all doing pushups in the hangar before they left.

"Isaac probably set up the whole thing." Andre mulled it over. "Strung us along all the way here. I bet he's got it himself."

Zander shifted in his seat. "What would Isaac want with a nuke?"

Andre shrugged. "Who knows? He wasn't the teammate we trusted. He got you arrested and he wanted Nora to shoot him?" He shook his head. "That's not the guy we knew."

"You were on the plane with him."

Andre sighed.

"It's been a month," Zander said. "Maybe you should tell us now what he said to you."

He pressed his lips together.

"Andre. What did he say?"

When his commander gave an order, Andre was compelled to follow it. He'd been in the army way too long to react otherwise, even if he'd been out for years. Probably he needed a vacation—at Dean's therapy center in Last Chance. The guy was a licensed counselor now, and married. Even if he was a former Navy SEAL, Andre trusted him. They'd lived in the same house for years, until Dean married Ellie.

"You're rabbit-trailing in your head. Focus up and start talking."

Maybe Andre didn't need therapy. Maybe he was exactly where he needed to be.

He twisted to face Zander, not bothering to school his expression. Who cared? The truth of his feelings was how he honestly felt—for better or worse. "He betrayed us."

"I'm as pissed about that as you are. But I also figure he had his reasons."

"You mean excuses." Andre didn't want to fall into a tail spin. That was why he'd never become a pilot. "Isaac was hurt, and he was blathering. Probably feverish. Or they injected him with something."

"So he talked."

Andre nodded. The rest of the car was quiet. "Making

excuses, trying to explain it away. Like he *had to* because he had no choice. Well, you know what? There's always a choice."

Badger twisted around in the front seat. "Excuses like what?"

"*She* made him do it." Isaac had even shed a tear at one point. Though Andre had figured that was more down to the pain of being shot. Because Isaac had shot himself to make it look like Nora subdued him. "I figured he was talking about Nora, but now I have no idea. He was working for Gladstone and not his daughter."

Zander shook his head. "Gladstone gave up the fact the warhead is out there, along with a ton of his other plans. I figure there's more and he's just baiting the hook. He probably wants to negotiate for his release and a cushy setup in witness protection somewhere with a beach."

Andre hissed out a breath. "They wouldn't do that."

"Depends what he gives up. Especially if he can hand over intel that'll lead to the warhead."

"But he hasn't yet. So Isaac probably leaked this to give us the runaround. Keep us distracted."

Judah said, "From what?"

No one said anything.

Andre sighed. "I should care, but I really don't. He has nothing to do with us now. That's his choice."

"And if he comes to us for help?" Zander asked.

Andre stared through the windshield at the road in front of them. "Like I said, he made his choice."

Judah pulled into the local airport where they'd left the plane. "Looks clear."

Their lives were about constant vigilance. Maybe Andre did need a break. He was more exhausted than usual, and even with a month that'd been lower key than normal, he hadn't been able to shake the feeling.

Andre leaned his head back and closed his eyes as Judah

drove down the one lane road that circled the airport to the hangar where he'd parked.

Eas's voice rumbled to him from the back seat. "Maybe you should go find something to blow up. Release the feelings?"

Judah chuckled. "I'm guessing four semi wheels didn't cut it."

Andre kept his eyes closed. "You think I have feelings?"

They laughed, even though everyone knew he was full of it. He'd tried to feel nothing ever since he had his heart so thoroughly stomped on. He'd learned the truth and now he only trusted his brothers—the men who were here for him.

That was probably why Isaac's betrayal stung so badly.

These guys were his family. Not because they had to be, but because they wanted him in their lives in a way that healed the restlessness in him.

Still, part of Andre would always remain unsettled. Unfinished. Incomplete.

He'd long ago resigned himself to that fact.

Blowing something up might feel good for a second, but it wouldn't fix what was wrong with him. The same way Eas knew exorcising the feelings only helped for a while.

Judah parked the SUV, and they pushed open the doors.

Zander's phone rang as they walked to the open hangar. "O'Connell." He listened for a couple of seconds and then stopped.

The rest of them gathered around him while Zander frowned.

"One sec." He shifted the phone from his mouth and looked at Andre. "Ted has an assistant director from the FBI who wants to talk to you."

"Eric?" That was the only fed he knew.

Zander shook his head.

"About what?" Andre was a military guy who worked private jobs now. What did he have to do with the feds?

"Lucia DeSoto."

Andre didn't move. He couldn't, or he would react and they would know.

"Who's that?" Judah looked around.

He'd only told Zander and Badger the story, one night a long time ago when he'd been feeling sorry for himself. Since then he hadn't mentioned it.

Zander said, "I'll have him patched through."

"Who is Lucia DeSoto?" Judah wasn't going to back down.

"She's my wife."

3

———

Lydell pulled the truck to a stop outside a huge building. The whole compound seemed more established than it had from satellite pictures. Instead of a few buildings, this was more like a village.

Lucia let her head tip to one side and then back to the left, groaning as though barely conscious.

From under her lowered eyelids, she spotted people walking around. The night was lit up by streetlights, though where they got the power from was a mystery. This place wasn't on the grid.

He slammed the driver's door and seconds later yanked hers open. The door creaked, as though resisting allowing her to exit the vehicle. That would've been fine by her. But good fortune had never shone on her life that way.

He reached in and tugged her out by her armpits, hauling her over his shoulder so the joint dug into her stomach even despite the breadth of his shoulders.

In the distance, she heard the high-pitched scream of an animal. Like the cry of a midsize cat—a panther or cougar.

She couldn't hold back the shiver.

Her head spun as he jostled her with every footfall up the steps and into the building. It smelled musty and damp inside, the way the air did after a big storm. Lingering moisture hung around and chilled her skin with the nighttime temperature.

There was a shuffle, and a woman made a sound. But it wasn't Lucia. It had come from across the room, where footsteps now scurried away.

"What is this?"

She'd never heard that voice before, and didn't have time to think through who the man was before Lydell bent slightly and tipped her onto the floor.

It didn't take much to act as though that movement had jarred her back to consciousness. She blinked up at the ceiling, bare trestle beams overhead.

This had to be some kind of meeting room that no one had cleaned recently. The floor was gritty with a layer of dirt that needed to be swept.

"I want her to be mine." That was Lydell.

His words made a shudder move through Lucia, but she refused to let it out. She acted as though she couldn't get up if she wanted to, which wasn't much of a stretch. Her mind replayed the images of her colleagues, shot and falling to the ground. What had happened to the rest of them?

Were they all dead?

She wasn't going to assume rescue would be here to get her anytime soon. After all, who even knew to look for her? That investigation could take days, or even weeks. And the feds weren't exactly about to bust the door down just to get her back. As much as she wanted to believe they would. The greater good always came first, and Burgess was a high-value target.

So much for using Lydell as their way in. He'd turned the tables, and now she was in serious trouble.

"You know that's not how this works." A man approached, his long, measured footsteps indicating he was in no hurry. "Who is she?"

"One of the people we met with."

"I knew something was going on." It had to be Burgess himself.

Lucia had seen a photo of him, but only from a distance. She wasn't sure she could positively identify him if he'd changed his hair at all.

"And now you bring her here? How do you know there aren't going to be people looking for her? You have no idea who this woman is." He sounded angry, though the tone of his voice didn't change. Instead of growing louder and more agitated, it just sounded…tighter. "She could be bait, sent here to bring us down from the inside." It almost seemed as though he thought the idea was amusing.

Didn't think much of women? There was a huge surprise.

Lucia shifted and looked up at the man. It was probably Burgess, but she couldn't be sure.

"They're from California. Branching out into this market. They were going to buy the military surplus stuff from us."

"So instead of money, you bring me another mouth to feed."

"You don't need to worry about her being a burden."

She figured that either meant Lydell planned on not feeding her at all, or he was going to feed her out of his share.

Neither sounded particularly appealing.

"If you don't want me here"—she cleared her throat and tried to sound in control of her faculties rather than scared out of her mind—"I could just go. It's no problem."

"That'd be where you're wrong," Burgess said to her. "Because you *are* a problem." He lifted his gaze to Lydell. "Did you search her for a wire?"

"I had a scanner on. She's clean."

They could tell if she was wired without checking? Some kind of scanner that picked up the signal being transmitted from any device she might be wearing. It was a good thing the assistant director had agreed to them not wearing wires.

"We'll see about that." Burgess stared down at her.

Lucia wanted to get up off the floor. That would be like accepting she was in this situation. Lying on her back while they stood over her, she could almost believe she was slightly removed from it.

In the distance, she could hear guns going off. But not a shootout. It was more rhythmic—the sound of an outside gun range down the street.

Lucia had seen a lot during her time as a DEA agent. The aftermath of terrible situations, and surveillance she'd done. Enough to give her a good idea of what to expect.

But a conflict between Burgess and Lydell could cause a rift in the entire compound. If there truly was a community here, and the second-in-command turned away or fell into bad favor, it could mean a huge upset.

"If you're the one in charge"—Lucia sat up—"then we should get to know each other. I'm sure I can convince you that I'm not going to cause you any trouble."

She didn't smile. Otherwise, she'd have betrayed how much of a lie those words were. A neutral expression gave away nothing.

Lydell grabbed a handful of her hair and pulled her head back against the outside of his leg. "I brought her here because she's mine."

All she needed was for Burgess to make a declaration, and she was pretty sure Lydell would start a war. Lucia wasn't exactly the greatest prize—something they were going to find out soon enough—but it turned out men hadn't changed in a thousand years. They were still willing to go to battle over their fleshly urges.

Women probably would as well, but it would be far more vicious or manipulative than a fistfight.

Anyone who tried to tell her she had a negative view of humanity was going to hear a few of her stories of exactly how horrible people could be. Once in a while she had to go to a city park and watch families and children play, their pets running around. Everyone happy, enjoying the sunshine.

In times like these the memory of those days was what kept her sane.

She heard the snick of a weapon being removed from its holster a second before Burgess lifted a gun and fired at Lydell's chest.

Lucia flinched. His hold on her hair pulled her back as he fell to the ground.

"Get up."

She said nothing as she rolled to her front and pushed off the floor to stand. Her head swam. She hissed out a breath and straightened to face Burgess. She wasn't about to look at the dead man on the floor. She'd seen enough of that tonight, and her ability to compose herself was worn.

Eventually it would snap. After that she would be curled up on the floor in the fetal position, crying her eyes out.

But she wasn't past hope yet. Not if she could keep a hold of herself.

He eyed her. "Who are you really?"

"Fine. I'm not from California." She switched to Spanish. "I was born in Mexico City." Keeping to the truth as much as possible was going to help her stay grounded. Lucia went back to English. "What is this place?"

He spread his arms wide, palms facing her. "This is my kingdom."

Great. He was exactly as crazy as everyone said.

He was probably in his fifties. Long light-brown hair like all those pictures of Jesus where they pretended he was a white guy who just happened to have been born in the Middle East but didn't look like it one bit.

"What do you want with me?" Lucia wanted information. As much as they were willing to give so she could manage her reactions to what was happening.

"Like I said, we'll get to that." He glanced aside at someone she hadn't seen there before. More than one man stood around the room.

He ordered, "Strip her."

ANDRE DESCENDED the plane steps first. It had taken far too much time to detour to Wyoming, but they were here now—and the black SUV waiting for them was property of the US Government.

From the research Ted had done during their flight, Lucia was DEA on a task force that included FBI, ATF, US Marshals, and several police officers, including a detective and a lieutenant. The subject of the task force? Franklin Burgess, ecowarrior, wildlife conservationist turned cult leader, complete with his own militia and a few side businesses growing and selling illicit substances and trading in weapons and tactical gear.

So an all-around bad guy who needed to be taken down.

And the real-time updates Ted had discovered indicated something went down on their operation tonight. Hours ago now, since it was almost dawn.

Zander said it was a God-thing that they'd contacted Andre as the next of kin. Especially if Lucia had been hurt, instead of the worst that could've happened—her being killed.

At least if she was alive, there was a shot they could save her.

A suited man strode over from the SUV. Badge on his belt, and graying hair. He worked out. He held out his hand and Andre assessed the man's handshake. He definitely worked out. This was a guy whose strength was more than it appeared to be.

"Assistant Director Campbell. You can call me Pierce."

"Where is she?" The sick feeling in his stomach hadn't evaporated yet.

"This is Andre Martinez." Zander shook Campbell's hand. "I'm Zander O'Connell."

He didn't introduce the rest of the guys, but Andre knew

Badger stood behind them with Judah. Eas was still on the plane, out of sight just in case the FBI agent recognized him—which was entirely possible.

What this guy thought of them, Andre didn't know. Didn't care. If there was something to do here, they would do it.

Campbell studied them. "I see I should've looked up who you were, rather than simply calling Special Agent DeSoto's next of kin and asking to talk."

Nora had called the guy back and told him where they would be.

"To inform me of what?" Andre needed information and fast. If she was missing, every hour counted. If she was dead? Andre didn't know what he'd do after hearing that. Part of him had always believed he'd see her again. But wishing for it was pointless when it would be torturous to his peace of mind.

She'd made her choice. He wasn't part of her life anymore.

"I don't normally do this." Campbell frowned. "And probably shouldn't, but…"

"Spit it out." Andre was ready to shake some sense into this guy. Who cared if they weren't cleared to hear about this?

They'd find out one way or the other.

"Four agents were killed on the operation." Campbell's expression darkened. "She was kidnapped after the surveillance van exploded killing two of the agents inside. The other two were with her, making the buy. It appears the target we were after, second-in-command to Burgess, had his eye on her *and* the wherewithal to set up the whole situation. They thought they were walking into a buy, getting their hands on tactical gear he stole from the military."

"He had other plans?"

"We were nearby, ready to move in and arrest him, when the van exploded and he took her from the scene. Our intelligence confirms he brought her to the compound where Burgess reigns supreme."

"So you know where she is." Andre nodded. "That's good."

"I really should have googled you at least."

"Yeah," Zander said. "You probably should've."

Andre figured that wasn't the point. Campbell wouldn't have found anything that way, though maybe he'd have stumbled over the company website. All spit and polish, a group of decorated former military soldiers who'd gone into business together providing security for people who had the money to pay for their level of skill.

It didn't completely cover what they did, but it was close enough.

They had enough to go on from Campbell if they were going to get her back.

"Normally I wouldn't provide operational details to the next of kin." Campbell sighed. "However, in this case it might prove prudent."

Andre lifted his chin. "Why's that?"

"A plan to rescue Special Agent DeSoto has been shelved for the time being. My boss believes jumping the gun would be detrimental to taking down Burgess. There's another agency with a man inside—one I know nothing about." He shook his head. "I don't even know who it is, but they aren't federal."

Andre didn't like the sound of this at all.

"Due to that, my hands are tied. I don't have the authorization to go after Lydell for killing my agents and abducting Special Agent DeSoto." He cocked his head to the side. "What is your relationship to her?"

Andre would have to explain at some point, but he didn't want to waste time right now. Judah had asked a ton of questions on the plane. Andre had blown him off, too worried about Lucia to be distracted. Zander had prayed, but he and Badger knew the highlights.

"She's my wife. We're estranged, and it's been that way for years." He'd checked they were still married. She hadn't managed to untangle that mess on her end.

"She never mentioned you."

Andre didn't want to get into that any more than the rest of it. He just wanted to make her safe so he could get on with the rest of his life—the one he lived *without* her.

"This is a courtesy. Nothing more." Campbell shook his head. "Despite the fact that you all seem…capable. Your job is to wait for further information. As soon as Special Agent DeSoto is recovered, we'll contact you."

That didn't sound good. Campbell had to cover himself, make sure he said all the things he was legally required to in order to absolve himself of anything Andre and the team might do. So he could say he'd warned them.

Andre figured they could make a call and get grafted onto this task force. Annexed.

He'd do whatever it took, considering Lucia was in danger.

Still, Andre couldn't help thinking there was more Campbell hadn't said. "You can't go get her?"

"My hands are tied," Campbell said. "As much as I want to initiate a rescue, I have four visits to make today to tell agent's families their loved one is dead. I can't go after her because I haven't been given the authorization to do that. I'm supposed to let it play out for the sake of the case."

To his credit, it seemed to genuinely bother him that he was leaving Lucia to the wolves—literally, considering what all Burgess had in that compound.

Still, hadn't this guy ever heard of defying orders? It was why Andre no longer served in the army. He'd taken his medals and his honorable discharge and gone to work for Zander about two seconds after Zander did the same. Badger had been right behind him. The three of them had been a team for years.

Now they had other members, providing unique skills to add to the foundation they had.

"Shame your hands are tied." Andre folded his arms. "Except maybe from sending me everything your task force has on Burgess and his entire setup."

"Of course I can't do that."

"Sure." Legally, he absolutely couldn't. But he could leave it somewhere for Ted to find—if he assumed they had someone like Ted on their payroll. "I understand."

Time would tell how helpful this guy might prove to be.

"When you said you'd be flying in," Campbell began, "I wasn't sure what to expect. Now I see Special Agent DeSoto is in good hands."

"She is," Zander said. "Because we'll be praying for her."

Andre knew that was true. Zander wouldn't lie about it. However, he also knew they'd be doing a whole lot more than that.

"Thank you for doing us the courtesy of coming here to speak to Andre." Zander ushered him toward his SUV.

"I believe it was your uh…*team* who came to me."

"Team? We're friends." Zander didn't elaborate. "I'm sure you have a lot of work to do." He practically shoved Campbell into his vehicle.

Then Zander turned to them.

Badger moved to Andre's side.

Judah took up the space on the other side.

"Well?" Badger asked.

"We're going after her?" Andre waited for Zander's word.

"Of course we are."

4

——————

Lucia's head pounded over the bustle of noise in the cafeteria. The floor under her bare feet was sticky, and gritty with crumbs. A couple of skinny dogs with matted hair wandered the room, sniffing at the tables and the corners. Looking for scraps.

Breakfast consisted of a slop-like oatmeal they'd given her, not allowing her any of the eggs and sausage the others were having. Predominantly the men. Most of the women in the room, and there were at least six aside from her, had the same bowl she did.

Lucia ate a bite, not bothering to sniff to see what it smelled like. She supposed it was meant to be cinnamon oatmeal, but it didn't taste like any breakfast she'd ever had. Or even a terrible bran muffin.

It was much worse than that, but still the least of her problems.

Two of the women were in different stages of pregnancy. All wore dirty, threadbare clothes. She was the only one with no shoes and no sweater. They'd barely left her with the jeans and tank top she'd been wearing.

The air chilled her skin, raising goosebumps down her arms.

She didn't bother to try to rub some warmth back into them. Her hands were colder.

At this point, she'd have liked her knife, because that carafe in the corner—the one she figured had coffee in it? She'd probably have stabbed someone just for a cup.

They hadn't allowed her to sleep, though some of the men from her welcoming committee had mentioned a room she would be staying in. She figured it was nothing better than a prison cell given the state of the women here. None of them looked like they were anywhere they wanted to be.

Supposedly checking for a wire, her captors had stared at her in her underwear, taking turns rubbing and squeezing her. Freaking animals. Once they got done, they'd sent her in here for "breakfast." The treatment wasn't enough to make her lose her will. But this oatmeal was enough to cause her to want to lift the bowl and fling it against the wall.

Regardless of what happened afterward.

Four men were stationed around the room, holding guns. One wandered to the next, whispering. She heard the word *mission* but didn't know for sure that's what she'd heard.

As much as it burned in her to start a fight, there would be consequences to doing so. She stayed with her backside on the hard bench seat of the long table and kept to herself while others whispered in their seats, and people drifted in and out.

On the wall were images of Burgess.

Of the planet and animals.

Slogans like, "Wilderness is for the wild," and, "Save the planet." One commanded her to take action, for the greater good.

She wondered exactly how far they would go to get the end they wanted.

Also, given the fact they'd been selling stolen military weapons, she figured their tactics were a little more like domestic terrorism than your average tree hugger.

She was surprised there were no Ten Commandments

According to Burgess. Dictates of their lord and master that everyone adhered to when they felt like it—or when he was watching.

And if she could get out of here without completely losing her mind? That would be a rousing success. A solid victory. Bringing down this entire operation and everyone involved in it would be only slightly less difficult than that.

Lucia stirred the oatmeal around her bowl. She wasn't even hungry. Was that surprising, given the night she'd had? Fatigue weighed like a thousand-pound bar across her shoulders, making her eyes burn and her thoughts sluggish. Not that she wanted to have any particular thoughts. All that would do is lead to her wondering about her dead colleagues. The status of the rest of the team.

And the one man she tried never to think about.

Better to use the cold to keep her awake. Concentrate on observing everything, and taking in the movements of the guards.

She knew what they were doing. Wearing her down, keeping her awake far longer than she should be so she was mentally and physically exhausted and they could begin to dehumanize her. Break her down until she had no resistance left.

She could see it in the eyes of the women in the room.

One carried a tray from the kitchen, a single bowl. No drink. She shuffled down the aisle between the long tables.

A man approached her back and slid an arm around her waist to pull her against his body. She stiffened. There was not one ounce of appreciation or affection on her face. She looked like she would rather be anywhere but here.

Lucia couldn't tear her eyes away as the man leaned down and whispered in her ear. The woman flinched.

The man said something else. Eventually, she gave a small nod.

The man took a squeeze of her for himself, then shoved her

toward a table. She stumbled and nearly dumped the contents of the bowl.

Movement drew her attention.

Across the room, one of the dogs set its front paws on the bench seat and lifted to sniff at a woman's tray. The dog began to lick up the unfinished contents of her bowl. The woman sat completely still and began to cry…until she was yelled at by one of the guards and told to finish her food.

The dog was kicked and sent away.

In all their investigation into Burgess and his compound, no one had ever gotten eyes inside. This was the federal government's first look at the truth of what he was up to. Lucia had to remember that. She wasn't one woman, alone in this situation. No allies, no backup. She was an agent of the DEA, and now a direct witness of what was going on here.

No matter what happened, she had to hold that close and keep a grasp on it.

The compound was thousands of acres. The buildings around this one only took up maybe a handful of that. Lucia needed to figure a way to find out what was happening on the rest of the land. Especially behind that high fence.

She was going to shine a light into all the dark places here. And then she would drag the truth out where everyone could see it. Where the full force of the justice system could come down on these people.

Lucia became aware the moment someone approached her back. She took a bite of oatmeal, did her best not to gag, and managed to swallow it while she pretended she hadn't noticed there was someone back there.

Until the person swept hair off her shoulder.

She shot to her feet and turned around.

The grungy looking man grinned. "This one has fire in her, I think."

She didn't need to wonder what his intentions were. Not when it was plain on his face, and she could read the room enough to know what this was. These women might have come by choice, believing in the cause that Burgess claimed to stand for—which seemed to be encapsulated in saving the planet and allowing wild animals and nature to have free reign of the land they occupied. Or they might have been abducted as she was.

Either way, now that they understood the reality of what this was, it was the last place they wanted to be.

She started to say something. The man grabbed her hand and twisted her. He tugged her wrist up between her shoulder blades and slammed her front onto the table.

Her head bounced off the corner of her tray, and she hissed out a breath between clenched teeth.

He leaned close. "Let's go have some fun, little firecracker."

Lucia tried to move the fingers of her other hand, smashed between her body and the table. He yanked her back upright. She spun, the handle of the broken spoon between her fingers.

Lucia stabbed it into his abdomen.

The man cried out and let go of her to clutch his stomach where her plastic spoon protruded from his skin and blood dampened his T-shirt.

"Sorry. Reflexes."

He launched at her, spewing a foul name. There was nowhere to go. She literally had her back to the table. One guy, a blond she wasn't going to mess with, grabbed him. "Get to the infirmary before that goes septic."

Four guys stood around him. The injured man stumbled through them.

Across the room she heard a shouted command. "Get her to the arena." Burgess sipped from a mug, his expression disinterested.

Two men grabbed her and dragged her to the door.

ANDRE RESTED his elbows on the dirt and looked through the binoculars, flat on his stomach on a hilltop overlooking the compound.

"So we're not even going to talk about how she's your wife?" Judah's voice drifted through the comms earbud like he was right next to Andre.

The team was spread out around the complex. Badger with Andre, and Zander with Eas and Judah.

Andre scanned the open area between buildings. "It was a long time ago. We were practically kids, and I haven't seen her since that summer."

Plenty of people milled around in the graveled area that ran between the village of buildings. Mostly men, but a few women. A couple of dogs.

Horses had been corralled behind a fence on one side. Skinny, bedraggled things that needed to be fed and cared for a whole lot better than they were.

He didn't see any children, thankfully, but supposed there were at least some.

Andre wondered aloud, "How long has this place been here?"

"Ted's research suggested it's been about two years," Zander replied. "He also said in the area to the north that's fenced off, he saw a whole lot of animals showing up as heat signatures on the satellite imagery he obtained."

Beside Andre, Badger said, "And we're not supposed to ask how he got ahold of that, I guess." Andre heard him shift his position on the ground. "Vegas?"

Whether he told them what had happened between him and Lucia, or not, the guys would still help him go in and get her out. Not to mention unravel the mess of whatever this was that Burgess had going on. They could pass the feds whatever information they needed. Their hands were tied by interdepartmental bickering, or whoever had an operation going on inside.

Andre and the team weren't the kind of men who left anyone behind, let alone someone one of them cared about.

Even if it had been years ago.

Andre sighed. "Her dad didn't like the idea of us being married. I left for basic training Monday after the wedding. When I got back, she wasn't at home. I tracked her down, and she told me she wasn't interested anymore."

He winced. Not exactly true, given she'd screamed in his face.

And yet, neither of them had ever annulled the marriage or filed for divorce. At least not to his knowledge.

If he'd met someone else in the years since, he might have tracked her down and put the paperwork through to dissolve the nothing their marriage had been. Except for those couple of days of bliss before he left town. He sighed again. No point dwelling on that when Lucia was in trouble. Her team had been decimated, and she'd been captured. What else was he going to do except show up here and get her out?

Sure, he still cared about her. But what had been between them was so long ago now that it didn't even factor.

She needed to be safe. Afterward he would go back to his life, and she could get on with hers.

"I'm not liking this at all." Judah sounded the way he got when it was clear a woman was in trouble. "I'm thinking we go in and start smacking some of these guys around."

"What do you see?" Zander asked.

"Two of them have a woman cornered in an alley. She's not having a good day." Judah's British accent thickened to hard edges. "Consequently, I'm not having a good day. That means someone's going to get hurt."

Andre's stomach knotted. "Not much better over here from what I can see."

As he watched, the doors to one of the buildings flung open and a crowd of men pushed out, dragging a woman with them.

"That's her." He gave them all the specifics of her location. "Looks like they're headed across the open area."

But to where? And what were they doing with her?

He studied her as she moved, but the image blurred. He couldn't see much. It had been too long for him to guess her physical state from her facial features, even if he had been able to make them out with any kind of clarity. She didn't have any visible bleeding wounds on the rest of her body. She walked with enough fluidity he knew she had no major injuries. And yet, they propelled her along, giving her no choice but to go with them.

One flung open a gate that led to the horse exercise ring. Horses that seem to be treated about as well as the women here were.

A dog raced in after the crowd and danced around outside.

Lucia was shoved to the middle, where she fell to one knee before standing back upright.

"She's strong."

Zander's assessment of her might be true, but it didn't mean she was going to survive this.

"We need to go in there." That was Judah, speaking the words that were on Andre's tongue.

"I'm bringing my knives," Eas said.

It would have comforted Andre to know that if he weren't watching two men circle Lucia.

Badger had a good idea. "Let's just go."

Andre was about to get up when Zander said, "We can't just walk in there. Not with who we are, and what it means when we're together. They'll clock us as a threat the second we show up. This needs to be finessed."

"What are you talking about?" Judah asked. "I'm the king of finesse."

Badger, still beside him, said something Andre didn't catch when he was too busy staring intently at Lucia, being circled by two of the men. The others watched on and jeered. He could see them shifting as they clapped and punched fists in the air.

It didn't seem as though the two circling her had weapons.

But ganging up on her?

Hot anger gathered low in his stomach. He wanted to run in there like Judah had suggested. Punch and shoot his way through to get to her. What he would do after that, Andre had no idea.

He also didn't really care.

If he had to do the same to get out, and wound up killing everyone down there in the process, he wasn't exactly going to be upset about it.

The weight on his back registered. His backpack.

"Couple of well-placed explosions should do the trick. Distract everyone, and perform an extraction." He figured it was a pretty good idea.

"I want alternative options from everyone." Zander did this often, asking for a plan of action from each team member. Sometimes they doubled up and came up with something together. Usually they chose which was the right course of action as a team, even if Zander had the final say.

One of the men circling Lucia kicked out at her leg. She didn't respond, continuing to move so she kept the men in sight at the same time.

In the years since he'd known her, someone had trained Lucia to defend herself. Likely the DEA. How effective that would be in this situation, he didn't know.

Not with that many men around her. Tormenting her. Prolonging it before they attacked. Exhausting her, wearing her down. They were like a pack of wolves with a deer. However it came about, dinner was already on the table.

Andre wanted to just get down there right away. He said to Badger, "I'm going for a closer look."

At least with that, his friend wasn't liable to realize what he was actually up to.

"Dude—"

Andre didn't hang around for the rest of what Badger was going to say. He sprinted as fast as he could, going downhill and making sure he retained his footing. Falling was the last thing he needed to do.

Moving too fast because he was desperate to get to her was also a bad idea. He'd wind up breaking his leg.

Andre took a few long breaths and pushed each one out slowly as he ran. Pacing his inhale and exhale with every other footfall.

He found an overturned tree, probably downed by a storm. It should have been cut down and cleared out, but someone had left it here. Good for him, it acted as a cover blind so he could watch from a closer vantage point. Through gates that were guarded by two men with AR-15s.

"Andre, come back." That was Zander, probably wanting an update as to his location and the situation.

He lifted the binoculars and looked again. One of the men punched Lucia in the side of her head. She collapsed to her knees, pushed off the ground, and swung out with her leg. Even dazed she managed to kick the man's thigh.

She spun and did the same to the other man.

Definitely trained.

But the men gathered around her. Not just two, but the rest of them as well.

"She's not going to last long." In the same situation, none of them would.

Andre had to get in there fast.

He swung the backpack from his shoulders and emptied it of anything that wouldn't solidify the story he was going to tell. Then he pulled his knife and cut a slit in his T-shirt, before he tore the sleeves away to reveal the tattoos on the outside of both arms.

The last thing he did was remove the earbud and leave it with the stuff tucked behind the tree.

Then he emerged from behind the cover blind and headed for the gate as though he'd simply strode out of the woods to the compound.

"What do you want?" One of the men approached, rifle pointed at him, but kept a safe distance.

Andre lifted both hands. "I wanna join."

5

———

Two hands shoved at Lucia's back. She stumbled, but didn't go down. The one in front pulled back his arm and balled his fist. With enough warning, Lucia bobbed out of the way. She spun around straight into another fist that hammered her skull.

She blinked and found herself on her hands and knees. A lump rose in her throat, and she swallowed it back down. She tried to take a breath, pretending this was just like any other training session she'd been in.

Lucia rocked back on the balls of her feet and pushed up. As she did, she ducked to the side and turned out of their reach. Out from between them, but that put her back to the crowd that'd gathered around them. It put her combatants in front of her. She was still surrounded, completely cut off from anything and anyone.

Beyond rescue.

When she was on the ground, all alone, her dad had taught her how to stand. He'd drilled into her the ability to take care of herself. He had been completely healthy—or so they'd thought—right up until he clutched his chest and keeled over.

She had chosen a life for herself, and it had broken his heart.

Lucia shifted her feet on the dirt, keeping in motion. She

would be ready to react instead of remaining static. All the while her head swam, and the little breakfast she'd eaten threatened to come back up. Though, given how it had tasted, that wasn't entirely surprising.

The circle tightened.

She assessed each man. She didn't see any weapons among the ones crowded around her. That at least was good. She figured this was payback for the injury she'd dished out to one of their friends. A way to get recompense. Or maybe they did this to every new person they got among them. Particularly the women.

Who knew? Maybe she was just unique in this, because they'd seen something in her. Because she'd had the gall to stab one of them with the handle of a plastic spoon.

Lucia didn't plan on being here long enough to find out everyone's story. She figured she didn't need to know when it was the court's job to sift through everything and bring charges. All she needed was enough evidence and a way to escape. She had to do her job here. This wasn't personal, and they had no idea who she was.

Maybe they would find out, but that would be after she left —probably on some kind of delivery truck leaving the compound.

The idea of stowing away on a vehicle headed out gave her strength and a rush of energy. She could do this. She could get out of here in one piece, clutching what she needed in her hand as she escaped.

She straightened her shoulders.

Two men from behind grabbed her arms. They held her steady while a man approached her front.

A knot tightened in her stomach.

"This is hardly fair. Holding me still." They had to see, somewhere deep down where their souls were supposed to be, that this was completely wrong. But trying to fight for some semblance of reason in a situation like this wasn't going to do her any good.

She could either defend herself physically, or she couldn't. They didn't care what words she used. Only that they either got whatever they wanted, or made the statement they were planning on making by trying to beat her black and blue.

It didn't matter. She was going to escape no matter what.

He said nothing, just pulled back his arm and smashed his fist into her stomach.

Air exploded from her mouth. She felt like she'd been hit by a baseball bat.

Guess that's why they chose him.

She pulled at the men grasping her arms, wriggling and trying to get free while the one in front of her hammered her breastbone this time.

She hissed out a breath, catching the cry before it escaped. She was pretty sure he had cracked something.

"Don't mess her up too bad. She'll be useless for days." A practical man. She could almost appreciate that from the guy on her right.

The one to her left had bad breath.

Another punch came, this time at her stomach. She turned her head a second before he slammed his fist into her abdomen and saw movement between two of the spectators.

She spotted a dark head of hair on a tall man. One she knew extremely well. Some might even say, intimately.

She blinked. The man punched her again.

No, she hadn't seen him. That was insane.

There was no way Andre was here.

Her husband? After all this time? That was ridiculous.

"She's delirious."

"She's about to pass out, and we're supposed…"

"…meeting."

The voices swam around her head. They were still holding her up on her feet, but now her chin touched her chest and she couldn't lift it back upright. Couldn't see what they were going to do next.

How could Andre have possibly gotten here so fast?

The man kicked this time, slamming his boot into her thigh. Pain exploded in her femur. Her leg collapsed. Her knee slammed on the dirt to jar even more pain up to her hip.

She hadn't seen him. Andre wasn't here, because that was impossible. It was just a figment of her imagination, conjuring him at the moment she most needed the one person in the world she would actually trust while she was unable to help herself.

Another kick at the other leg. She toppled to the side and hit the dirt. More than one person kicked her. Stomach. Back. The back of her thighs. Someone stomped on her shin, and another on her wrist. Pain blasted, white hot.

"That's enough," a stern voice spoke. "What did I say about putting her out of commission, huh?"

She wanted it to be Andre, but of course it wasn't. It didn't matter how much she needed the impossible to happen right now, the truth remained. Impossible did not become possible just because she might wish differently.

Her father had taught her to rely on reality. On measured expectations that kept her from being disappointed.

Andre didn't want to be in her life. He didn't care about her, didn't love her. Not after she had pushed him away. Everything that was between them, she had destroyed it. Ended the way she had ended her father's life the night she told him she'd married Andre.

Steady hands lifted her from the ground, pulling her up into a man's arms. She could tell it was a man by the feel of his chest against her. She could smell dirt from the arena, and blood.

"Try not to talk." He took long strides, barely jostling her. But it still hurt. More than she cared to admit to herself.

"I saw Andre." She muttered the words more to herself than to him. He didn't know who she was talking about. Lucia tried to grasp a single thought floating around in her mind, swimming like her whole head seemed to be doing inside her skull.

"Maybe I didn't see him." She spoke as he ascended some steps. "I probably just made it up."

Now after trying not to think about him for years, she apparently couldn't help herself. Probably because despite the work she'd put into being an independent woman, down deep inside she wanted a pair of strong arms wrapped around her. Someone to tell her everything was going to be all right.

And bring her a cupcake.

A chocolate one, with a mountain of frosting.

"I prefer vanilla." The man reached down, still carrying her in his arms, and opened the door.

She tried to look up at his face and saw only blond hair. She couldn't make out his features while her eyes refused to focus. "Who are you?"

He shook his head.

"You're different than the rest of them."

He deposited her on a thin mattress on a cot in the corner. "I'm not your friend. But I might be your ally."

ANDRE HEADED down the hallway inside the main building where he'd seen her carried, moving with purpose but not as quickly as he would if he was on the clock. Never mind that every second passed by with an urgency he'd never felt. It didn't take a genius to realize it was because this situation involved Lucia.

The mission was more important than how he felt about any of this. Whether or not he was in denial about her.

He turned the corner at the end.

Two hands grabbed him and slammed him against the wall.

Andre pulled a hidden blade and pressed it against his assailant's throat.

"What, no hello?"

He lifted his gaze and nearly sliced the man across the throat just for the principle of it. He hissed, "Isaac."

"Guess I don't need to ask how you feel about me now." He narrowed his eyes and flashed a calculating gaze Andre had only ever seen him use with the target. Never with a fellow teammate. "What are you doing here?"

"I needed to use the bathroom." At least, that was the story he'd given those guys who wanted to take him straight to Burgess. He figured he'd have Lucia and be halfway to the nearest exit before they realized he was making a run for it.

He also had zero intention of explaining all that to Isaac, the teammate who had betrayed them just a few weeks ago. Or precisely what his relationship was with her.

Isaac said, "You know I mean, what are you doing in this compound?"

Andre said nothing.

"At least lower the knife. I'm getting nervous with you holding that thing so close to my throat."

He lowered the knife and turned his wrist so the end of the handle faced Isaac. Then he punched the hilt into his former friend's shoulder. Isaac folded almost double.

Andre lowered the knife, and Isaac groaned louder than Andre figured he would've if anyone not a member of Zander's team had been around. "I'm guessing the gunshot wound hasn't quite healed yet."

Isaac straightened. "I know I deserved that. But don't you even want to know why I had to walk away?"

"No." Andre shook his head.

Deep down he might want an answer. Enough to consider shaking his friend and demanding one. But Isaac dealt in information the way most people struck a bargain, or just straight up blackmailed one another. He was a former CIA agent. They were masters of manipulation.

If Isaac even told him the truth, how did he know it was the whole truth? It was better if Andre and the boys found out for themselves, through their own channels.

So far they had nothing. But it wasn't the point, was it? They would get to the bottom eventually.

Isaac took a step back. "She's in her room. Second on the right."

"Just like that?"

"As much as you think otherwise, I'm not your enemy, Andre."

"You aren't my friend either."

Isaac shook his head. "So that's how it's going to be?"

Andre shrugged. "It's how you made it. I didn't have anything to do with it."

Isaac worked his mouth back and forth.

Even when they'd been on that airplane together, working to protect the former president from an assassination attempt, Isaac hadn't been forthcoming about what was going on. Beyond that business about it being "her" fault. Because "she" made him do it. But that was it.

Anytime Andre tried to get further answers from him, Isaac shut the conversation down and told him to focus on saving the former president.

Then he'd simply disappeared. After the airplane exploded and Isaac had been stabbed, he'd just been…gone.

Ted had followed up with the ambulance that had taken Isaac from the scene. But the journey had been intercepted before the ambulance could reach the hospital.

The EMT they'd spoken to told them the vehicle had been disabled and men in black fatigues and masks, carrying guns, had hit them with stun guns. When they'd awoken, Isaac was gone. Even the blood on the sheets of the stretcher. The empty packets they'd used to staunch the bleeding.

Any trace he had been there at all had been taken with him.

As though Isaac didn't exist.

Or, someone wanted it to be impossible to prove he was ever there.

"I know who she is to you. Maybe not right away when I saw her, but I know now." Isaac looked almost sad.

Andre knew he had heartbreak in his past. But then again, so did everyone in the world. Life wasn't about saving yourself from being hurt. It was about how you got back up and kept going when those things inevitably happened.

He said, "Did you tell Burgess?"

Isaac shook his head. "That doesn't mean you shouldn't be careful. He's got his eye on her."

"What is he up to?" If Andre could take some useful intel back to Zander, that would help.

Isaac studied him for a second. Then he pulled something out of his pocket and held it out. A flash drive. "I was going to hand this off to—that doesn't matter. It's better off in your hands, anyway."

"Are you the reason the feds' hands are tied coming in here?"

"I can't talk about it."

Andre wanted to roll his eyes. But he'd dealt enough with top-secret missions to know that brushing off the seriousness didn't help anyone.

If Isaac was still in the employ of the government, something that would surprise all of Andre's teammates to hear, then it was likely at a high enough level they could dictate operations to the feds.

Andre had no interest in getting in the middle of a turf war. He also didn't like anyone except Zander telling him what to do —and that rarely happened anyway. At least not stuff Andre wouldn't have happily chosen anyway.

He figured he was a grown enough man that was unlikely to change.

Take this situation, for example.

"I should get going." Andre didn't like taking even this much time to talk to Isaac. He held up the flash drive. "You're going to get in trouble for giving me this?"

"Probably." Isaac shrugged. "But when I bring them Burgess, or everything they need to take him down, I'll be forgiven."

"Okay." Andre couldn't imagine living that kind of life. "Now tell me how to get out of here."

Isaac grinned. "You're not gonna like this."

Andre nearly groaned. "Just tell me how to get her away from this place."

Isaac nodded, a knowing expression on his face. "She doesn't need to be here. Whoever she is."

Andre knew he was trying to fish for information, but didn't say anything about Lucia's job.

Isaac held out a cell phone this time, along with a gun. "Both are untraceable. Have Zander pick you up."

"From where?"

Isaac pointed down the hall. "Take the exit door at the end. Go left, hug the wall so you're out of view of the cameras. Fifteen steps, and you go diagonal at a thirty-degree angle. No one will see you until you reach the fence. Climb over into the wilderness area."

The one Ted had told them was full of animals?

Isaac continued, "There's a clearing in the middle. Have Zander pick you up."

The helicopter. That was going to make a serious commotion everyone in the entire compound would see. "And when they catch up to us before we take off?"

Isaac leaned in a fraction. "Make sure they don't." Then he wandered off, ambling down the hallway as though he was out for a stroll.

Andre jimmied the lock until he could bump it open. He rushed to the bed and saw she was unconscious. The wave of relief had him collapsing to one knee. He brushed the hair back from her face and winced.

When she regained consciousness, she was going to be in a lot of discomfort.

He lifted her into his arms. She let out a small moan and curled against him, tucking her forehead in his neck.

Andre carried her from the room and headed to the exit door Isaac had told him about. Mostly just trying not to think about how it felt having her in his arms again. It had been so long. He should think about her like any other woman in the world who needed saving. How he felt about her should be irrelevant.

As he pushed outside, the fire alarm sounded. Commotion exploded from every corner of the compound.

"Isaac."

His friend hadn't settled for one betrayal. He had done it all over again.

Several buildings away, the door flung open. A stream of women ran out, all headed for the wilderness area. He didn't have much information about this place other than what Ted had managed to pull together in a short amount of time.

But apparently tonight was the night they were all going to escape.

6

———————

Lucia slapped his shoulder. She might not be firing on all cylinders, but she had the wherewithal to know what she wanted. "Put me down."

The man carrying her grunted.

She knew who he was. She just didn't want to admit it to herself, or even begin to think about why he was here.

He wasn't some construction of her imagination, brought to her when she was admittedly at a low point. But hadn't she been in worse situations than captive at a scary compound? Maybe, or maybe not, she couldn't exactly remember right now. But she was pretty sure her life wasn't exactly cupcakes and roses.

I prefer vanilla.

The other man's voice rolled through her memories. Just a flash of remembrance, then it was gone. She had no idea who that had been, the blond guy, but it wasn't the man carrying her now because he smelled completely different. And utterly familiar.

Fifteen years. There was no way he should smell the same. But, given his essence had nothing to do with cologne, and everything to do with the fact he was one hundred fifty percent *man*, maybe it wasn't so strange.

"Just a little farther."

She tried to look around. He had one arm under her knees and one behind her back. Carrying her like a bride over a threshold. Something, incidentally, he had *not* done.

"You're going to throw your back out carrying me like this."

He grunted again. "Don't worry about it."

Part of that one hundred fifty percent man included a healthy ability to push himself beyond what was reasonable, just to prove a point. Or maybe it was just a guy thing, being so stubborn you refused to listen to what was reasonable.

He ducked his head and carried her under a low-hanging branch before he settled her on the ground behind the cover of a huge bush. No one would be able to see her here.

"Are they following us?" She glanced around, brushing hair back from her face. When she looked back at him, he was staring at her. "What?"

"That's it?" He shrugged. "Just 'what'?"

She really didn't want to get into this. "Maybe it's not the time for an emotional reunion, or an awkward one. Whichever it's going to be, we should probably get out of this situation first. Right?"

"I forgot you're grumpy when you wake up."

Now that she was sitting, and not distracted by the fact she was being carried by a man who'd always wanted to be her hero, the reality of her situation crept back in. Aches and pains made themselves known. Her cheek throbbed, and her head hurt more than that. Her chest, and abdomen. Breathing hurt, but she blew out an exhale anyway. It was that or pass out—which sounded pretty good right now.

"You okay?"

Lucia drew her right arm to her front and ignored the way her stomach rolled. If she didn't pay attention to controlling her pain level, she was going to be sick.

"We need to get you out of here." He shifted and pulled out

a phone, which was when she realized he had a gun in his other hand.

"Where did you get those?"

A dark expression crossed his face, and she figured he was about to tell her that he didn't want to talk about it. He'd always been good at keeping things close to the vest. Holding his emotions in check by stuffing them down inside him and carrying on regardless. Distracting himself, the way she did. But with him it was more like he never wanted to feel those emotions, rather than the way she held off and processed it later when she was in a safe place.

He'd been her safe place for a long time. During those days when she believed there was a future for her that was good.

Now she knew life wasn't like that at all.

For people like her, there was no happily ever after.

If there was, then her dad would never have died. Andre would never have left.

He tapped the screen of the phone and lifted it to his ear. After a second he said, "Yeah, it's me." He paused. "It worked, didn't it? And there's more. Isaac is in there." Another pause. "That is the point, when I know Ted is already tracing this call and you guys are mobilizing to come and pick up Lucia and me." He rolled his eyes. "I know, it's *Lucia and I*. Whatever, just come and get us."

He hung up the phone and stowed it in his back pocket.

"Mind if I use that?" She wouldn't mind checking in with her boss right now. After all, she had no idea what'd happened to her team, or her backup.

The mental image of each one being hit by a bullet, after which they fell to the ground and bled out, rolled through her mind. The weight of their deaths pressed on her along with exhaustion. She started to slump to the side, but Andre's strong arms were there. His hands held her from smashing her face on the dirt.

"Careful."

She glanced away so he didn't see the sheen of tears in her eyes. It was dark, so he probably wouldn't be able to anyway. But why admit she was in more than just physical pain? He might be here, rescuing her, but that didn't mean… "Why are you here?"

"You'd rather I'd left you there to get beat on some more, and then whatever they planned to do with you after?"

She wanted to wince, but moving her face that much was going to hurt. "I'm supposed to say thank you for getting me out of there and ruining our biggest shot at actually closing this case? I'm a DEA agent now."

How much of the investigation could be salvaged, she wasn't exactly sure. Not when agents were dead and it wouldn't be long before her cover was blown. She doubted they'd have been able to get someone in to make contact with her, or get her a way to contact her new handler.

If there was even anyone left on the task force to be her contact while she was undercover in Burgess's compound.

Assuming she'd have survived being undercover.

"I know what you do."

She heard the implication in his words—that maybe she had no idea what he did.

"What I don't know is why I was still listed as your next of kin?"

She swallowed. "You are my next of kin, aren't you?"

He'd refused to give her divorce when she'd asked for one— maybe more like screamed it at him—and she'd figured that meant he was entitled to live up to his responsibilities.

The fact there was no one else in the world to be her emergency contact except a couple of friends she saw every few months when she finally got around to checking in with them wasn't exactly the point, was it?

She'd wanted out, so he'd given her what she wanted. It had only taken fifteen years for her to prove her point in person rather than knowing she'd proved it was the right decision and him having zero idea.

In the distance, a woman screamed.

Lucia shifted around to look, but couldn't see anything in the dense trees. A shiver rolled through her. It was chilly out, pitch-black except in the direction where the compound was and the shimmer of moonlight coming from the clear sky.

Her eyes were starting to adjust to the dark. But she still couldn't make out much.

Andre said, "We should keep moving until I get the call for where they'll pick us up."

"So we can get out, and whoever that was out there who screamed can be recaptured?" She understood what was happening here. Someone else had escaped as well. "Did they come after us?" Maybe that was how another woman ended up in danger.

"It won't be long before Burgess mobilizes the entire community, Lucia. We've gotta move."

That wasn't exactly an answer to her question. She figured if they hadn't set out after her and Andre yet, then they would soon. She tried to wrack her brain and figure out what was going on. "We're in the wilderness part of the compound, right?"

He shook his head. "What does that have to do with anything?"

"Only that they'll be running this recapture mission a whole lot differently than you think."

She'd seen the posters and overheard conversations enough to know more than Andre did, apparently.

She continued, "This place is full of animals, and he lets them run wild. That's the whole point. He doesn't interfere with nature. Burgess left this place to be overrun by plants and animals. Who knows what's out here?"

"It's just a forest. In America. So there are a few mountain lions…and maybe a bear?"

Lucia pointed out the ground beside her. "Then what is that?"

ANDRE STARED at the print impression in the dirt. *Not good.* "Some kind of cat." She didn't need to know if he was worried. Which he wasn't. Yet.

"Yeah, and it's a really big cat." She pushed herself up to standing, unable to hide the wince.

He wanted to reach out a hand and assist her, but Lucia had never been one to admit she needed help. Even when it was plainly obvious to anyone and everyone in view that she could use it. If she was just going to be stubborn, then he would keep things as professional as she wanted them.

He glanced around. "We're going the opposite direction from the compound. Let's get as much distance from those guys as possible. We have the means to defend ourselves if necessary. Zander should be calling back in a minute. He's probably fired up the chopper by now, and is on his way."

"Who is Zander?"

He set off, assuming she would follow him. "My boss."

The one who had just reamed him for going in by himself and blowing the whole recon mission. As if that'd ever been what it was—at least not as far as he was concerned. Andre couldn't pinpoint the exact moment he'd decided he would go in and get her out, but it had likely been early on. Maybe from the very moment he heard she'd been captured.

He glanced back over his shoulder and saw she was keeping up with him. "I'm sorry about your friends. Your colleagues."

She sniffed and glanced to the side. "It's part of the job, which I'm sure you know from being in the military."

And yet, both of them had survived until now. Fifteen years and they were here. Together again.

He refused to believe that was some kind of ultimate design.

Otherwise, they would never have separated for this long in the first place. Who had ever heard of anyone getting married and then being estranged for fifteen years with no contact, and no resolution to the relationship? He'd known exactly why she asked for a divorce. That day when she'd screamed at him, facing off with him on the college quad. Her dad had just died. He'd shown up with a bandage on the side of his head, and she'd freaked.

Shut down and refused to entertain anything. Not even a conversation with him. Kind of like the way she always talked herself out of dealing with things. Refusing to admit in the moment that it was happening, so she could process it later.

He checked over his shoulder to see if she was currently willing to embrace reality. She kept her wary eyes scanning around them. Looking for what?

He'd clocked the animal prints early on. Three sets, all different-sized big cats. She didn't even like going to the zoo. At any other time he figured she'd probably have agreed with Burgess about the need for wild things to be wild. But only because Lucia didn't like the way people sometimes treated animals rather than just leaving them alone.

Maybe these days she knew what Andre did—that man treated man in much the same way, often for lousy reasons.

The roar of a big cat echoed through the trees.

A woman screamed, the sound coming from a different direction than it had before. It was followed by several wolves calling to one another.

He heard Lucia shift behind him, then her hand brushed against his. Her fingers threaded between his. Andre held onto her as much as he knew she wanted to hold onto him, but would never allow herself to. Because he felt exactly the same way.

Just because he was a man didn't mean he was immune to fear. He didn't want to meet one of these big cats that apparently roamed the woods out here. Where Burgess had gotten them from, Andre could only guess. But it didn't matter because they were here—between Andre and Lucia, and their way out.

"Come on." He gave her hand a slight squeeze, but didn't let go.

"Do you have a rendezvous point?" She kept her voice low as he had done.

"No, but Isaac said to come this way." Another betrayal? He didn't want to believe that about his friend. But what was the point in denying reality when Isaac had ditched their team, gone off on his own, and now he was here. For what?

Andre didn't understand the guy at all. It seemed as though he'd wanted to say more than he did. But there was no time to wait around for an explanation, even if Isaac had anything that would even remotely convince Andre he'd done the right thing. Or at least something that made any sense at all. Because from where he was sitting, it didn't compute in the least.

"We just need to get to the clearing," Andre said.

"Because you have a chopper?" Before he could respond, she continued, "Does that mean you aren't with the army anymore?"

He got them moving at a decent clip, watching because she wouldn't admit when she needed to take a break. He had to keep an eye on her pace and her gait. The last thing they needed was for her to injure herself.

He could carry her some more. He just preferred not to have to do it. Especially if he came across Burgess or any of his guys, or one of the wild animals out here. Equally as dangerous, just in different ways.

A gunshot echoed in the distance.

He flinched, only realizing afterward that he had. At the same time he realized Lucia had huddled against his back. He glanced down at her. She looked up at him.

"Sorry." She took a half step back, still tethered to him by their clasped hands. "We should keep moving."

As though she was in charge here, instead of the one being

rescued. "You know," he said as they walked, "your boss called me pretty quickly. I don't think they'd have notified any random next of kin as fast as they told me. Why do you think that is?"

"How am I supposed to know?" She frowned. "There was a sniper at the scene who shot Lydell's guy. But we didn't have one. So who was it?"

"I thought maybe you'd told them about me." After all, it was pretty handy for her that he just happened to be highly trained in protection. Negotiation. Hostage retrieval. Personal security. Explosives were his favorite. "The guy who came to see me pretty much handed me this mission."

"Who?"

"Assistant Director Campbell."

"He's alive?" She blinked. "He gave you the rescue mission? I figured since I was in Burgess's compound, I might as well find the evidence we need to take him down."

"He told me someone else had a mission here. A man inside." Isaac. It had to be. "No one was coming to get you because they didn't have the authorization to blow that other mission by storming the gates and pulling you out."

She was quiet for long enough he glanced back.

"You okay?"

She shrugged. "Why wouldn't I be? They only would've left me here like one of those other women and never pulled me out."

"I don't know about never, but their hands were tied when they told me. Which made me wonder if they knew what I do for a living."

"And what is that?"

She really had no idea? He'd been following her career for the last fifteen years. He'd read the case files of some of her biggest missions and knew the time she'd been reprimanded for disobeying orders. Lately it'd been murky what she was up to—apparently working with a task force.

Ted had drawn the line at hacking into her therapist files

and getting copies of their session notes. Andre might not have liked that decision, but he also didn't admit it to anyone else. Ted was probably right that it was over the line. But Andre had seen too much evil to worry about scruples when a person's protection was at stake.

A shuffle in front of them, probably twenty feet away, made him halt his stride.

Lucia caught herself before she slammed into his back. As much as he might have wanted her pressed up against him at one point in his life, that was a long time ago now. He didn't need to be distracted on a mission. Normally not a problem, he was having to fight to concentrate right now.

"What is it?" she whispered in the dark.

Andre had to redouble his efforts not to be distracted by her. "Stay here."

She didn't like it, but he gave her the phone and crept forward. Toward the noise.

As he approached, he could make out a figure in the moonlight. A woman, and she was definitely pregnant given the rounded belly on her slim body. Malnourished. Treated the way the rest of them were by Burgess, and his men.

She rose with a blade in one hand. On the ground was a lump big enough to be an animal. A wolf, panther, or cougar.

He was about to ask her if she needed help when she spun and threw the knife at him.

7

———

Lucia heard a grunt, then the sound of a heavy body hitting the forest floor. She hurried over and saw a woman flee through the trees.

"Whoa." Andre.

Lucia caught herself before she tripped over him, but momentum had her stumbling to the ground. "Andre?"

She used the flashlight on the phone to illuminate where he lay on the ground. The second she saw the knife, she gasped and reached for it.

"Nope." He shoved her hands away.

"Shouldn't we get it out?" He'd been stabbed. In his shoulder, outside in the fleshy part of his upper arm. "That looks nasty. What happened?"

"She probably thought I was one of Burgess's men. She just threw it and ran off." He gritted his teeth and shifted the flashlight away from his face. "Turn that off. It'll kill your night vision."

"I needed to see you."

"And now you have."

She tapped the phone screen to turn the light off.

He reached for the blade handle, sucked in a breath, and

pulled it out.

"Andre." She wanted to say so much more, but couldn't choose which expression to use first. Probably all of them she'd have to repent over. Even if this situation was extreme, and maybe warranted that kind of reaction. "What are we going to do?" It wasn't a question she needed an answer to. She just had to say *something*.

Being a federal agent was a lot like what she imagined being in the military was like. They saw enough to need an outlet, and often that came in the form of cussing and off-color jokes. Like a pressure cooker release valve, they had to let go of the stress and tension that built up after seeing the horrible things people did to each other. Or to children. Those were always the worst.

There were perpetrators who cared nothing for other people's feelings. Or the pain they caused. The truly wicked people in the world. Like Burgess, who saw others as less than human and treated them as such.

"You take the knife." He held it out to her.

Lucia flinched away from it. "I'm not touching that. It stabbed you."

"Well, I'm not giving you the gun. So if you want something to defend yourself, this is what we have."

Before she could argue, the phone started to ring in her hand. He reached for it but Lucia backed up and stood before he could grab it. She swiped the screen and answered. "Special Agent DeSoto."

"Does that mean Andre's incapacitated?" The man's voice was solid, and strong. It rang with authority but also a hint of worry. For his friend, or simply a coworker?

"Well, he's been stabbed, but I wouldn't call that incapacitated." The phone buzzed in her hand. She lowered and looked at the screen. "A location to meet you?"

"What do you mean stabbed?"

This guy was really worried about Andre. He seemed to

genuinely care about a man who was her husband. Who she hardly knew.

Andre had an entire life that was nothing to do with her. Friends. Maybe even a family, although legally they were still married. She'd been asked out. Work took up so much of her time there wasn't much point entertaining the idea of dating, even if she had been available. Which she wasn't.

Had he done the same? They'd always been similar in their outlook enough to not have to wonder what the other was thinking, or how they would feel about something. Once in a while they surprised each other. But the fact was they were compatible. Being with him had been the easiest thing in her life, something she'd yearned for.

Even after it was gone—because she'd destroyed all of it.

The way she did with everything.

"Special Agent DeSoto." He barked her name.

She'd drifted off into her thoughts. And now that she tried to speak again, the words got stuck in her throat.

Then Andre was there, in front of her. He touched her hand gently. "Give me the phone, Luce."

She allowed him to take it from her, and he lifted it to his ear. "It's me. I'm fine enough to get out of here."

He reached for her, as though intending to tug her to his side. Maybe hug her, or at least hold her. Lucia stumbled away. She didn't look at him, but knew what would be on his face. Confusion. Maybe even that hurt she'd seen in the quad outside her dorm.

"Copy that. We'll be there."

Lucia walked far enough away she found a dead animal on the grass. Cut up so that the wounds had caused the animal to bleed out and die. She stared at it and tears filled her eyes. Before she knew it, they were rolling down her face, and she had to gasp for her next breath.

"Hey." The soft tone of his voice undid her. The last thing she wanted to do was lose it.

She shook her head and backed up again. Both hands raised. Palms facing him. "No. Don't."

"It's okay to not be okay."

"Not right now it isn't. Burgess and his guys are probably going to hunt us through these woods. We'll get eaten by some wild animal, or something else will happen." *I'll lose you all over again.*

The unspoken words hung between them.

Andre just stared at her.

It was easier to believe he thought she was an idiot, or some overly emotional wimp. Even though she knew he would never think that about her. At least, the man he had been at eighteen wouldn't have. She didn't know who he was now.

Lucia swiped the tears from her face. "Let's get moving. This day has been long enough."

She needed a hot bath and a good cry, and she would lay there until the water was cold. Then she would sleep in a cold bed. Until the dreams of this place resurged, or she saw her father clutch his chest and collapse to the floor.

"Fine." He took her hand again, regardless of the fact she didn't need him to do that. It was probably more about making sure she stuck with him. "They'll be here in two minutes anyway."

He moved with efficiency, even with the knife wound in his shoulder. They might know each other, but this was a job and he was going to do it to the best of his ability.

She knew that much about him hadn't changed. Something she'd always appreciated. Whether it was a favor for a friend, or finishing a science project. Andre was the kind of guy who could push away everything else and focus on the task at hand.

He'd even taught her how to do it—which was how they'd ended up married. She'd done it anyway, even knowing her dad would hit the roof. Fully aware it would suck when Andre was gone at boot camp while she lived her life at home with her dad. Waiting for him to come home.

They'd hardly known what life would bring, and yet they'd made that world changing decision to tie themselves together.

She knew what it meant now. The enormity of the action they'd taken. After all, she'd been living with the consequences of it for the last fifteen years.

More tears rolled down her cheeks, and she swept them away as well even though her wrist hurt. He kept moving, despite the fact he had a bleeding wound in his shoulder. It was like he didn't even notice. Or he knew it wasn't going to slow them down. *He* wasn't going to slow them down.

She wanted to barf her wrist hurt so bad.

She needed to think the same as he did and not give in to everything trying to crash down on her right now. But reality crept in the dark like a demon waiting to pounce. Soon enough she was going to be devoured.

And how would she ever come back from that?

Her colleagues were dead. Burgess was free to do whatever he wanted. Andre was here, and the past had returned in full force because he was right in front of her. His presence was strong enough it swallowed up nearly everything until she couldn't focus on anything but him.

The way it had always been.

Maybe, right now, that was actually a good thing.

"Hello?" The voice was tentative, and female.

"It's okay." Despite Andre's words, the woman, whoever she was, whimpered.

Lucia called out, "He's a friend of mine. It's really okay. He's here to help me." If she needed help then she had to believe Andre wasn't one of Burgess's men. "Do you need help as well?"

"I don't know what to do."

Lucia headed for the sound of the voice and found a woman crouched beside a tree.

"I saw a bunch of wolves. I think they smelled me."

Lucia held out her free hand. "Come on. You can stick with us, and we'll all get out of here together."

She shook her head, matted strands of her dark hair swishing from side to side. "There's a fence. We won't be able to climb out. There's nowhere for any of us to go."

Lucia frowned. "How many of us are out here?" Solidarity might induce this woman to trust her. But she had no idea.

"All of us got out."

"How many?" Andre's voice made the woman flinch.

"Maybe ten?"

ANDRE KEPT his reaction to himself, not wanting either of the women to see the truth of his thoughts. The chopper was coming. But it wasn't nearly big enough to hold that many people if this woman was right, and there were ten out here in the woods trying to escape Burgess.

If they were going to get everyone out, that meant more than one trip.

The second group trying to escape would likely run up against Burgess and his men. Unless they could get far enough into this wilderness that Burgess wouldn't have time to catch up. It was a long shot, but all the chance they had.

What he wouldn't give for his backpack right then, but he'd left all the good stuff out and Burgess's guys had taken the rest. A few well-placed explosive charges, and some other weapons for them to defend themselves, and they'd have had a lot better chance to get out of here.

"Come on." He motioned for the woman to stand and held his hand out just in case she wanted to take it. He didn't think she was likely to accept his help given the way she'd probably been treated. And it turned out he was right. "We need to get moving."

"He's right." Lucia nodded. "Being sitting ducks is putting us in more danger than we need to be."

She was right enough about that. Andre might've escaped from some crazy situations in the last few years, but this was probably going to turn out to be one of the worst. Maybe even top five of all time.

"Which direction are we going?" Lucia gave the woman a reassuring smile.

Andre pointed north. "Zander said there's a clearing big enough for the helicopter to land, but it's about a mile or so from here." More like two, but these ladies didn't need to know that. It wasn't lying in a situation like this. Not if it motivated them to keep moving.

"You guys have a helicopter?" The woman gasped, moving as though her side hurt.

"It's a long story. But it's a way out of here."

Andre was glad Lucia took point on responding to that. And her answer was a good one.

He didn't want it getting back to Burgess in any way exactly who he or Lucia were. Not that he much cared if their covers were blown considering they'd likely be long gone soon enough. And he didn't exactly plan on coming back and trying to get friendly with the man again. Lucia probably felt the same way, though she seemed intent on completing the "mission." Still, there was a slight possibility they might need Burgess to be unaware of her ties to the DEA and the particulars of his career.

Another wolf howled. He saw Lucia shiver out the corner of his eye. The woman with them whimpered, and he honestly couldn't have said he felt any differently about this.

There was more than one wolf out there.

Maybe even more than one pack.

If they got any closer, things could get seriously messy. Andre slid the clip from the gun and confirmed how many bullets he had remaining before he shoved it back in. There was a limit to the amount of damage he could do with this weapon.

"How's your shoulder?"

He glanced over at Lucia. "Not the worst injury I've ever had. And it isn't even going to slow us down."

This wasn't an attempt to prove himself as being overly macho. She probably thought it was, but in time she would get to know him again well enough to understand what he was capable of.

Or, they would go their separate ways again and she wouldn't.

There was no time for him to figure out whether he wanted her in his life anymore, or not. He figured his actions said enough.

He wasn't willing to let anything happen to her if he could do something about it. But that didn't mean he needed to go about rekindling what had been between them a long time ago. They'd been barely adults, and hardly able to understand the depth of everything that had gone on between them.

This woman was a whole lot different than the one he'd known years ago. He could honestly say she intrigued him enough he might want her to stick around. At least so they could talk.

There had to be a reason why life had flung them into each other's paths again. Maybe it was about teaming up to take down Burgess. Or maybe God had a far more personal idea in mind.

Andre hadn't often wondered what the Creator wanted, or had planned. Now that Zander was working on rekindling his faith, Andre had considered the idea as well. And if this was God's doing, he was willing to see it through.

Assuming they got out of here alive.

A woman screamed. He realized there were two of them, huddled together.

Lucia said, "It's okay. We're getting out of here. Come with us."

One of the women gasped. "He's one of them. I know it."

Lucia shook her head. "He came in to get me out. He's one of the good guys."

Andre tried to look unassuming, or unthreatening. He figured it was almost pointless because he looked in the mirror on a daily basis and knew exactly what people's impression of him was. Even with a nasty wound in his shoulder he looked like he fit in with Burgess's guys.

Some disgruntled army vet. Probably unstable.

There were plenty of reasons to be unstable. He just chose to channel his frustration into working for Zander.

He knew trying to come across as nonthreatening didn't work when the women glanced at him, then back at Lucia. It was clear they didn't believe her that he was good.

She said, "We're getting out of here. Come with us, or don't."

Lucia and the first woman they'd found followed him as he led the way north, avoiding the trail that meandered between the trees. Not a trail carved in the terrain by man. No, this was a trail made by animals.

What kinds, he couldn't tell in the dark. And what did it matter? They were getting out of here either way.

The two women whispered behind them, keeping pace well enough.

Five of them. Potentially another five or six somewhere out here in these woods.

A couple of gunshots were squeezed off in rapid succession, and a woman screamed.

"Stay quiet!" he ordered them.

It was far enough away he took note of the direction but didn't worry they would be in the path of a bullet anytime soon.

One of the women whimpered, and he was glad they didn't

scream outright. Whoever had been found by the shooter was beyond their help now.

Two more shots rang out.

One of the women said something. Lucia shifted behind him as they walked, one hand around his elbow. "We can't. We're too far away, and we don't have enough firepower to hold off Burgess's men. I'm sorry, but we just need to keep moving so they don't catch up to *us*."

Andre saw something out the corner of his eye. A shift, and some movement. He halted.

The women stopped behind him and whispered some more to each other.

"Hush."

Anyone else, and he'd have used an entirely different phrase. But he knew he had to go gentle with these women. Unless it was a matter of life or death, he was going to speak and act with care like a real man. Not one of those monsters Burgess called friends.

"What is it?" Lucia whispered the question beside his ear.

He pushed away the sensation of what it meant to have her with him again. The last thing he needed right now was this attraction trying to set all his nerve endings on fire. Probably it was just adrenaline, and the fact he was bleeding down his arm quite badly now. Not because he still felt anything for her.

Those feelings were long gone.

A woman ran across the path in front of them. Andre started to call out when she glanced back over her shoulder and screamed.

Two big wolves jumped from the grass and took her down while she screamed and writhed.

One of the women brushed past him. He grabbed her, arms around her waist, before he realized it was Lucia.

"We have to help her." She kept her voice to a whisper.

The others whimpered, but did a decent job remaining quiet.

"There's nothing we can do." He said it as much to her as he did to the others. "The situation you're in is horrible. But we're going to get out of it. Understand?"

The two women behind him nodded. Lucia did the same, her face against his good shoulder.

The last woman was nowhere to be found.

8

———

Lucia's whole body shivered, tucked up against Andre. The warmth coming off him was almost too much against the chill in the air. As soon as he let go, she was going to be even colder than she'd been before he held onto her.

Yes, she'd rushed toward that woman being killed by the wolves. Purely on instinct she'd moved to help. To protect.

But only because if anything happened to Lucia, there wasn't anyone to mourn the loss.

Maybe that made her push boundaries she shouldn't otherwise push. At least, her team leader thought so. That was what every review of her performance said. And it was the topic of every counseling session she had when they finally moved away from the psychologist attempting to get her to talk about either Andre, or her father.

Lucia didn't need anyone in her life. There were plenty of people in the world who had no one. She was the one who stood in the gap for those people, and she made sure they had somebody who would help them. That was why she'd joined the DEA.

To protect the ones who had no one else.

These days her mission was something different, but it boiled down to her original "why."

Andre dragged her to the side, off the path and into the trees. Away from where the wolves decimated that woman's body.

All that woman had been trying to do was get to safety. Now she was food, the way the rest of them might be if they didn't get out of here fast enough.

She glanced at the other women. "Come on." She kept her voice quiet, the whisper still carrying in the night air. "Quickly. Come on."

Andre gave her a squeeze, almost a thank-you for helping him with these women. He didn't need to do that, but she appreciated it anyway.

They made their way quickly through the trees. She felt prickly bushes tug at the legs of her pants, the slashes and swipes of thorns. Given all her other injuries, and the state of these women, it didn't mean much. It wasn't going to slow her down.

Overhead, helicopter rotors whomped in the distance.

The relief at hearing that sound was akin to how she felt realizing it was Andre carrying her. As much as she didn't want him in her life, least of all now and in a situation like this, she was still glad he was here. Of all the people in the world, he was the one she didn't have to pretend with, or explain herself to. They'd always understood each other.

The fact he had access to backup that involved a helicopter was a seriously good thing. Whoever he was. Probably some kind of fed like her.

Why else would the assistant director have contacted him? Someone in the mix knew who he was. Knew he'd drop what he was doing and come to get her.

He'd gotten here faster than she thought her team would. If they were still alive. Campbell had survived, but what about the others?

"It's not much farther." He ushered them all along.

This huddle of women seemed to be as scared of him as they were of the animals and the men chasing them. Lucia wasn't, because she knew Andre. But she also hadn't been in the compound as long as these women had been, or subjected to who knew what.

Lucia had worked with trafficking victims before, and the work that organizations who rescued those victims did was an unimaginable good in the world.

Those who were trained to walk a victim through healing and recovery back to a life they could be proud of and happy with were the real heroes as far as she was concerned. Lucia's job taking down the bad guys and making sure they were put in prison wasn't something she discounted. It was her role. That of protector and warrior. But those who stayed beside the victims for years? They were the ones who brought restoration.

Moonlight washed the clearing up ahead in white light.

Then a flash, and the sound of an ordinance whizzed in the sky.

"That isn't good."

Andre squeezed her hand. "I see it." He seemed to not be overly worried about it, though. Or that was simply his attempt at not freaking the rest of them out. Maybe inside, he was as terrified as her. "Hold up here for a second."

She walked the girls to a spot hidden beside a couple of trees that had grown close together. There wasn't much in terms of coverage, and with the animals roaming about they didn't need to be worried so much about being seen. Not when their scents were now all over this area.

"Stay still. And quiet." She touched the two on the outside of the huddle on the shoulder and gave them a small squeeze.

Andre had his phone out. The dim glow lit the side of his face and the frown on his brows. "Yeah, I saw it. You guys good?" He paused, still frowning. "Copy that." He hung up and glanced at her. "They'll be here in a second, and then we're going to have to make a run for it."

She thought there was more to this, but didn't want to ask with the other women in earshot.

Lucia watched as the helicopter came closer. No more ordinances blew through the sky. She hadn't even been aware that Burgess had access to that kind of firepower. If the person shooting it was trained, another shot might net them a success. It could bring that helicopter to the ground.

She bit the inside of her lip and watched the helicopter approach from outside the fence of the wildlife area. "The animals are going to move away from that noise, because they'll be scared of it."

She didn't know if she was asking a question or making a statement. Did it matter? They would either get out of here, or they wouldn't. She would either have the chance to talk to Andre about real, personal things.

Or she would not.

What she wanted, or how she felt, usually didn't factor into the truth or the reality of the world she lived in. There had always been that dissonance between what was inside her and everything else.

Only Andre had ever cracked the shell. The time they'd spent together, even if they'd both been teens, were some of the richest in her life. When she felt at peace and completely understood.

But then it'd all been destroyed. There hadn't been enough to sustain what life threw at them when reality finally crashed in.

The helicopter descended to the ground, far slower than she wanted it to move. The sound was deafening. Wind whipped at her hair and clothes.

"Let's go." Andre shoved them in front of him and ran behind. The rearguard, he held his gun and glanced around to make sure no one tried to attack them before they got to safety.

The animals might run away, but Burgess and his men were

closing in fast. They had likely already taken down at least one of the women. She didn't want them to get these, as well.

As they ran, two more women emerged from the tree line to their right. Both screamed as they crossed the grass of the clearing toward the helicopter. Two of Lucia's group started to run faster. Another woman emerged on the left—a pregnant woman, running with both hands on her distended belly.

A man followed the two on the right. Andre swung his gun around and fired a single shot. It wouldn't be enough to take the man down, even if he had hit him square in the chest. She knew how impossible that was when running.

But someone in the helicopter leaned out with an AR-15 and squeezed off a steady stream of bullets that forced the man to the ground. It seemed as though whoever Andre ran with wasn't taking any chances.

Lucia bit back the whimper of relief that wanted to escape her lips.

The first two women climbed onto the helicopter.

Two men helped the pregnant woman get on, one smaller and one broad-shouldered. Both wore black clothing and beanies pulled low over their ears, disguising their hair. Another man was behind them, the one with the AR-15. The fourth flew the helicopter.

Men who rushed here to save Andre.

She reached the helicopter. Two more women rushed up to them. Lucia helped them on, realizing the chopper was quickly filling up.

Before she could yell to the nearest person if that was going to be a problem, Andre said, "We aren't going to fit." He turned and fired off two shots. "Go, Lucia."

"Get in." The words were spoken by the guy in front of her, accented though she couldn't tell the origin. Maybe British? He was kind of…captivating. If she was willing to admit that to herself.

"Lucia." Andre shoved at her shoulder.

A shot slammed into the side of the helicopter. Everyone flinched and ducked their heads. She spotted a gun under the bench seat, slid it out, and turned.

She braced her feet and squeezed off a shot, then another. Then more. All this in less than a second so the shooter didn't even have time to fire before she put three bullets in his chest. He dropped to the ground.

Someone yelled, "I think I just fell in love," over the sound of the helicopter rotors.

More men emerged from the trees.

There was no point trying to get on.

"Come on." She grabbed the back of Andre's shirt and tugged him toward the front of the helicopter.

The chopper was going to have trouble lifting off with the extra weight. As much as she wanted to jump aboard, there were some guys down on the ground she would like to have a chat with now that she was fully armed.

Adding a bulletproof vest would be better, but she would take what she could get.

* * *

I THINK I just fell in love.

Judah's words rang in Andre's head. When they had a conversation later, Andre was going to explain the reality of that man developing a crush on his wife.

Not that he'd been much of a husband. Or her, in her own role toward him. But that wasn't the point. The bro code was clear.

The helicopter lifted off, whipping his shirt to his armpits as it rose overhead. He wanted to provide cover fire, but they were exposed out here. "Go."

Lucia was already running ahead of him.

He followed her, disappointed he couldn't take a moment to admire the spectacular view. Not with this many armed men by the trees.

A shot hit the helicopter, and someone yelped.

When Andre turned to look, Judah leaned out of the open chopper door and opened fire. On the other side, Eas rappelled down a rope with a weapon of his own and shot at the men trying to hamper their escape.

Why Lucia didn't want to get on that chopper, he wasn't able to say. But he was pretty sure he had an idea. Now that she had a weapon, she felt strong. Like liquid courage, but it came in the form of solid metal in your hands. The ability to rain vengeance down upon those who had wronged you.

He still preferred explosive ordinance.

The chopper swung overhead. In front of Lucia a huge duffel bag landed on the ground with a thump.

She slowed.

Andre called out, "I'll get it."

He didn't need her trying to lift it when the thing would only slow her down. As it was, Andre had to brace himself. He switched the gun to his injured arm and used his momentum to swing the duffel up behind him onto his shoulder.

They broke through the trees, and he followed to where she'd found a good cover spot. Not right by the clearing, but farther in where it would take time for these men to find them.

She crouched.

"You okay?" he asked.

Lucia checked the weapon was loaded and ready to fire. "Would you ask me that if I was one of your guys?"

"Yeah, but I would expect a sarcastic answer."

He could see that surprised her. They weren't some uptight military unit anymore—even though he'd served with two of the members of his current team in Delta Force. Now they were more of a ragtag band of glorified mercenaries. Their government contracts were on hiatus because they'd discovered the former director of the Department of Clandestine Service had been running his own side business making money selling weapons, among other things.

Now the government wanted to save face, and there was some Goody Two-shoes in the role that none of them had ever met. But Zander's woman was determined to win the guy over. She was a class act, and Andre figured if anyone could do it then it was Nora—even if the former director was her father.

He looked up at the chopper and saw it swing low again. All the alarms on the dashboard would be blaring in Zander's face. And still, his team leader would be cool and calm. Perfectly in control while everyone on board screamed inwardly for their lives, convinced they were going to die any second.

The rope Eas hung onto swung under the helicopter.

The aircraft dipped again, and when it rose there was no one on the rope. "Eas."

"What was that?"

"One of my guys is down here as well." A second later, Andre got a text from Ted with a new location. They had to get over the fence, and there was a vehicle waiting for them.

He texted back.

Easier said than done.

The reply text he got back consisted of only emojis, so he didn't bother replying to that. Ted knew he was busy right now.

Andre unzipped the duffel. "We should move quickly."

Before they did that, he pulled out a vest for himself and one for Lucia. They pulled them on over their shirts, and he dug again in the bag, just in case there was a sweater or jacket for her. But there wasn't.

What he did find was a couple of grenades and several extra clips for the gun he held. He tucked a second gun—a tranquilizer—in the back of his waistband just in case they ran into any animals. And extra clips for everything into his pockets. Flashlight. He handed that to Lucia, saying, "Only turn it on when I tell you to."

"I'm not going to give away our position. I have training. Probably as much as you do."

He wasn't going to argue with her that there was no way she did. It wasn't arrogance—it was simply a cataloging of all he was capable of. And he knew exactly what he could handle and when he needed a team to back him up. Or a bomb.

Sure, she was a highly capable federal agent. But she hadn't gone through special forces training. Or years in service, followed by Zander's special training, which he didn't even want to get started thinking about.

His phone buzzed again. A text from Zander.

Clear.

So they were good, and Zander was getting the occupants of the helicopter to safety—which included the woman who had stabbed him. He wasn't going to fault a pregnant woman who had to fight against an animal in the wild for her life. Not even when she then turned around and threw the knife at him. She'd been in kill-or-be-killed mode.

He was glad the woman and her child would be safe now, where she could get the help she needed. Not with Burgess anymore.

Andre swung the duffel over his shoulder again.

"Need me to carry anything?"

Given her injuries, the answer was definitely no. He figured her wrist might be broken, but if he said no to her, she would get mad and tell him how capable she was. So he said, "Maybe later."

She wasn't convinced, but there was no time for her to argue and they both knew it.

They headed for the fence line at a run, racing to get out. No way was Andre going to allow these guys to get their hands on Lucia. Not after what he'd seen them do to her. Isaac could take care of himself. He'd made his choice, and it wasn't their team so Andre owed him nothing.

He spotted movement to his right.

Andre let out a couple of short whistles. No reply. Whoever —or whatever—was there, it wasn't Eas.

Animal? Or man?

"Cut left."

The terrain was about to steepen. They could head around the elevation and hopefully skirt out of scent range. Avoid detection. Though, if they kept crashing through the brush, whoever hunted them only needed to listen for the noise. Now that the chopper had gone, his hearing seemed heightened.

Andre shifted the gun in his hand and let his instincts lead him. There was definitely something out there.

He swapped the weapon to his off hand and slid the tranq gun from the back of his waistband.

He barely got it raised before the animal burst from behind a bush and leaped toward Lucia. Andre squeezed the trigger.

The animal's body jerked, and it fell to the ground with a pained cry.

She started to slow down.

"Go!"

Lucia didn't waste much time before she picked up her pace again. He could tell she wasn't okay, her injuries hurting her more than she wanted to admit. She should be on the chopper. Not out here, and for what? He used the irritation to fuel his resolve. To energize his muscles into running faster than he would've without it. He pushed away the nagging pain in his shoulder, the same way he knew Lucia pushed aside whatever she felt in her middle and her wrist.

He'd seen her beaten.

She wasn't fine.

A gunshot cracked.

Fire hit his thigh a split second after he recognized the sound. Andre stumbled and fell to his knees, pushed off his good foot, and kept going.

He slammed into Lucia's back. She'd stopped. He held on, winding his arms around her waist so they could hold each other up while his thigh screamed. Some instinct he wasn't aware of had flared. He knew why when he realized the number of men who approached.

His vision blurred them, but there were several.

"She's ours." The man's voice rang out. "You've cost us enough tonight. Now you pay. In blood."

9

———

Lucia's mind washed with the image of blood. Her coworkers falling to the ground. Andre, the same. He'd been shot, but barely missed a beat. It seemed he was more concerned with her being safe than with the fact his leg now had a bullet hole through it.

Surrounded by these men and their guns, she hugged the weapon to her front. Andre's arm around her. He had a weapon as well.

What else could they use?

It wouldn't be possible to shoot their way out of this. They were outmanned and outgunned.

"Drop your weapons."

It wasn't Burgess talking, but one of his men. The number two guy, Lydell, had been shot in front of her. Yet another death she'd seen on this longest day of her life—or couple of days. She'd lost all track of time at this point. Who was this?

The man motioned with his gun toward Andre. "Back away from her. She comes with us."

Lucia shuddered. Andre's arm around her tightened, because he'd felt the fear roll through her. That was the last thing she wanted, to be some overwhelmed liability who would slow him down and make the situation worse. She had to push aside the fear and get control.

There was no point arguing with these men. Or yelling that she would never go with them willingly. It wasn't like they were going to listen to her.

Before he could speak again, a high-pitched whistle sounded somewhere from their right.

She felt the tiny shift in Andre's muscles, pressed against her back. Something was about to happen. But the men around them didn't notice.

Andre tapped her side, just above her hip. She shook her head very slightly. If she went left, the way he'd indicated, that would put her on the same side as his gun. She couldn't get in the way of his free hand like that. Not that she thought he would shoot her, but it made things more complicated if he had to shift his weapon to his uninjured side to not risk shooting her.

Lucia moved her gun to the side. As though she were going to drop it to the ground. Instead, she put it in Andre's free hand.

"I said drop—"

The man's head jerked at the force of a bullet, the sound almost simultaneous.

Andre moved both arms and started firing at the same time Lucia turned around and pressed her front to his. She reached around to pull the tranq gun from his waistband. It was the only way to not interfere with his arms and the aim he had—the way he squeezed both triggers at the same time, holding both guns outstretched.

He started to turn, taking out more guys.

Whoever was in the trees shot as well. Each of the men around them fell to the ground. A couple got off shots, and Lucia flinched against Andre's front. She lifted to the balls of her feet and peered over his shoulder. She spotted a man behind him and aimed a tranquilizer dart at his chest.

He looked down at the projectile sticking in the front of his shirt.

Andre's chest heaved.

It took her a second to realize the shooting had stopped. The dart gun fell from her fingers onto the ground, and she grasped Andre's shirt to keep from falling. Then remembered he had a gunshot wound in his leg.

She let go with a jerk and nearly fell backward.

He wound his arms around her again, and she felt the butt of a gun pressed against her hip.

"Don't." She shook her head. He shouldn't hold her up. She needed to take her weight off him, not become some burden he had to bear.

Andre frowned down at her and stepped back. "Sorry."

She nearly stumbled, but managed to turn and survey the area around them. All of these guys were dead or breathing their last. She recognized that horrible death rattle that came seconds before a person lost their life.

She hated that sound.

A man emerged from between two trees, a mask covering his face. Lucia grasped for one of Andre's guns. Didn't he know this man was here?

"Hey."

She realized then that she'd screamed. Andre dropped one of the guns and hugged her to him again. "It's okay. He's a friend."

She shook her head.

"You need to trust me right now. It's okay."

Lucia wasn't sure it would ever be okay again.

His face came close to hers. His breath warm on her face. "Look at me. You need to breathe, Luce."

They still had to get out of here. There were more men on the way. Surely the gun battle had drawn much too much attention to them, and it would be only minutes before Burgess and more of his guys showed up.

"You aren't calming down."

"Because I don't want to." She huffed out a breath, trying to act like she had an attitude and not like she wanted to continue freaking out. Losing it wasn't going to help them. Even if it was tempting to let go and fall into the whirlpool of uncontrollable emotions.

"There you are."

"Yes. You're so observant." She even lifted her chin. "I am, in fact, right here. Where we're stuck with a bunch of wild animals, guys with more guns than us, and you've been shot in the leg. Plus the helicopter just left us here—"

"You could have gotten on it. And my leg was just grazed."

"—and now we have to climb over the fence. Or dig our way out with our bare hands."

"You guys really are married," the masked man said.

He still freaked her out. She knew she'd reacted to this stranger's presence when Andre squeezed her shoulder. She ignored his attempt to get her attention and asked him, "Who are you?"

"Doesn't matter. Because I was never here." The masked man turned and walked off, flicking two fingers over his shoulder as he went.

"I know," Andre called out to him.

"He's just leaving us here?"

"Good idea." Andre stowed the pistol in his waistband. "Keep getting angry about stuff. It'll help you stay alert."

"What you mean is it will keep me from freaking out." She waited for him to hand over a gun, but he didn't. "Give me my weapon back."

He looked down at the AR-15 in his hands. "No, I don't think I'm going to." He motioned to one of the dead men with his chin. "Get that guy's gun."

"Because you need two?"

"You think I only have two?" Andre swept up the duffel and slung it over his shoulder. "Let's get moving."

He started to walk away. Lucia stared at his back while she stood in the middle of a circle of dead guys. When would the wolf pack roaming this forest show up? Probably soon enough, considering the scent of blood was now on the breeze.

That thought was enough to shake her out of her—she didn't know what it was. Exhaustion, maybe. Among a whole bunch of other things she didn't want to dwell on. Brushing it off wasn't going to work.

He was almost to the trees. A few steps, and he would be out of sight.

And then what?

It had been years since Lucia willingly followed Andre. Caught up in his wake, pulled along by the sheer force of his presence in her life. These days she had her own life. Did she need to get sucked into his once again?

If she'd been in an entirely different mood, Lucia might believe that coming full circle like this—back to Andre being in her life—was destiny. The path she was always supposed to have been on. Generally she fell into that mood on sleepless nights when she watched too many romantic movies back to back. Nostalgia wasn't a good look on her. All it did was remind her that even if life had some grand plan for her to follow, she'd definitely gone and messed that up.

Murderers didn't deserve a happily ever after.

"Let's go, DeSoto."

Now there was an instruction she could follow. All that musing about destiny? Andre was only here because it was something he and his friends—or his teammates and coworkers, whatever they were—did for work.

Which meant to him she was only a job.

Lucia had to remember that this was a professional operation for him, just the way it was for her. Why mess things up by making it personal? That had never worked for them before. Why would it suddenly start to work now?

She grabbed up the nearest gun, checked it was loaded and ready to fire with a decent amount of bullets still, and headed after him. Whoever his colleague was didn't matter. Why Andre was here didn't matter.

What mattered was avenging her dead coworkers

Getting justice.

Taking down Burgess before he could enact whatever plan he had in the works.

ANDRE WAS ACHINGLY aware of two things—the wound from the bullet on the outside of his thigh, and the fact Lucia was behind him. She'd been through so much in the last few hours that he hadn't been surprised she was on the verge of freaking out. No one would blame her for that. In terms of high-stress situations, this had been a bad one.

He'd seen guys in the military lose it for far less. He was proud of her for holding it together, and glad he could help at that moment.

Now the stubbornness and the fire she had in her kept her going. The way his innate stubbornness meant he could push aside the pain in his leg, or at least acknowledge it with each step and still manage to keep going. It wasn't a foolproof plan. Sooner or later his leg would give out and he wouldn't be able to walk anymore. But the truth he'd learned in his years of active service was that a single bullet usually didn't incapacitate a person. The human body could withstand a serious amount of damage before the person even succumbed to unconsciousness. Let alone death.

It was incredibly messy business. But it was the life he'd chosen for himself. One Lucia hadn't wanted any part of. And yet, here she was doing the job of a federal agent.

He wanted to be proud of her about that as well. But just the idea of speaking those words left a bitter taste in his mouth.

"How far is it?"

He glanced over his shoulder. "To the fence?"

"If that's where we're going." She shrugged, still trudging along behind him. "Though, it's electrified right?"

"Probably. If he doesn't want the animals to get out."

"So we can't climb over it."

Andre nodded. "There's some stuff in the duffel bag that'll make a hole in the fence."

They would wind up drawing attention to themselves yet again. But if they moved fast enough and made a break for it on the other side of the fence, then they had a chance at getting out of there.

His phone buzzed in his pocket, so he dug it out. His foot clipped a rock, and he gritted his teeth, unable to hide how much that hurt. Walking was one thing. Jarring his wound by stumbling was going to be a whole other ballgame.

Andre answered the phone, not bothering to hide his pain and frustration. "What?"

"Now I regret wanting to call and ask if you need help."

"Ted." Andre pushed out a breath. "Needing help and wanting it are two different things."

"It is with you guys."

"Sorry I barked at you," Andre said.

"Like I'm not used to it? It's literally how you guys communicate with each other." Ted chuckled to himself. "Considering my dad was passive-aggressive and manipulative, you guys being straight talkers who don't hold back isn't exactly a chore to deal with."

"Glad we could help."

Andre knew Ted had another job in the corporate world, and the stories he told about those clients made everyone's eyebrows rise. Talk about adult-sized babies. At least the team didn't whine about every little thing. "Speaking of help, Lucia would like to know how much farther it is to the fence if you wouldn't mind."

"Let me run your GPS on this number." Ted shuffled on the other end of the line, a rustling against Andre's ear. Then he said, "It won't be mega accurate, but I can give you a rough estimate."

"I thought you had satellite imagery, like thermal?"

He heard Lucia make a noise in her throat behind him. Not a scared noise, but more like a question she didn't voice. The woman was getting a crash course in him and his team. If she wanted to know *everything*, she was going to have to sign a nondisclosure agreement.

Ted said, "I lost access to the satellite. It started fritzing, then shut off. And if I hack in again, then someone will notice."

"So you can't tell me if anyone is approaching?"

"Sorry, but you'll have to use your special ops senses for that."

"I have our friend out here with me." Andre still wasn't sure if Eas had fallen from the helicopter, or simply jumped so they could fly away faster with less weight.

The guy always wanted to be in the thick of the fight. Something that gave Andre pause, as it was a little too close for comfort to him having a straight-up death wish.

Anytime Andre tried to ask him why he was like that, Eas always changed the subject.

Kind of like the way Badger avoided anything personal right now.

Andre hadn't exactly been a happy camper, churned up about Isaac's betrayal of their team.

Zander was the only one who was happy, given his new relationship. But then there was Judah, who never seemed to want to give up his laissez-faire outlook on the world.

The team needed to sit down and hash out their issues. Or go play a few rounds of paintball and work out their stress.

"Near as I can figure," Ted said, "it's about half a mile, give or take, to the fence."

Andre glanced over his shoulder. "Half a mile, or thereabouts." Lucia had stopped. He backtracked to her. "What is it?"

She pointed at the ground. "That spider is ginormous."

"That's just a hole in the ground."

"Yeah, and it belongs to a wolf spider. A huge one."

On the other end of the phone, he could hear Ted chuckle. "Tell her I agree with her about spiders."

Andre wasn't about to encourage her. "Let's just get out of here, okay?"

She nodded, and they set off again.

Still carrying the duffel bag and the AR-15, he had her go in front of him as he held the phone to his ear. His leg hurt enough he wanted to say it out loud, just to acknowledge it. But neither Ted nor Lucia needed to know how much it hurt.

Or precisely how adorable he thought Lucia was. The woman went up against gunmen and didn't seem to lose it over packs of rabid wolves. But one spider and she was ready to run screaming.

He figured he would go to his grave—hopefully in many years, when he was wrinkly and gray—still not understanding women.

Andre sighed. He had to push one foot in front of the other with each step. He was mad enough about the injury that he wanted to blow something up right now. That would make him feel better, though it wouldn't take away the pain in his leg.

Maybe he should get Lucia out, then backtrack and blow up Burgess's house. Or the entire compound. After he pulled the fire alarm—if they had one. All those people would scurry out of their houses, and he could watch the buildings explode into smithereens.

"I see it." Lucia picked up her pace.

Andre would've done the same if his legs were capable of moving faster. He had to maintain this steady pace, or he'd lose his step and wind up falling on his face. Or landing on the duffel bag and setting off an explosive.

Then it wouldn't matter if he learned to understand women.

"...the plan."

He realized Ted was talking to him. "What's that?"

"I was asking if you had a plan to take down the fence. But you should know you're getting a text message."

Andre had asked him once how Ted knew that. The explanation had been about as technical as Ted pointing out when a smart watch started to ring a second before the phone did, and Andre still didn't understand it. Though, he didn't need the technical details. Ted was used to having to dumb down how smart he was.

Andre already knew he was a C-average student and an army grunt—Lucia's father's description of him—so it didn't bother him that Ted was smarter. If God wanted him to be more intelligent than he was, then He'd have made Andre smarter. But He'd given him exactly what he needed.

The strength to walk away from Lucia while his heart was breaking.

"I'm going to blow the fence. How far away is the vehicle?" The phone beeped against his ear.

Ted said, "The text is a video. And it depends on your blast radius."

"Grenade?" Andre stared at the fence, assessing.

"As long as you don't do anything fun. Because I can't see it." Ted paused a second. "I'm sending this video to Zander."

Andre lowered the phone, pulled up the text and played the video hoping it wasn't long. It was time to get out of here.

Lucia shifted close to his side and looked at the phone with him.

Burgess was in the middle of speaking. "…found. Dead or alive, you bring them to me. I don't care what condition they're in. Find out who that chopper belongs to. All of them are *dead*."

She shifted, nervousness moving through her body language.

Before he could say anything, the video shifted to the wall beyond Burgess, and the image zoomed in.

"Is that a map?" she asked.

Andre studied the image. "Looks like a bunch of houses, or buildings."

Overlaid on it was a red circle.

Lucia gasped. "He's going to target a neighborhood?"

Andre's stomach clenched. "Let's get out of here. Then we can figure it out." He put two fingers in his mouth and whistled for Eas. It was time to go.

His friend met them at the fence, evidently done covering them from a hidden spot. Eas said nothing, but motioned to the tall, electrified construction with a nod of his head. As though Andre could simply set a charge and blow something like this.

Lucia shifted closer to him. "How are we going to get out?"

"I'm going to set a charge and blow it." Andre crouched and rummaged one-handed in the duffel. He started to pull out supplies. "Hold this."

Eas grasped the block of C4.

"Here." Andre handed a detonator.

"Uh…"

"Two minutes and we're out."

Lucia said, "You might want to make that faster."

Eas turned away, palming a knife.

Andre made it in ninety seconds. They were crouched behind a downed tree outside the blast radius when the sky exploded in a rush of orange and heat.

He tugged Lucia to her feet, ignoring the sting in his leg wound. "Let's go."

10

Lucia opened her eyes as the car came to a stop. She sucked in a panicked breath before realizing they were outside a house and no longer at the compound.

She blinked. It was no longer night. The sun had risen, and everything that had happened before she passed out asleep rushed back at her.

Andre had set an explosive charge and blown out a section of the fence. After that, they'd run for the vehicle parked on the other side. The second man, the one wearing that mask, had opened the back door of the car for Andre and had him lay down. Not wanting to be stuck in the back seat with the man she was married to, Lucia had climbed in the front passenger side.

Instead of making conversation with the masked guy, she closed her eyes.

Now that she was awake again, she glanced over at him. He turned off the car and got out. Still wearing that mask. He didn't even glance at her when he slammed the door shut and walked away from the vehicle toward the house they were parked in front of.

The place was a huge ranch-style house surrounded by pine trees and a hill. She couldn't even tell where they were, but it felt protected by the landscape all around them. "Are we still in Wyoming?"

"Does it matter?"

She didn't say anything else because he sounded like he was in serious pain. Or he didn't trust her enough to tell her. Or it was both.

She figured at least this was somewhere that got a decent amount of rain so it was all a deep green. Not a desert climate. That was about all she could tell before the front door of the house opened and several people ran out. Three guys, and a woman. All of them ran to the back seat of the car.

Andre grunted. "Great."

The blonde woman stopped by Lucia's door and reached for the handle. The big man who stood close to her intervened before she could open the door.

Lucia pulled the handle herself and shoved the door open. Both of them had to step back while the other two men, ones she recognized from the helicopter, opened the back and hauled out Andre.

"Easy, fellas. I'm not a sack of potatoes."

The black guy grinned a handsome smile. "Could've fooled me." He frowned down at Andre's leg. "I thought you guys said it was bad?"

"Bad enough." Andre didn't argue much though. It almost seemed like the black guy was trying to bring levity to the situation. But the man she had married wasn't amused.

Ugh. Lucia needed to stop thinking of him that way. It wasn't helping anything to keep reminding herself that they were tied together. The years since she last saw him had been spent purposely *not* thinking about him or their connection.

Now it seemed to be the only thing her mind wanted to dwell on.

"Hello." The blonde smiled, though it appeared tentative. As though she wasn't quite sure how to be in the situation.

The big man beside her slid an arm around her shoulders and tugged her to his side.

"I'm Nora. This is Zander." She pointed at the two men helping Andre. "Those are Badger…and Judah."

The two men each lifted a hand at her. Andre didn't even glance over, though it appeared he was attempting to walk and not give away exactly how much his leg hurt. Lucia needed to draw attention from him if he wanted to accomplish that. These people, especially the man whose name was Zander, were entirely too astute given the way their attention landed on her.

If she even tried to pull one over on these people, Zander was the one who would figure it out.

"I'm DEA Special Agent Lucia DeSoto."

The one named Badger called back over his shoulder. "Yeah. Andre's *wife*."

She hardly knew how to respond to that. It was one thing for her to have to deal with it. These people meant something to Andre, and she didn't know what that was or how it worked between them. Her coworkers didn't even know her history.

She could tell by the way Badger and Judah assisted Andre to the house. Walking and ribbing him at the same time. As though trying to distract him while they helped.

Zander twisted and called out to Andre, "As soon as you're done with the doc, we need to talk."

There was a slight shift in Andre's gait. She wasn't sure the rest of them even noticed. Except for Zander, who frowned.

Lucia said, "Is there some kind of problem?"

Nora smiled. The way she held her shoulders back and straight made Lucia want to stand up a little taller. To correct her posture the way this woman seemed to do naturally. "I'm sure if there is, it will be sorted out soon enough. And once Andre is done with the doctor, you could see Windermere as well. If you'd like to."

It was a gentle way of asking if she was okay. Lucia was glad the woman hadn't just asked her straight out. The way Andre did it was one thing. Anyone else? Lucia wasn't accustomed to admitting her weaknesses. It had been a long time since she was safe enough to tell anyone how she felt.

"Sure." Lucia glanced around. "I shouldn't stay long though, and I really need to check in with my team."

Now that she'd had a few hours of sleep, it made sense to get back to work and find out exactly what the damage was to the rest of her colleagues. Then they would figure out how to bring Burgess down for good.

"Let's go inside first."

Before Nora could say more, Zander offered, "I'll find you a clean phone, and you can make that call."

Nora nodded, as though the need for a clean phone was a perfectly normal occurrence.

Lucia's mind whirred around the idea they thought she might inadvertently give away their location—or their identities. "Who are you guys?"

Nora frowned. "Andre didn't tell you?"

Lucia shrugged. "There wasn't exactly time."

"If he'd wanted to tell you," Zander said, "then you would know. He'd have made the time."

They headed inside the house while Lucia tried to absorb that. The implication hung between them. There was a reason why Andre hadn't shared who he was now with her.

Zander held himself like a military-trained guy. A couple of the other men she'd seen here did the same. The masked one wasn't exactly readable.

She figured they were some kind of unit. A team. Maybe mercenaries? She'd have to do research later if she was going to find out. After all, she couldn't see how they'd give away the truth themselves.

Not to an unknown.

As a federal agent, she wasn't exactly accustomed to being the person that was distrusted in a situation. Being in Burgess's compound was the first time she'd ever gone undercover, such as it was. Now she was in this house with these people who weren't willing to share who they were with her? It almost felt like she was still on an operation.

Maybe talking to Andre would cure her of that. Probably it was only her overactive imagination. All her nerve endings remained on edge, along with the lingering adrenaline in her system. Maybe she would shake the feeling after another few hours of good sleep and some coffee.

Or maybe she wouldn't.

The feeling might grow, and she'd end up realizing they were the bad guys.

"You can rest in here, if you'd like." The room Nora led her into was small. A single twin bed and a small dresser. "The bathroom is down the hall, and I can find you some clothes to change into if you'd like to shower."

Lucia nodded. "That would be amazing. I feel like it's been days since I was clean."

Nora surveyed her face. "Some of your bruises look like they could use attention. You have a couple of cuts. And your arm?"

Lucia looked down. That was better than lifting her hand. Her right wrist was now twice the size of the other one. "It doesn't really hurt."

"Now that I've drawn your attention to it, probably it will." Nora winced. "Sorry about that."

Lucia shook her head. "Don't worry."

Unlike the rest of the guys, Nora gave off an air of honesty and graciousness. Lucia didn't see a lot of that in her life. This woman was welcoming her, a stranger.

Andre was here.

His teammates were…whatever they were.

"I really do need to use the phone." The sooner she could get back to reality, the better.

Nothing about this was familiar.

She had to remember that this wasn't, and would never be, her life.

ANDRE LOOKED at the dining table. "I'm not climbing up there."

"Well, the doctor needs to look at your leg."

Windermere, the team's doctor, strode past Judah. "Just take your pants off, and I'll have a look."

Andre didn't move. He glanced at Judah.

Badger smacked Judah on the outside of his shoulder. "Come on. He doesn't want us staring at his hairy legs."

Judah made some comment that was probably supposed to be funny, and the two wandered off toward the kitchen. Considering the whole place was open plan, that didn't give him much privacy.

"Make me a sandwich." Andre hoped it would involve bacon and a fried egg. "But no ketchup."

Judah always insisted on putting ketchup on his bacon. Why, Andre had no idea. Except that it might be another one of those weird British things.

Badger called back, "You'll get what you get."

Windermere shook his head.

Andre unbuckled his belt and slid his pants off. "I can get on the table if you want me to."

"Unless you're going to pass out and fall over, you can stand if you want." Windermere pulled up a chair and sat so Andre's thigh was at eye level.

The bullet had cut a slice on the outside of his left thigh. Thankfully—or not, depending on how he decided he was going to look at it—the tattoo on the front of his thigh remained intact. Judah had never seen the insignia, but Badger knew it was there, which was why he'd covered for Andre.

There was no reason why Judah needed to know that part of his service history with the army. Certain things were private. Badger and Zander knew on sight what the emblem meant, and they'd put together what he did before Delta Force. But for the rest of them, it would be a source of curiosity to see the insignia for a unit that was little more than a legend in military circles. Andre didn't want to answer any questions about the things he'd seen and done beyond Delta Force. That was enough.

"Hmm." The doctor felt around the wound with his gloved hands. "I'll get you some crutches."

"Just sew it up and stick me with a needle." As if he needed six weeks of recovery time.

Andre knew bullets were filthy. He would probably have a fever in a day or two, and feel like junk enough he might take a nap for once. Other than that, he didn't plan on this thing slowing him down much.

"Two needles. One for antibiotics, and the other with pain medicine in it."

"No—"

"Narcotics." The doctor sighed. "I got it."

After the fool Badger had made of himself while hopped up on pain meds after his knee surgery, Andre had no intention of getting loopy like that and doing the same. Though, he didn't even have Bitmojis on his phone, so it wasn't likely he would send them to everyone and completely embarrass himself.

Not to mention the fact Lucia was here. He needed to be on his A-game, and not medicated to deal with that situation. Not just fielding questions from the guys on the team. He had to traverse the minefield that was any interaction he had with her.

As much as he might want to avoid a conversation altogether, he wasn't sure that was going to be possible. And the idea she might leave the house before he even got to talk to her made him curl his fists at his sides.

"Don't tense up." Windermere stuck the needle in the skin around the bullet wound and sewed it up. "When I'm done, you need to clean up. Then you need a meal and a nap. If you want help to fall asleep, I can give you something."

Andre didn't even answer that. Not that it was a question. The doctor would probably put it in the needle anyway, regardless of what Andre thought. A team like theirs? They paid the doctor to make medical decisions. And sometimes that meant doing what was best for someone rather than listening to what they said.

Windermere was good at reading between the lines.

If Andre didn't actually want help falling asleep, he would have said so and Windermere would have listened. But he knew himself, and how hard it usually was to rest.

"Turn around so I can get to the back."

Andre said nothing. He turned his back on the doctor and stood still while Windermere sewed up the end of the graze at the back of his leg. He wanted to close his eyes and let his mind drift, but it would inevitably go back to Lucia and how it had felt having her close to him. Holding her.

It was a nice enough thought he could probably drift away standing on his feet, dreaming of the comfort that kind of intimacy brought. The peace that was found in sharing closeness with another person and had nothing to do with sex, but everything to do with contentment.

They'd been good at that once. Maybe they'd been good at both, but he knew which one they could use right now. The rest of it was far too complicated to broach the subject when he wasn't at a hundred percent capacity.

When he opened his eyes, he spotted Zander on the other side of the room.

Before his team leader could say anything, Andre said, "I was supposed to get a sandwich."

"The boys are on it."

He would much prefer Zander was the one to cook. He was far better at it than the rest of them, making sure they were not only fueled up more than adequately for missions and training sessions, but that they all actually enjoyed what they were eating. Home-cooked meals were better than days on days of takeout.

"You're drifting." Zander chuckled.

Andre shrugged one shoulder.

"No coffee," Windermere said. "He needs to rest."

Andre made a face the doctor couldn't see. Zander grinned.

Then Andre blinked, and the humor was gone from Zander's face, replaced by a hard stare. "You walked in there by yourself. Unarmed. No backup. No plan."

Andre stared back. Until the doctor started to poke at his shoulder.

Zander said, "What am I supposed to do with that?"

Andre stood there while the doc sewed the cut in his shoulder shut. Just a few stitches.

He gritted his teeth.

Finally, the doctor shifted. "I'm done."

Andre realized the doctor had wrapped a bandage around his leg. He wanted to leave, but only had the strength to brace himself on the table and plant his behind in the nearest chair.

"You need to be careful until it's healed." The doc took off his gloves. "Or you'll rip your stitches, and it'll start bleeding everywhere again."

The doctor drew out two needles and stabbed Andre with both, punching the ends into his leg and depressing the plungers while Andre gritted his teeth.

And then he was on his way to the door.

"Don't expect a tip."

The doctor glanced over his shoulder at the doorway. "Your sunny demeanor is gratitude enough."

Andre shifted his gaze to Zander. He wasn't going to defend himself because Zander had already known all about Lucia even before he walked into that compound by himself.

Zander walked over with his phone and showed Andre the picture on the screen. The guy in the photo wasn't anyone he knew, but he got why Zander showed it to him.

On screen the man's mustache curled over his lip and down both sides of his mouth to his chin.

Andre said, "Seriously?"

Judah called over from the kitchen. "Fair's fair."

As if that was the point.

Andre sighed. He was going to have to grow a nasty mustache for his transgression.

He bent and grabbed his pants from the floor, rummaging in the pocket. He held the flash drive out. "Isaac gave me this."

Zander strode over. "Can't say that's what I expected you to tell me."

"I'm not going to apologize for going after Lucia." They'd all seen what those men were doing to her. "If I'd waited?" Andre winced, unable to even consider what more of that hell she'd have gone through. "A few of those women were pregnant."

Zander nodded. "They're all at the hospital now. Safe, because you went in there and got Lucia out." His tone was clear. The mustache still stood.

Andre said, "Not all of them."

"Sometimes the best we can do has to be enough. Otherwise, you'll tear yourself in knots regretting what you weren't able to control."

Andre could only nod.

"You don't go anywhere unless I tell you to. Until the doc gives you the all clear to be back out with the team."

"You're benching me?"

"The injury aside?" Zander paused. "Judah and Eas are new at this. They don't have the dynamic you and I have, or even Badger for that matter. Everyone has to know there are consequences to going rogue." Zander waved the phone. "Fair's fair."

Andre leaned back in the chair and blew out a breath.

"After you've eaten and rested, I have some things for you to do."

"Scrub the shower and clean the toilet?" Those were favorite punishments given by their commanding officers in the military. Not that Andre had ever experienced screwing up and suffering the consequences of it. *Of course not.*

"As if you'd willingly do those anyway?" Zander left the room on that quip, taking the flash drive with him. Not offering to look at it with Andre. No, he was going to shut Andre out until the other guys realized he was serious about them following orders.

Andre knew his team leader. There would be a mission to take out Burgess. A man who ran a compound that held captives and had no regard for human life? No way was Zander going to let that fly.

Andre just had to figure out how he was going to get in on the action.

11

───────

Lucia toweled off her hair, fully dressed as she paced the bedroom. Her wrist hurt. But it didn't feel like it had the one time she'd broken it so she didn't think it was so bad. The rest of her just ached.

Whoever these people were she'd never met anyone like them. The woman, Nora, didn't exactly fit with the rest. This bunch of mercenary guys Andre had attached himself to.

The more she paced, the more outlandish scenarios her mind came up with as to who these people were that Andre ran with now.

She'd turned down the offer of their doctor taking a look at her. Nora had been nice enough, sweet even. But Lucia would rather be seen by an actual medical professional than whoever this Windermere man was.

Not that any of them here gave off a weird vibe, as if they couldn't be trusted. She just didn't get the sense she was completely safe.

Probably lingering from her recent experience.

Once she got back to work and what was left of her team went after Burgess, Lucia could help bring about his demise one way or another, and she'd feel a whole lot better.

Which was why she needed them to bring her that clean phone now. The sooner she checked in with her team, the better. She didn't even know right now who was dead or alive except for Campbell. She shuddered at the thought of the sheer number of funerals she was going to have to attend. The debriefings and explanations. All the reports she would have to write. The aftermath of a mission gone so horribly wrong.

The door eased open. Lucia lowered the towel, expecting Nora. Instead it was Andre who limped in. He wore a pair of basketball shorts, weighted down on one side by what looked like a cell phone. Clean T-shirt.

"Hey." She didn't know what else to say, so she finished drying her hair and put the towel over the back of the chair in the corner.

A million questions went through her mind in the split second in which he stared at her, as though the same thing were happening to him.

"Hey, yourself." His eyelids lowered in a blink that seemed sluggish.

She nearly smiled. That was what he'd used to say to her, more than a lifetime ago now. And yet, everything about him was familiar enough to birth an ache in her. But wanting what she couldn't—and shouldn't—have wasn't going to do her any favors.

And it wouldn't bring Burgess or any of his guys to justice.

"Getting settled in?" He glanced around the room.

Lucia shrugged one shoulder. "Nora is bringing me a phone so I can call into work."

He didn't offer her his phone, or respond to what she'd said in any way. He blinked, his eyes closing for almost a whole second before he opened them again.

"Are you okay? What did the doctor say about your leg?"

He leaned against the wall, easing the door closed behind him. "He just sewed me up."

"Oh. Good."

"Did he come and see you?"

"I don't need anything." She had found a bandage under the sink in the bathroom. Now that Andre was here, she retrieved it from the end table. She moved to him and held it out. "Will you wrap my wrist?"

Andre took the bandage and held her hand. "You probably need an X-ray."

"When the swelling goes down, I'll see my doctor." She wasn't sure what the damage was, but the fact she could still rotate her wrist reasonably well meant it couldn't be terrible. And all the bruises ached but she could move okay.

All she wanted was to shut herself away in a quiet place. Cry for longer than she had in the shower, where a few tears had slipped out despite the fact she tried to hold them back.

"They beat you. Badly."

Tears burned in her eyes. "I'm alive, aren't I?"

Lucia didn't want to be poked and prodded when she'd rather just get on with the operation. After that, she would take every day of her vacation time and find somewhere with no one else that she could spend enough days to read every book on her shelf that she hadn't gotten around to starting yet.

He wrapped the bandage around her wrist.

Lucia tried not to dwell too much on how it felt to have him touching her hand. Such a simple gesture, and yet it reminded her far too much of everything they'd shared.

He sighed, still leaning against the wall.

"You want to sit down?" She didn't exactly mean in here, but he crossed the room to the bed and eased to sit on the edge. Not the chair. The twin bed in this room, the one hardly big enough for his body. Not that she even contemplated the idea of sharing it with him. Even if they weren't married, that wasn't exactly a helpful place for them to go.

He blew out a long breath, his eyes closing for a second. Still sitting up.

"You look dead on your feet."

"Sitting now." The edge of a smile curled his lips for a second.

In the room, lit by the overhead light and the daylight streaming in through the blinds over the window, he seemed so much different than he had in the dark of night. In the woods with those wild animals. All the gunmen, and the blood.

He turned and glanced at the pillow. "This isn't my room." The words were slurred. "But you're here."

"I am here." If he needed to rest somewhere, she didn't mind watching over him while he did. Exhaustion tugged at the edges of her senses still, even after the nap she had taken in the car, and he occupied the only bed in the room.

She just didn't know why he was here. They needed to talk, but now wasn't the time if he was this out of it. She couldn't press him and get any straight answers. Even if no part of her wanted to dredge up a past she had avoided for years, leaving it buried in the grave along with her dad's body.

Absent of life. Kind of like their marriage. DOA days after it began.

"What are you doing?" she whispered, but he didn't seem to hear the question.

Andre tugged over the pillow and lay down, scooting so his back was against the wall. He lifted his hand and held it out.

His eyes closed. "Lucia."

It was an invitation.

A temptation she should avoid. A gift she shouldn't accept.

And yet she stared at his hand, a million thoughts rolling through her mind while she looked at the skin of his palm. The strength in his muscles. That face, the one she had fallen in love with. Now it bore the lines of years of combat, stress, and high-tension situations. He probably had scars, as she did.

A history she had nothing to do with. One she had no business asking about, and no right to know—as much as she might wish otherwise.

Part of her wanted to tell him everything. But what would

that do? It wasn't going to change the past, or fix anything. Life might have thrown them back together, but it wasn't for them to have a shot at healing anything.

"Come here." His voice was a whisper, as though he were already half asleep. "You'll keep the nightmares away."

Lucia had plenty of those. She knew exactly what that was like after years of sleeping alone. Fighting by herself.

She lay down beside him, wincing as the movement shifted her bruised abdomen. Andre slid his arm around her waist and set his hand by her waist. She laced her fingers in his and heard him blow out a long sigh as he drifted away into sleep.

The phone in his pocket pressed against the back of her leg now. Lucia reached back with her other hand and slid it out.

Tomorrow she might regret this. Never mind, she would *definitely* regret this tomorrow. He probably wouldn't even remember, but there wasn't much chance they would wake up and not have second thoughts about sleeping in the same bed. Even if nothing else was happening.

She didn't even want to think about that.

Right then she felt lousy enough she wanted to be selfish for once in her life. Or at least for once in a very long time. She wanted to have her dream before she went back to her real life.

Lucia used his phone to send a text to her boss. Even while sleep tugged her down beside him, and she let herself drift away, knowing soon enough it would be over.

Again.

They would go their separate ways. Torn apart by life, and the reality that she wasn't the kind of person who could have this. Not permanently.

Andre would learn the truth. Those old hurts would rear their heads and snap like the wolves, tearing innocent flesh. She would have to leave knowing she had shredded him.

Again.

ANDRE WOKE with the knowledge that they still needed to have a conversation utmost in his mind. He had no idea how much sleep he'd gotten, but doubted it was more than an hour or so even with the medicine he knew the doctor had given him.

Thinking about their impending conversation and the fact it was important they have it before they parted ways again didn't exactly stop him from thinking about how it felt to have her sleeping beside him.

There wasn't even room for Andre to roll to his back in the tiny bed. His leg didn't hurt a whole lot, but he also wasn't inclined to move it much. He'd have been able to tell even without the tight bandage that it wasn't free of injury. That was his biggest issue with pain meds. They didn't take away the injury—they only masked your brain's ability to feel the pain. Sometimes pain was good, because it told you exactly how deep the wound went.

Like the pain of feeling his wife tucked against him after all this time.

At least she was asleep, not yelling at him like the last time he'd seen her. Before the compound and everything that happened there. That was how he knew this wasn't real.

He wanted to hate himself for the fact he was so content right now. His entire body was relaxed, comfortable with her here. Even while his mind screamed that wasn't right.

They were kidding themselves if either of them thought this was a good idea. Let alone that it would work more than for today. When she woke up it would only be awkward, and they would tiptoe around each other, trying not to set off the ticking time bomb that was their relationship and bring in its inevitable destruction.

Part of him wondered if he was going to regret this anyway, that maybe he shouldn't get whatever he could out of seeing her before then? Not that either of them were in tip-top shape. And he didn't want to add shame to the regret, knowing he'd convinced her to do more than she wanted to purely for his own selfish gain. A momentary physical release wasn't going to heal what was wrong between them—even if either of them actually wanted to fix it.

Which he wasn't sure he did.

There was so much time lost between them. So much water under that bridge, the one she'd burned and he had blown up. Andre figured he'd be better off getting divorce papers written up and having her sign them.

That way both of them could move on once and for all.

And yet, there was a reason why neither of them had done it yet. Probably the same reason why it felt so familiar to have her with him now, despite how long it had been.

He turned his head and looked at the ceiling, staring up at the bland paint. Tiny imperfections marred the surface. If only his life was like that, instead of being nothing but a destroyed mess. A shell of something that had once been half decent, but was now only rubble.

His phone buzzed. It took him a second to locate it on the nightstand, where he didn't remember putting it. Whoever it was, they could wait. Andre wanted to let his eyes close again and soak up as much as he could of a peace he rarely felt.

The fact he only ever seemed to be able to feel it when Lucia was with him was going to make this hurt all the more later. When she was gone again.

Instead of wallowing, he reached over and grabbed the phone from the nightstand. Thankfully that didn't involve too much movement. Otherwise, he was going to wake her. Andre needed to slide his arm out from under her and ease off the bed with as little jostling as possible. Then he'd be able to get out of the room before she even woke up.

But that meant tugging his hand from hers, where their fingers were intertwined.

He wondered who had initiated that. Her—or him.

Andre used his thumb to unlock the phone, which took him

to the messages. The last that had been sent was a new thread with a number he didn't know.

Lucia had used his phone before she fell asleep? She'd sent a message to someone asking them to come and pick her up. His entire body tensed.

Someone was coming.

Andre moved his fingers to the power and volume down buttons and held both for three seconds. The entire phone flashed, and he let go of the buttons.

Lucia had breached security.

That was what was important here, not the fact she wasn't going to rely on their team to help her. Or work with them to take down Burgess. She might not know who they were, but wasn't it obvious how capable they were of doing this?

She wasn't going to trust them. She'd already made her choice, and it was to go back to her old life. Probably without having the conversation they needed to have.

His phone buzzed with an incoming text from Zander.

WE KNOW. THEY'RE ALREADY HERE.

Andre sat up in bed and slid his arm out from under her. He scooted to the foot of the bed so he could stand without climbing over her. Lucia stirred and blinked. He couldn't acknowledge even in his mind how she looked, lying there all contented. Her eyes cloudy with sleep. "Who did you text?"

They'd replied less than a minute later, given the timestamp on the thread. Immediately agreeing to come and pick her up.

Surely Ted had seen that. He could've warned the others that they had people incoming.

His team would have to pack up and leave here when they hadn't planned to, something they were accustomed to doing, but it didn't make it okay. Each of them knew how to roll with changes, but a breach of security from an outside source wasn't much better than a member of the team causing them trouble.

The way Isaac had driven a wedge, then walked away.

Even if this was the feds she'd worked with, their team had strict rules they lived by. Eas was here. If anyone saw him…

"Never mind. It doesn't matter now." Andre stowed the phone in his pocket. "They're already here."

She sat up fast and looked around. What for, he didn't know. "How long were we asleep?"

"The clock has run out, like we knew it would."

She looked like she wanted to say something. Andre didn't exactly want to hear it, so he opened the door and headed for the hall.

He heard her shuffle and a little mew of pain he refused to let sway him. Then she called out, "Andre!"

He was about to turn when someone rounded the corner and walked into view. Eas, not wearing his mask. Headed somewhere quickly—probably to find his face covering so he'd be able to disguise his identity when whoever Lucia had called showed up.

Behind him, he heard her gasp.

Eas ducked back out of view. Andre turned back and closed the space between them. He covered her mouth with his fingertips. "Don't."

He could see in her eyes. She knew exactly who Eas was.

It had taken him some time to figure it out, but he'd put the pieces together on the current status of his teammate—if not the man's whole story. Andre knew the reason he could never show his face in public. Only with their team, where he knew he was safe.

"That was—"

"Don't." He knew he was just repeating what he'd already said. "You've already done enough damage."

She flinched. "What are you talking about?"

"Zander said the cavalry is here. Whoever you called didn't waste any time coming to your rescue."

She looked down at the floor, then back up at him. "I can't lay around here any longer than I already have. This isn't my life, and I need to get back to work. I need to take down Burgess. To stop whatever he has planning, because I know he's planning something and it's big. I'm not just going to indulge in whatever I feel like doing when justice needs to be done."

"So you go back to your life, and I go back to mine?"

"I appreciate you rescuing me, I really do." She sighed. "I know at least in part what it cost you. You didn't have to come, but you did anyway."

He shrugged one shoulder, even though it felt wrong. "I'm your next of kin, remember?"

She scrunched up her nose, looking as if she wanted to cry. "This wasn't how I wanted things to go."

"We don't often get what we want." He knew that more than anyone, maybe. After all, it'd been Lucia's choice that he go away and stay out of her life. That cold, lonely life where she sought justice, never spending an afternoon the way they just had was exactly that. Her choice.

He wasn't going to let it bother him.

"Get the paperwork drawn up." A sharp pain moved through his chest. "Give me a divorce."

"Andre—"

He cut her off. "You need to cut me loose, Lucia."

Pain sliced through her expression, but he turned away so she wouldn't know he felt the same way. It was for the best.

From somewhere in the house someone called out, "Special Agent DeSoto!"

12

Lucia headed for the front of the house, resisting the urge to shove Andre out of the way and get there before him. His long strides took him there much faster than she could.

Her mind reeled with the identity of his friend. She'd recognized the man immediately, and these people were harboring him? She couldn't believe it.

At any other time she would have literally called a halt to everything going on in order to deal with it. However, she had bigger fish to fry right now. Her boss was actually here.

When she emerged into the wide foyer, a group awaited her: Andre's friends, Nora—a woman Lucia wouldn't mind getting to know, even if they were visibly completely different—and her boss in his usual suit, standing inside the front door. Something in her unknotted a fraction seeing a familiar face, even if it was the head of the task force. "Assistant Director Campbell."

"Special Agent DeSoto. I have to say, it's good to see you in one piece"—he glanced around—"thanks to these people." There was a slight edge to his words, as though he didn't entirely trust the intentions of Andre and his friends. He looked like he wanted to say more, but didn't.

Maybe about the fact Andre was her husband and she had never told anyone?

"What happened to the rest of the team on the mission?" She knew the two with her were dead. Lydell shot them before one of his men had been killed by a rooftop gunman.

But given the explosion, there had to have been more casualties.

How was he here?

Campbell shifted slightly, a consideration toward the gravity of the situation. He expressed himself in infinitesimal degrees. His ability to hide how he was truly feeling had impressed her from the beginning, but she had learned those telltale signs that gave away what he had to hold back.

"Four dead," he replied. "The two with you, and two others who were in the van. Three more in the hospital, but they only have minor injuries." He shifted slightly, and she knew that meant he also had been injured. Maybe he was one of the three. "As I said, it's good to see you in one piece. We'll need a full debrief. If you could gather your things and come with me."

She shrugged. "I had nothing on me when I was captured. I don't have any things."

"You didn't manage to gather any evidence?"

She knew it wasn't a slight, or criticism. It was simply a question, and that was how he meant it. But given the way everyone in the room shifted except for her and Campbell, she figured the others didn't exactly take it that way. "Unfortunately, no."

"As if she would've been able to?" Andre said. "Should she have been interrogating them while they were beating her?"

"Andre—"

He cut her off. "They weren't going to go in and get you back. Their hands were tied. That's why I had to go in there."

"And we're grateful for that," Campbell said. "In all honesty, I was aware of who you are. I received a detailed email and pieced that together with chatter I've heard about some of your team's more…recent dealings. If anyone could get Special Agent DeSoto back from Burgess, I knew it was you and your team."

She could tell Andre didn't like it. Not that he gave away any more than Campbell did.

Lucia would have put a hand on Andre's arm if he'd been anyone else. She was used to dealing with witnesses. Or uncooperative suspects. He would probably explode if she tried to placate him—or if he thought that was what she was doing.

She said, "If the task force's hands were tied, there's nothing they could've done. And if you'd left me in there, then I would have gathered evidence. But you pulled me out fast. Not that I'm not grateful for that, but I was there to do my job. And I would have done it."

Andre folded his arms. "You were there because Burgess's number two hijacked a meeting and kidnapped you."

"We had no idea that was going to happen when we went to the meeting." She wasn't sure if he thought she needed to apologize for it. "Things happen. You just roll with it, and you get the job done."

He stared at her. She could tell from the expression on Andre's face that he was wondering who on earth she was, though he didn't say anything.

"If you're ready then?" Campbell motioned to the door. "I have a car outside. You'll be placed under protective detail until Burgess is brought to justice."

Zander shifted. "Is there some kind of threat in play?"

Protective custody wasn't necessary in all cases. Still, she hadn't ever heard of a situation quite like this.

If Campbell thought she needed to be kept safe, then it was for a good reason. There was no doubt a whole lot of work to do. Paperwork to fill out, and funerals to attend. She was already exhausted and needed some recovery time as well. It could take weeks before whoever was assigned to continue looking into Burgess was able to make an arrest, time she could spend recuperating and getting some desk work done.

Then there was the fact Burgess would now be on high alert. Someone had infiltrated his compound, and he was likely considering the fact they might be cops. If he was gunning for them, it was only a matter of time before he figured out who they were.

If he had a plan in place to do something big, they could have just inadvertently accelerated the timetable.

Campbell said, "It's my understanding that if your team would like to participate in the investigation, the Department of Justice is willing to accommodate you as consultants."

Someone snorted.

Zander tipped his head to the side. "Is that right?"

"However, in cases that are sensitive, like this one, we have to tread carefully. That will take finesse." Campbell was all but accusing Zander and his team of operating more like bulls charging through a market. "We could certainly use your expertise, though. The more heads we have working this one, the quicker we can bring down Burgess."

Campbell glanced at her. "We should go now. Burgess put a call out to every unsavory character he knows in this part of the country. There is a price on your head. And that of your friend here." He waved dismissively at Andre.

"I can take care of myself." Andre still had his arms folded.

Part of her wanted to know if he was willing to have her remain with him. But Andre wasn't even offering it as an option. Sure, she had to get back to work. That didn't mean she wasn't interested in him at least holding out his hand to her again. Offering an olive branch where they could have time together. More than sleeping, and a short but awkward conversation.

She and Andre had always burned hot, and some of their fights had been explosive. She'd always thought things would mellow with time. That they would settle into a peaceful cohabitation. Life hadn't given them the chance to find out if their relationship would have survived long term.

Now it seemed as though Andre wasn't interested in even talking.

He'd asked her for a divorce, and now was practically shoving her out the door.

Campbell said to Andre, "I'm sure between you and your friends, everything here will be copacetic."

Lucia wasn't willing to leave it to wishful thinking. She turned to him. "Be careful. Please." She'd seen firsthand what Burgess was capable of, and the setup of his compound with the community and the wild area made her want to shudder all over again just thinking about it.

If Andre was hurt, or killed, by Burgess and his guys, then they would never get to have that conversation. Maybe their lives weren't compatible at all. But part of her at least wanted to try.

He studied her face. She thought for a second he would dismiss what she said, but he nodded.

Zander answered his phone.

Lucia pushed away the desire to say something else to Andre. It wouldn't go down well, whatever she chose. Words had never been her strong point. Not when action was so much more impactful.

She crossed to him, lifted on the balls of her feet, and pressed a kiss to his cheek.

He didn't even move. She didn't make eye contact, not wanting to see whatever expression would be on his face. Maybe it was better that they didn't talk. That they just left the past to lie where it was and moved on with their lives. She could get the paperwork done and send it to him while she recuperated.

Lucia went to the door, wondering how it would feel to finally let him go.

"Understood." Zander paused a second. "Campbell, one second."

She didn't have time to look at Zander to see what he wanted before the crack of the gun firing exploded in the foyer. The bullet hit Campbell's forehead, and he dropped to the floor, leaving them all standing there, and Zander holding a smoking gun.

ANDRE SPUN around to his team leader. "He was dirty?"

"Ted told me he's been in contact with Burgess. The two guys outside are also on the take." Zander glanced around. "Chartreuse, two minutes."

"What about the guys outside?" Badger motioned to the door. "We should take care of them, right?"

Andre didn't like the tone of his voice. Badger had been entirely too reckless since Isaac betrayed them. While Andre held his anger and frustration inside, simply wanting to pummel the guy's face the next time he saw him, Badger had soured.

And judging by the look on Zander's face, he felt the same way.

"I'll take care of it." Eas strode across the foyer to the front door, his mask back on. As he passed Lucia, she flinched.

Andre realized she hadn't moved since the assistant director hit the ground. "Luce."

If they were going to get out of here fast, she had to come with him.

She sucked in a breath. "You just killed an FBI assistant director. The head of a task force!"

Andre moved to her, reached out, and grabbed her hand. He turned and headed back through the foyer to the hallway.

Backpack first, then car.

She tugged on his hand in an attempt to slow him down.

He ignored it. "We can talk about this later." As if Andre was going to put all their lives in danger just to appease her shock. "I know that was intense, and you didn't know he was working with Burgess. But now you do."

Andre needed to figure out who'd told Campbell about the team, and how that played into the whole Burgess thing.

"So we just move on?" She sounded like she had no intention of doing that.

He glanced over his shoulder. "What we *do* is get out of here before the two guys out front realize Campbell is dead and not one of Zander's team members. That way we're not next."

She inhaled. "This is insane. That man was a federal agent. You can't just kill a guy like that and walk away."

And yet they were. "We'll leave all the pertinent evidence here. No one's going to come and clean it up. When the police get here and find him, they'll know what killed him."

"Zander's bullet."

Andre shook his head. "Untraceable."

He slowed and entered the bedroom.

"Do you guys…do this often?"

"If you mean kill people, that's the wrong question to ask." He didn't glance at her, just pulled the sheets from the bed where they'd slept and bundled them into a heap with the pillowcase. "But when we found out the director of the Department of Clandestine Service was running a side business that turned out to be an illegal empire, we participated in getting the evidence to bring him down. Now he's in prison, and he'll be there for a long time."

"Director Gladstone?"

He went to stand at the door, facing her. "You didn't figure out who Nora is?"

She opened her mouth, but it was a second before she said, "Nora Gladstone."

"Not anymore, but yeah. The way things were going with her and Zander, it wasn't likely to be long before she was Mrs. Nora O'Connell. Turned out we were right." They'd gotten married a couple of weeks ago.

"Nora Gladstone. This is a lot to absorb."

Andre shrugged. "Par for the course, as far as I can see."

She still appeared to be in a state of shock, pale and slightly glassy-eyed. He didn't like that look on her at all. But given all she'd been through, it wasn't entirely surprising. Andre preferred the Lucia who pushed back. Fought back. Stood up for herself and didn't accept anything she didn't want.

She might have been beaten down a little recently, but the truth was, the woman he knew was who she was inside. This woman reminded him more of the one who'd screamed that she never wanted to see him again.

He wondered what she thought of herself. Which made him wonder what she thought of him, and the man he was now. She didn't have the first clue about the things he'd seen and done.

Maybe when she discovered the truth, she would hate who he was.

"We need to go."

She nodded. "I should call into my boss. The one I had before I was assigned to the task force. Tell him everything that's happened."

Something moved in her expression, but he couldn't tell what.

He said, "I'll get you a phone, and you can send an email." He wasn't going to keep her from her job, but they needed to do this in a way that kept all of them safe.

"Are you mad at me because I sent that text?"

"It's done." They couldn't change what had already happened, so what was the point in dwelling on it? "You didn't know Campbell was dirty. Now we have to go."

That thing he couldn't pinpoint in her expression flashed again, but was gone as quick as he spotted it. "Because I put everyone in danger?" she said.

He led her through the door and down the hallway. "You didn't know he was dirty, Luce."

Kind of like the way they hadn't anticipated Isaac would

betray them. Now he was in Burgess's compound. Doing what, Andre had no idea. He had to be working for some kind of organization, even the CIA, as he had before he'd joined the team.

On a job.

Which made Andre wonder if Isaac had been on a job when he was assigned to their team. It could be their entire working relationship was only a mission to Isaac. They hadn't meant anything to him but that he did his job.

Meanwhile, the rest of them had actually trusted him.

"No, I didn't know he was dirty."

"You can give yourself a break." He was still thinking about Isaac. "None of us is immune to being tricked."

"Sounds like you know firsthand about that."

Andre pushed the door open into the garage and grabbed a set of keys from a hook on the wall. Zander and Nora were already pulling out. He heard a couple of gunshots from a distance and figured the guys out front hadn't been willing to surrender. That meant they were dead now. Within minutes there would be no trace of this team here in the house.

Andre shoved the bundle of sheets in the trunk of the car and held the door for Lucia to get in the passenger side. As soon as she pulled her foot in, he closed the door and moved around the hood to the driver's side, ignoring the pull in his leg wound. Or the bandages on his shoulder.

As he reversed out of the garage, she said, "If you asked me a week ago, I'd never have believed you if you'd have told me I would be in a car with you. Both of us injured."

He shoved the car into drive and hit the gas. "I can honestly say I agree with that."

They'd essentially been avoiding each other for the last fifteen years. Why now? What they had was far too complicated and messed up for them to untangle everything and get it all straightened out.

Let alone build something from that.

All he needed to do was get her safe and make sure she was free of danger. Then she could go back to her life. He would go back to his. Things would move on.

"Do you really want me to get you divorce papers?"

His stomach flipped just at the idea of severing the connection between them. "That is what I said."

But now? She was in danger.

"Let's just focus on neutralizing Burgess."

"And ending whatever plan he has in place."

Andre frowned. Up ahead, Zander took a left turn onto a highway that would lead east. He continued on this road to the freeway that would take them west.

His phone buzzed in his pocket. Then again.

Then twice more in quick succession.

Everyone was out of the house.

Isaac might have given him a flash drive, but they still hadn't had time to find out what was on it. He needed to call Ted and get an update. Maybe by now their tech guy knew what the target on that neighborhood meant, and if it all added together to an actual lead they could move on.

Possibly they could wrap this up in a day or two.

"What do you mean about Burgess having a plan?"

"The mission." She paused a second, considering. "I didn't hear much about it, but they were whispering, and it seemed like everyone was gearing up for this big thing."

"But you don't know what, or when?"

Lucia sighed.

"Don't worry, the team will take care of it. You just need to stay safe in the meantime." Didn't she know he was going to do everything he could to keep her safe? She would learn pretty quickly the team got results. They might have methods she wasn't used to, but they got the job done.

"And when Burgess finds out who you are and sends his army?"

"Doesn't matter. You'll be safe."

"You think I'm not going to worry about you?" she said.

"I'm just saying you don't need to."

She sighed again and turned to the window. Andre blew out a breath. He'd been right that there was too much complication between them to ever figure out their deal. That was what he had to concentrate on—the mission.

She was in danger, and he was the one who was going to keep her safe.

13

———

"This way."

Lucia jerked around to Andre and saw him motion toward an airplane with the steps down. Some kind of private plane.

No one had questioned their entry into a side gate of the airport they'd driven to. The security guard had noted down the details of Andre's driver's license and then ushered them through quickly, as though he didn't want to be the one to hold them up.

"This is Zander's plane. It's the team plane."

She frowned, closed the car door behind her, and didn't move. "Who are you guys? I thought you joined the army."

"I got out two years ago. Zander, Badger, and I all served together. When I left, Zander asked if I wanted to join his team."

His expression didn't betray anything. It wasn't like he was being cagey, but he also wasn't elaborating. Just giving her basic information. "Never mind. Sorry I even asked."

Clearly he thought she had no right to any of his personal information. Even though it stung, she figured that meant she wasn't at liberty to divulge anything about her own life in return.

She didn't like that things were so weird between them. But what did she expect? It wasn't like she could snap her fingers and they'd be able to communicate the way they used to, almost without words.

She'd been able to read him then. He had always called her on it, anytime she tried to hide the truth. He'd wanted to wade into the mess that had been her life with her dad.

Now it seemed like he couldn't have cared less than he did now.

"Why don't you just give me the keys, and I'll take the car." She figured it wasn't his. Probably a rental, or a team vehicle. "I can take care of myself."

"Yeah?" His eyebrows rose. "Do you have a gun?"

"Maybe I don't need one. Carrying a gun just draws attention, and that's not the plan here."

He reached for her, but she took a step back and slammed up against the car door. The last thing she needed was for him to grab her hand again. Or put his arm around her shoulders.

After all, falling asleep beside him was one thing. It didn't mean that had to be a recurring event. Not when the mess between them was so confusing.

Nora came into view in the open airplane door. A second later, she glanced at whoever was inside and then disappeared out of sight again.

"Let's go, DeSoto." Andre jerked a thumb over his shoulder. "The plane needs to be wheels up as soon as possible."

When she didn't move, Andre frowned.

"You don't trust me?"

"You said it." She lifted her chin. "I don't even know you."

"And you know those people you work with, like that assistant director who was working for Burgess? He was going to take you back to the compound, right?" Before she could even react to the idea of that, he continued, "You think I'd have been able to get you out a second time?"

She wanted to ask why he'd gotten her out in the first place. But the fact was, she would always be grateful that he had. Andre had put his life on the line to save her.

He looked around now, his gaze wary. As though someone else would show up imminently, attempting to take her from him. "We really should go."

Lucia strode past him to the airplane stairs and trotted up as quickly as her bruised body wanted to move. Not exactly fighting form, but she'd learned the hard way she had to allow her body time to recuperate and not simply jump back into the fray. That would only make her fall harder when she couldn't push any longer.

Nora waited just inside the airplane door. Zander passed her, giving his wife a squeeze as he made his way with Andre to the rear of the plane.

She wanted to be in that conversation, but figured they weren't about to allow her to be privy to team information. As far as they were concerned, Lucia was the one who needed to be protected. She was the victim, the one they had rescued.

A blond guy moved to stand beside Nora. Before either of them could speak he stuck his hand out. "I'm Badger."

"I remember."

Nora smiled. "That's not his real name. It's just what everyone calls him."

After Lucia had shaken hands with Badger, Nora stuck her own hand out. "Nora O'Connell."

Formerly Gladstone. Now Nora wore a beautiful diamond on her left ring finger and was married to Zander. All this *after* their team had taken down her father.

Lucia knew the story surrounding Director Gladstone. She'd read about it in the newspaper. But the reporter had been clear that these were only allegations. What did this team, and Nora herself, know about her dad that the world wouldn't until he got to trial?

Whatever it was, it had led to Zander and Nora falling in love.

"I'm sure you had a long few days, and you want to rest now." Nora winced. The team had just killed her former boss. "I can show you to a seat if you'd like?"

"Thank you." She wasn't sure what else to say, so she simply followed Nora to the chair the woman indicated and settled in. Thinking about resting just made her mind go back to sharing a bed with Andre.

But then he'd asked for a divorce.

His boss had shot hers. Because Campbell was dirty.

Lucia's head wouldn't stop spinning. It kept coming back to lying snuggled up with Andre, something she probably needed to quit dwelling on so much. Sure, it had been nice. Just sleeping, and being there with each other so they could rest. She wondered if Andre had needed it as much as she felt like she did.

So many years apart. At this point she was probably starved for physical affection. And wasn't that a recipe for something disastrous to happen?

She pushed away the thought and considered her situation here. Her task force team decimated. Her boss, on the take with the person they should be bringing to justice.

Lucia wondered if Zander and the guys would even let her know where the plane was headed. Or was that a secret, as well? Privileged team information she wasn't allowed to know.

The door to the plane shut, and Lucia realized it was only her and Nora on board. Everyone else had gone, though she had no idea where.

Before she could ask, Nora said, "You should put your seat belt on. We'll be taking off soon."

"It doesn't bother you?"

Nora shook her head. "I'm sorry, I don't know what you mean. What doesn't bother me?"

This woman was all class and sophistication. In comparison, Lucia felt like some street kid invited to a banquet. She had no idea which fork to use.

Nora said, "As soon as we're in the air, I can get you coffee and something to eat."

"You can just show me where it all is. You don't have to wait on me." Lucia would feel strange if she did.

Nora smiled. "Typical guys, leaving us to fend for ourselves."

"That's what I meant." Lucia gave her a small smile in return. "What are they even doing?"

There was nothing funny about the situation, but the fact that the guys had parked her and Nora in this airplane and then disappeared absolutely meant they were up to something.

"They didn't all leave. Andre is talking to the pilot, and then he'll be back here. That's when we're leaving." A small shadow of worry crossed Nora's face. "The guys went back to the compound to have a look around. The friend of theirs, that's who we think was on the inside, the reason the feds couldn't go in and get you out? They want to talk to him about what he handed over to Andre."

"Burgess isn't going to like it if a bunch of people show up."

Nora gave a small shrug. "Zander told me it's just recon. But they have ways of contacting Isaac."

She knew who that was. The man's face swam in her mind, the blond one who'd taken her back to her room. The truth was, he probably saved her from whatever those guys had planned next.

"I do worry about them," Nora said. "They're good at what they do. Actually, they're the best. And that's not bragging."

"But they're not official, right? Andre said he's out of the military."

"They are private contractors. And if anyone can get to the bottom of what Burgess is up to, it's them."

Lucia looked at the tarmac out the window. This was supposed to have been her case, and now it had fallen apart. Andre might not have gone with the others. But what if one of them was killed before Burgess was brought in?

She should have simply climbed in that car of his and driven away.

His team needed to let this go and allow the feds to take the case to its conclusion. Otherwise, she would have to absorb the risk of him dying because of her.

Just like her father.

"Okay, I see you." Andre adjusted the headset and clipped his seatbelt. The plane was already rolling down the runway. "Can you hear me?"

"Loud and clear." A rustling sound came through the headset speaker, and he knew Zander made his way down the hill toward the compound. It matched what Andre could see on the screen of the laptop perched on his knees, the feed from his body cam.

Across the aisle, Nora read a paperback while Lucia had her eyes closed. When he'd emerged from the cockpit, he'd found them exactly this way. Nora had waved her fingers and mouthed a couple of questions silently. Lucia hadn't even opened her eyes.

Considering he wasn't sure at all what to do with her, that was fine by him. Andre didn't even know what to say at this point. They weren't going to fix what was upside down between them without a long conversation. And this was hardly the time for it.

Once the situation with Burgess was resolved, they could think about doing that. Until then it would only prove frustrating to try.

"Approaching the perimeter." That was Badger, who had

jumped at the chance to get off the plane and out in the field again.

The kid had never opened up about what frustrated him. This time, with Isaac in the mix, Badger was even more reticent. Another conversation Andre needed to have but couldn't right then.

At least Zander was aware as well. Even Judah, who usually didn't let anything bother him, had noticed Badger wasn't his normal happy self. Judah had chalked that up to woman troubles. Namely, a certain New York police detective who may or may not be Nora's biological sister, and the fact she hadn't called him back yet. Badger had spent some time with her a few weeks ago, and now nothing. She was communicating with Nora, but that didn't stop her from even sending a text to his friend, surely.

"I see you." Andre had them all on camera. They didn't always use body cams, but it was frequent. Usually the government wanted an electronic record of the things they had seen and done on a mission. When it was necessary to have confirmation the mission was complete in a way that could be added to official files.

Occasionally, it was simply so they could watch the footage later and learn from any mistakes that had been made. Figure out ways to improve. That was always part of Zander's training plan, pushing them to be the best they could be. Something none of them had a problem with even if once in a while it bordered on obsessive.

At least with the appearance of Nora and her role in their lives now, that had calmed down to an extent.

"Seems kind of empty." Judah's British-accented voice filled the line. "This place was buzzing with people last time we were here."

Andre frowned. "Who is on the main entrance?"

"I see the gate," Eas replied. "Not too many cars inside, and I don't see any people."

"Maybe they're holed up in one of the buildings?" Zander asked Andre, "Did Ted manage to get back on that satellite footage?"

That would have been handy. However, the kid was still having problems. "He said it's too risky. Whoever noticed he was in there the first time, and managed to kick him out, will likely be watching for if he shows back up again."

Ted was seriously skilled in the arena of communications, and even electronic forensic analysis. However, Andre knew it wasn't a foolproof method of getting what they needed. Too much reliance on being able to hack something, or get around any surveillance, could make them take a risk that wound up backfiring.

He much preferred good old-fashioned methods that involved kicking down doors and interrogating suspects into giving over the whereabouts of their leader and details of their plan. The fact he couldn't do it on this particular day, because of the bullet graze on his leg and the knife wound, wasn't something that sat well with him. It also wasn't something he could change, so there was no point worrying about it. Going out and inserting himself into the mission meant he'd be a liability.

They trusted each other not to do that.

"Huh."

When Zander said nothing else, Andre asked, "What is it?"

He peered closer at the screen but couldn't see anything amiss. In fact, there wasn't much at all there except the terrain itself.

"Hold up." Zander barked the command loud enough Andre winced.

He said nothing, not wanting to break anyone's concentration. The same way the rest of the guys kept quiet. They all waited for Zander to continue.

It took a cool minute, and then he said, "There's a pack of wolves walking down the main street."

Andre frowned. "Someone left the gate open?" Or they

hadn't closed it after the breach. Whichever it was, anyone down there was now in serious danger. He and Lucia had seen those wolves tear apart one woman. "Be careful. They're vicious."

"If anyone was down there still, wouldn't we know it?" Badger said. "I mean, they'd be running around screaming, right?" Andre could picture the look on his face.

"Unless they're hiding inside a building with nowhere to go." Andre blew out a breath.

That was not a place he'd want to be. But the idea of going with his team on a building-to-building search, rooting out anyone who needed assistance and taking care of the animals, would be a day spent doing a worthy activity.

Zander told Andre, "Call the state wildlife authority."

"Copy that." He opened a new window on his browser and did a quick Google search for the number. "You're thinking they need to come in and round up all these animals?"

"They'll know what to do to catch and release them back into the wild, where they should be. They can also find anyone still inside."

Zander was probably right. The state would have a whole lot more personnel at their disposal, not to mention the resources and know-how. His team would likely wind up hurting some of the animals just to keep their own lives.

No matter how vicious the animals were, shooting them was a whole lot different than taking out a person who had chosen to end the life of another. Animals were only doing what nature dictated. A person who had given up their soul, disregarding the value of another human life, was a whole different ballgame.

"I'm making that call." Andre removed his headset and called the number for the state wildlife office. He got the runaround through a couple of people, then managed to confirm that the compound existed where he said it did. He also sent an email to someone they knew at the FBI, so he could get a team down here. Andre had no interest in talking to some random fed who had no clue. And he couldn't call any of Lucia's former colleagues.

Not now that they knew the assistant director over her task force had been dirty.

He put the headset back on. "It's on their radar, at least. As for trying to save anyone in there, do you guys have any ideas?"

Eas chimed in. "I can do a quick search. It should only take me an hour or two."

Andre didn't know if that was quick, but given the size of this place, he figured it was probably accurate.

Zander said, "You can get in and out without being noticed by any of these animals?"

"It would be easier if you had some lion urine. But I will be fine."

Judah groaned. "Do I even want to know what that's supposed to mean?"

Zander said, "I want to know if anyone in there needs help."

Andre agreed with him. Though he didn't know if he'd be volunteering if he was on the ground with them instead of being thousands of feet up in the air. Zander always made sure there were no innocent lives at risk where they operated. It wouldn't sit right with any of them to simply leave the situation like this.

Andre reached up and squeezed the back of his neck. "You seriously think Burgess and all of his people cleared out?"

"That's what it looks like," Zander said. "The whole place seems to have been abandoned."

Andre frowned. "We need to know where he went, and what he's up to."

Sure that was a completely obvious statement, but it had to be said aloud. That was how Andre focused on the task at hand, building a plan in his mind of what to do next.

"Get on with Ted. Find out if he has anything new." Zander didn't waste a beat before he added, "We'll meet you at home."

14

———

"Wakey, wakey."

Lucia succumbed to the shaking and opened her eyes. She didn't know how long she'd been asleep, but the plane wasn't moving. "Where are we?"

Andre stood in front of her. "We've arrived."

She couldn't decipher the look on his face. She wondered if there would ever be a point in the future when she could again, the way she'd been able to years ago. He turned away to the door of the plane and opened it, lowering the steps.

Nora came over and handed her a sling. "Here, this will help you not bump your arm around."

She helped Lucia put the strap over her head, and when her arm relaxed in the sling, Lucia let out a sigh. "That feels much better, thanks."

Nora gave her a smile that seemed more perfunctory than anything else. Then she was out, down the steps. Lucia met Andre at the door. Nora was already crossing to an SUV parked beside another identical one. The rest of Andre's team stood around the vehicles.

"You go first." He lifted the backpack he'd loaded at the house, then slung it over his shoulder.

"What's going on?" Lucia headed out and started down the steps since it didn't seem like he wanted her to delay anything.

"We're in the car over there."

Lucia got to it quick enough she could look at him over the roof of the car before he got in. The frown that drew his brows together was new. He hadn't been wearing that when she'd fallen asleep. He'd been about to get on a video call with Zander, where he would be able to see what happened on their mission. At least that's what Nora had told her. Instead of staying awake to listen in, Lucia had dozed off.

Did something happen on the mission? All the guys were here, so it wasn't that they'd been hurt.

Andre went first, and the other two SUVs followed his.

"Is this your car?" She didn't know much about cars, more than she figured any regular person knew. But she could tell this was a nice one. Upmarket. She figured he'd be the kind of guy to drive something a whole lot sportier.

He shrugged one shoulder as he drove. "The team has a few vehicles. We're in this one because there are two of us. The rest of the guys don't want to be in a back seat when they could sit in the captain's chair in the middle row of an SUV."

She looked out the window and realized this airport seemed completely devoid of people, or other airplanes even. The control tower was barely taller than the two-story building beside it. "What airport is this?"

"Just one close to where we have a house. It's easier to keep someone safe if you know the terrain, and the people who live around you. Rental houses can be anon—"

"Like the one we were in before?"

He nodded. "But when we need to be completely under the radar, we have safe houses."

She studied the mountains surrounding them. Kind of a strange place to put an airport, tucked in a basin surrounded by peaks. Snow sat atop the mountains even though it was late

September. But what did she know about landscapes? She'd grown up in Los Angeles County, in the concrete jungle where heat flickered off the asphalt in waves and traffic backed up at all hours of the day and night.

This place seemed kind of…rural.

Not off the grid completely, the way Burgess's compound had been. This place was the kind locals happily kept secret for fear it would be overrun and lose its innate rustic charm.

Pine trees covered the mountains, though on her side of the car much of the terrain was black ash. From a recent wildfire?

"What happened on the mission?" she asked. "I thought the guys were headed to the compound."

Andre pulled off the road that led down to the airport, onto the blacktop of the highway. Would the house they were headed to be in the middle of nowhere, the way she pictured it? Or were they going to some kind of town where she could get a decent cup of coffee and a bacon cheeseburger?

Since he didn't answer her question, she continued, "I should probably contact someone at the FBI, or on the task force." She tapped her index finger on her thigh. "Or my old boss at the DEA. They need to know that Assistant Director Campbell is back at that house." *Dead.*

"We made an anonymous tip." Andre didn't even look at her. "And as far as anyone is concerned, you were never there."

"So you're determined to keep me out of this, even though that's going to look incredibly suspicious? Someone will figure out I escaped from Burgess's compound. They're going to want me to account for my whereabouts after that."

He shrugged. "Tell them you were recovering. You saw a doctor, and you weren't ready to talk to anyone."

"How does that help me figure out how to get the evidence to take Burgess down? I'm not supposed to be lying low, and Campbell was at least right that I should go in for a debrief."

"Sure you want to do that?"

"Why are you being weird?" he said. It was more than just the issues between them rearing their heads, the way it happened when they'd both woken up. There was definitely something he wasn't telling her.

"I'm not being weird. I just don't think you should be so quick to contact your people."

"Because you think more of them are dirty like Campbell?"

"You tell me."

There was that weirdness again. She didn't know what to make of it, but there wasn't time to ask him before they pulled up outside a huge house. More like a mansion, with a giant barn or workshop beside it that was bigger than the house.

"This is it?" Now she was just asking redundant questions to fill the awkward silence.

He pushed out of his door, and she did the same. The rest of the team got out of the two SUVs that had parked behind them on the long gravel driveway. A Jeep was parked in front of the workshop. Someone else was already here.

"Get her locked down," Zander called out from beside his SUV.

Lucia opened her mouth to ask what he was talking about when Andre grasped her arm above her elbow. "Come with me."

He walked faster than she would have. Thankfully, he was tugging on her good arm. But that only meant she didn't have one to punch him with if necessary. Probably it was by design. He would know she wasn't going to hesitate to retaliate in order to break away.

He pushed open the front door ahead of them and tugged her through a living area, down the hall to some steps that led to a lower floor.

"Taking me to your creepy dungeon?" Even if she wanted to scream for help, she doubted there was anyone around willing to lend her a hand. Except maybe Nora. Although, given her relationship with Zander, Lucia figured even if the other woman wanted to help her that her husband wasn't about to let it happen.

She was out of luck.

Lucia dragged her feet. "What aren't you telling—"

He shoved her into a room. Thankfully it was better furnished than a prison cell, but not by much. Whoever decorated needed to contact a professional interior designer instead.

A man appeared in the doorway. Younger than her and Andre, he had dark hair that fell over his forehead. He handed a tablet to Andre, who brought it over and held it out in front of her.

She didn't take it. There was something about the way he stood that indicated he wasn't handing her the device.

There were a series of beeps, then a long tone.

The man at the doorway said, "She's clean."

Andre handed the tablet back to him and shut the door in his face. In the hallway, she heard the young man chuckle.

Lucia just stood staring at him. No matter how many times she asked questions, if he didn't want to explain then he wasn't going to.

"I had to check for electronic devices. Including bugs."

"You think I had something planted on me?"

Andre said, "I think we can't be too careful in a situation like this."

"Burgess doesn't operate using surveillance. Not unless you're talking about the scope on a rifle. Or the targeting system on a rocket launcher."

"After we found the compound cleared out with no trace of Burgess or his men, we looked into you. Someone cloned your phone before the mission you went on. They've been spying on you for a while. Your whole life was hacked." The skin around his mouth tightened. "If there is a leak in the task force, it's not just Campbell. It's you, too."

ANDRE HADN'T WANTED to begin the conversation in the car. Knowing she was clean, and not carrying any bugs or hidden devices, helped to plead her case. Knowingly or unknowingly, someone had given themselves access to her entire life.

He considered the fact it could've been Isaac. That was Ted's immediate response to the idea someone had hacked her. The kid had even gone so far as to suggest that Isaac had been aware Burgess's number two had a thing for Lucia. That their former teammate had done a deep dive into her life to put tabs on her just in case the number two made his move. Considering the move was exactly what had happened, he'd have been right to be cautious. But anything Isaac might have done to prevent it didn't help her one bit, so Andre wasn't so sure. Except for the fact Lucia had mentioned a sniper when she was kidnapped.

Had that been Isaac, trying to save her? Usually when Isaac got into something, no one could figure out the reason until he made it plain. Andre wasn't going to bother trying to figure it out.

Andre had considered the idea Lucia was dirty for about a second. Zander was still inclined to believe it, but that was only because he knew the whole story about how Lucia had ended things. Judah was on Lucia's side, but he was a sucker for a dark-featured woman. Badger knew the story of the end of their relationship as well, but he didn't think Lucia had anything to do with Burgess—other than as one of his victims.

Badger had stormed off, claiming he was going for a run.

Eas and Judah were crashing in their rooms so they could get some sleep.

Nora was probably going to clean the kitchen until she had wrestled out everything about this. Zander would help her, because this was a house full of guys and they were all processing in their own ways, but they still pulled together to do chores.

Andre turned to Lucia. "If I thought you were any part of this, I would never have brought you to my home. That would be reckless considering you could do something to hurt Nora."

She glanced around the room.

"This isn't my room. It's for guests, whether they're here by choice or not." He folded his arms. "Everything we found out when we looked into you points to the idea that you were under Campbell in a way it appears as though you knew exactly what he was up to."

"I…what?"

"It looks like you set up your teammates and went back to Burgess." It was a theory, one that would be fired at her in the coming days when she faced down her bosses at the DEA or the task force.

"And the plan involved them beating on me?"

He shrugged. She wasn't going to be shown any empathy. "Maybe you didn't anticipate that would happen."

"And if I told you the number two guy killed my colleagues and then captured me because he had a thing for me? He was probably stalking me if someone really did hack my life." She waved a hand. "I didn't think he knew I was DEA, though. If he did, then he wasn't about to share that information with Burgess. Maybe he was going to hold it over my head to get me to do whatever he wanted." She shuddered.

Andre pushed down the urge to do the same thing. "What do you mean he had a thing for you?"

"It's what happens when a guy finds a woman attractive and gets interested in her. Except in this case, he killed multiple people to obtain me and then wound up dead."

"*Attracted?*" Ire rose in him.

"I was surprised, too. It's been so long I figured I wasn't a viable candidate anymore." She lifted her chin, determination in her gaze. She was straight up challenging him. "It's good to know at least someone finds me attractive. Although, I could have done without the murder."

"What do you mean attracted?" That was why she'd ended up in Burgess's compound? She could have just told him that from the beginning, and this would have gone much differently. Now he knew she'd essentially had a stalker, he could prove to Zander she hadn't been in league with Campbell. "You really had no idea what the assistant director was doing?"

"Of course not." She practically yelled the words at him. "You think I'm in favor of anything Burgess has done, or plans to do? That's insane. And by that I mean clinically, legally nuts."

"Maybe I am." After all, it had been years and here he was. Back with her. Tied in knots all over again because of Lucia DeSoto, when by all logical reasoning he should have cut her loose when he walked away years ago. "He's dead now?" That's what she'd said about her stalker.

"Burgess shot him because he broke with the plan to sell us those stolen weapons and brought me to the compound."

"But he takes women, right?"

"Maybe it's more about Burgess needing to be in control of everything all the time." Andre squeezed the bridge of his nose.

"You said he's gone? Like completely cleared out of the compound?"

He lowered his hand and nodded. "We're looking into where he went."

"I'll call my boss at the DEA and get out of your hair. Obviously you don't want me here, considering you believed I was working with Campbell."

She thought he was going to let her leave? "I brought you to my home to keep you safe. There is no leaving."

"So I traded being captured by Burgess and held in his compound for being stuck here with you, and the equally unlikely chance I can leave. Is that it?"

"I didn't kidnap you."

"Depends on how I word it when I write my report." She lifted her chin.

"So that's how this is going to be?" First a man with evil intentions finds her attractive enough to murder people to take her, and now she thought he was just going to let her go gallivanting off where whoever was watching could take a potshot at her?

"I'm not hiding here."

"You don't have a choice," he said. "Campbell was right about you needing to be in protective custody. This place is safe. It's secure. And you can get on a video call with your bosses. Explain everything, including why you're not coming back until Burgess is taken down."

"Good." She nodded. "I'll help you guys do that."

He stared at her. The determination and drive in her were attractive, something he'd never seen before. The woman she'd become turned his head. Andre could admit that much to himself.

She'd thought she wasn't—what had she called it? A *viable candidate?*

Hearing that someone psycho had been attracted to her—even if the guy was dead now—stirred in him what would probably be labeled jealousy. But he didn't want to acknowledge that, even if it was only in his mind. He'd never shied away from ugly emotions, figuring it was easier just to be real with himself.

Take it or leave it, Andre had to feel what was in him. He'd deal wisely with the emotions in the end. But ignoring or bottling up his feelings just led to more problems later.

She lifted her chin another inch. "I'm not kidding, Andre. If you're going after Burgess, then I'll be right there with you."

He knew how she meant that statement. Still, having her here instead of going their separate ways? That only meant he was now fully cognizant of the fact she was still the kind of woman who turned his head.

Fine. She was the *only* woman in his life who had ever turned his head like this.

The sooner he got that straight, the better off he would be in the long run.

He stepped forward. She drew him like a magnet. The strength in her made him want to be as close as possible.

She eyed him. "The last man who had the same look that's on your face wound up dead. Like my father."

"You're talking about Burgess's guy?" As if he was twisted like that.

"Maybe you don't want to be associated with a guy like Lydell, but anyone in my orbit ends up dead and I—"

He didn't know what she was talking about. "You what?" The look on his face would lead to him dying? When she said nothing, he pointed out the obvious. "You care about me." After all, why else would she be upset at the idea he could die? It wasn't just that she'd have no emergency contact in her personnel file.

"You think I'm a bad guy," she pointed out. "As if I would ever betray the oath I've taken."

"Why not? You betrayed me."

His challenge was met with a challenging gaze in return. "Yeah? Did I?" she said.

She thought she hadn't betrayed him? They'd been married all this time. Did her words really mean she'd never fallen for anyone else?

Andre wasn't about to tell her that he hadn't fallen for anyone either. At least not until he was sure she would say the same.

He figured there was a way to tell easily enough, so he closed the gap between them.

Familiarity came back with the proximity, and he saw the realization flare in her eyes a second before his lips touched hers. For all their banter and the sparks that flashed between them, this was how they told the truth to each other. Speaking without words.

Andre tipped his head to the side and touched his lips to hers again.

The kiss was just getting interesting when she slid her hands to his chest. *Nice.*

She shoved him back and pointed at the door. "Get out."

15

———————

The door opened, and Lucia spun around.

"Look, we should talk about—"

It wasn't Andre. Instead, Nora took a couple of steps into the room and eyed her with a curious expression.

Lucia winced. "I thought you were someone else."

"Sorry, just me." Nora took a couple more steps, holding a tray that she deposited on the top of the dresser.

Lucia wondered if Nora could be described as "just" anything. But after that disastrous conversation with Andre, it was a welcome distraction.

"I brought you some lunch, in case you were hungry." Nora gave her a soft smile. "Sandwiches and heating soup are two of my specialties right now, although I'm working on omelets."

"You're learning to cook?"

"I know." Nora rolled her eyes. "I'm a grown woman. It's sad not to know how to cook. But with Zander being so good at it, there isn't much need. When he's here. It's when he's gone that I have to be able to fend for myself without just going into town and eating at the diner all the time." She patted her stomach.

Lucia had learned how to cook in elementary school. But

there were plenty of other things people could do that she had a hard time with. "I love those meal delivery services where they send you all the ingredients and the recipe."

Nora's eyes widened. "That's a great idea. If I have them send me a meal for two or four people, then I can have people over to visit while Zander is out of town."

"Do they go on missions often?"

Nora shrugged. "I don't exactly know what's normal. I never knew anybody in the line of work that they are in, but they're probably gone three weeks out of the month. There's another guy who lives here, the one who does tech support for the team. But he's engaged, and younger, so he doesn't exactly want to hang out with me." She gave a sheepish smile. "I've made some friends in town, though. The people here are really nice."

"Where is 'here'?" She thought the question was innocent enough. At some point Nora was going to realize that Lucia needed as much information about what was going on as possible. Then she needed to get to a phone so she could call into the agency she worked for.

Her task force boss had been killed, and the team decimated. Surely somebody wanted an accounting of what'd happened.

She figured they'd be going after Burgess now. Even if they weren't going to let Lucia participate in that operation, she was still a material witness in this investigation.

Getting back to work would be far better than sitting around here being the loose end. She needed to do something other than wallow in how it felt to kiss Andre finally, after all these years. She knew he'd been testing her. Their relationship had always been about the clash between them, the competition. Sure, there had been those sweet moments. But they challenged each other, and she loved that part of how they worked every day to make each other better than when they started.

These days she had to figure out how to challenge herself.

And when she made her goals? No one cared. Maybe that was why it didn't seem as satisfying as it should have.

Nora studied her. Probably trying to figure out if she was going to trust Lucia, or what exactly the boys had meant when they'd given her instructions on what to say and what not to.

Lucia glanced around. "It's not like I'm going anywhere."

If Nora was worried she was a breach of security, then she didn't need to be. After all, they'd given her no access to electronics, and when she'd tried the door, it had been unlocked—leading into a hallway with a door at the end that *was* locked.

For a minute, she'd wondered exactly what damage she could do from down here. Just so they knew what they had on their hands when they'd brought her here.

But she wasn't one to give in to spite. Or being petty.

Just so that Nora knew she had some information, Lucia asked, "Is this where you guys are based?" The question was a long shot, but she figured with a setup like this, Andre and his team had brought her to a familiar place where they controlled the terrain.

She didn't think they intended to keep her prisoner exactly. It was more that they were regrouping. Andre was injured, Lucia had more bruises than friends, and they needed a whole lot more information about Burgess. Whether or not they would go after him was a different question.

Of course, if they were going to ask *her*, they would discover she knew quite a lot about Burgess, even beyond spending time in his compound.

Lucia crossed to the tray of food and took a bite of the sandwich just to have something to focus on so she could attempt to purge those memories from her mind.

Or at least try.

"This is Last Chance County." Nora stood close to the door, as if not exactly scared of Lucia, but also not completely comfortable in this situation. She had been warned.

Which only made Lucia wonder again what they told her.

Nora blew out a breath. "I don't know why I'm so surprised that men would act like men."

Lucia eyed her.

"They are brothers in every sense of the word, and having a sister suddenly is different for everyone. But still..." Nora slumped into the armchair.

"You need girl time?"

"I don't know. What is that?"

Lucia shrugged. "I don't think I've ever done it before. Or had it. Or whatever."

Nora narrowed her eyes and grinned. "I guess we'll have to figure it out together. Zander and Andre are best friends. All the guys are. Sometimes it's hard to break through the bond they have, even if Zander and I are married now." Her grin turned into a wide smile. "We eloped two weeks ago and got married on the beach in Hawaii. All the guys came."

"Eloped?" That was alarmingly similar to what she and Andre had done. But they'd driven to Vegas at the end of summer the year they graduated high school.

What a disaster that had turned out to be.

Nora nodded, still exuding happiness. "Ry—uh, Badger— has been moody ever since, but he said it's not because we got married." She sighed. "And then on top of that, I just had a DNA test done with this woman. Her name is Hannah, and she's a police detective. You would probably like her a lot. Anyway, the results came back, and it turns out she's my half sister."

Lucia tried to keep up with the conversation.

"Can you believe that?" Nora lifted both her hands, palms up, then let them fall back to her lap. "I grew up with a father who wasn't exactly big on showing affection. Then it turned out he was this international criminal anyway, and now he's in jail awaiting trial. So then I had no family. Now I have a husband *and* a sister I didn't even know about."

"Wow."

"Stephen Gladstone is my father. The minute he became the subject of an investigation, he'd tried to blame everything on me."

"I'm sorry," Lucia said. "That's rough."

Nora nodded again. "That's why Zander and I got married, plus we didn't want to wait anyway. Now I'm Nora O'Connell, and I never have to hear the name Gladstone again if I don't want to."

Lucia could understand that. "I can't imagine finding out I had half sister I never knew about."

"It's crazy, right? I mean, I guess my dad had an affair. Which is totally possible because…" Nora made a face. "He told me my mom died. But maybe she's still out there?" She waved to the side. "Somewhere. Apparently uninterested in having a relationship with me. That's probably why I bonded so hard with the boys. I mean, it's not difficult to do that, because they're awesome."

Lucia couldn't help but smile. Nora had found a family here after a life trapped with a terrible father. Her team hadn't been like that at all, the kind of friends who made a family. Though she'd have said some of them were friends. Maybe.

She couldn't help wondering if Nora was, in her own way, issuing an invitation. But this woman had no idea the destruction that could result from going after Burgess. Not to mention what would happen if Lucia fell for Andre all over again.

The whole thing was extremely tempting, which only made her realize that it would be the worst thing for her *and* Nora. Stay here, and risk getting so close to Andre she never wanted to give him up again?

The most enticing things were usually *always* a bad idea.

All Lucia should do was stick around long enough to make sure it didn't turn into a giant disaster. She wasn't anything like Nora, a woman who deserved to be as happy as she was now.

Lucia needed a plan.

ALL THE GUYS sat around the dining table as Andre sipped his coffee and tried not to think about how much his leg hurt. He still had an hour before he could take more pain meds, according to the doctor.

Ted sat at the head of the table at one end and Zander at the other. He knew Nora was downstairs talking to Lucia and wanted to go down there. But only to make sure Nora was all right. Not because he'd kissed the woman who was his wife and she'd shoved him away. He wasn't all that surprised, or upset, by it. After all, he'd wanted to know if she still had strong emotions for him. Turned out she did. A woman who didn't care one bit wouldn't have been so affronted that she shoved him away.

Which told him he still meant something to her.

"…asking about Andre."

He lowered his cup. "What?" Ted had been talking about him, and now he was going to have to expose the fact he hadn't been listening at all. That wasn't going to go down well with Zander, especially on top of his existing punishment.

Andre scratched at the stubble now growing across his upper lip and down the sides of his mouth. He was going to look like a real creeper when the thing grew in all the way. On top of that he'd probably wind up doing extra workouts for the next month. Though, not until his leg and arm both healed.

Judah smirked. Eas took a sip of his tea, as though at some diplomatic meeting about the weather. Or the price of cheese. Badger didn't even look up from his phone.

"Who was asking about me?" Andre motioned at their teammate with a nod of his head. Asking one question and silently communicating about something else entirely.

Zander nodded back, frowning. He was in agreement that they needed to do something about Badger, who hadn't been himself since he'd hung out with a certain police detective a few weeks ago. Or since they'd all flown to Hawaii for Zander and

Nora's wedding. No one was sure when exactly it started. Despite the fact that Badger was on his phone, and had been almost constantly the last few days, he still hadn't called back the police detective they all now knew was Nora's half sister.

But they'd found that out *after* Badger didn't call her back. So it wasn't that.

What it was, was Badger being Badger. When there was a problem, he retreated into himself. The love-them-and-leave-them guy could joke with the best of them, but when it came to committing to something other than this team, he shut down and refused to get into it. He wanted everyone around him to believe the mask he put on.

Ted leaned back in his chair. "I got intel that Burgess has been putting out feelers online, and there's some chatter the FBI got ahold of from a confidential informant, or an undercover agent. I don't remember. But it mentioned you. Burgess wants to know who you really are."

"What about Lucia?" Andre asked.

Ted shrugged one shoulder. "Nothing, that I know of."

That was good, at least. "We're just going to ignore the fact Isaac was there?"

That got Badger to look up, but it didn't change his mood any.

Maybe the detective had shoved him away like Lucia had done to Andre, literally or figuratively. Didn't matter. Same result, either way.

Andre should drag him out for a run. Or, he would have if he could run right now instead of limping in a slow walk. Ted's brother Dean ran a center for people who needed counseling that was in the hills above town, mostly for veterans or those who had suffered trauma. But getting Badger to go voluntarily would be the tricky part.

Andre said, "Do we think Isaac is the guy on the inside?"

The feds hadn't been able to move in because of some kind of operation happening within the compound, specifically that some government department or organization had an asset planted within Burgess's group.

Badger looked at Zander. Their team leader shrugged. "It's certainly possible, though as far as we can tell he's not working with the CIA anymore. There's bad blood between them."

"So who's he working for?" Judah asked.

"And if he isn't working for the good guys, then is he going to tell Burgess who you are?" Badger glanced at Andre.

His friend didn't think Andre would be bothered about that, did he? "I'll be more surprised if he doesn't tell Burgess who I am." He hoped Isaac didn't tell Burgess where to find Andre. Intel didn't matter, but a location was entirely different if the guy was looking for payback. His compound had been compromised, and most of the people inside either escaped or relocated.

"If he does find out about me," Andre said, "will it be something other than that I'm a disgruntled veteran with an ax to grind?"

Ted said, "I threw up a fake profile online that matches what you told him. It won't stand up to much scrutiny, but I can work on strengthening it."

"Do we know if Burgess has compounds anywhere else?" Andre glanced at Ted. "A secondary location where they might have fled?"

Ted shook his head.

Zander said, "I'd like to believe he fled, but I'm not sure he's running scared. Maybe just inconvenienced. I'm assuming that if Burgess had a plan, then it's still on track."

"So we stop him." Andre didn't figure it needed to be more confusing than that. Still the guys, for some reason, thought he was amusing. Andre ignored them. "If he is looking for me, maybe I should show up again. Get back in, or have one of you hand me over and get in."

Zander shook his head. "Too dangerous."

Andre shot him a look. Given all the missions they'd been on together, it would hardly be the worst they had suffered. Especially since he held all pain and suffering up against the memory of Lucia screaming in his face for all to hear that she never wanted to see him again.

"You know what I mean," Zander said.

Andre nodded, because he at least understood that his friend didn't want to risk any of their lives if he could avoid it. The danger was inherent in their chosen career. He appreciated the way Zander watched all their backs and worked to mitigate the risk as much as he could.

After Lucia ended their relationship, he had chosen this life and these people to be his true family. Until now, he hadn't even considered the idea Lucia might come back into his life. That he could have her on top of all he had built.

But working through all the junk to get to their happily ever after meant opening up.

He would have to give up the grudge that had been his source of strength for years—the thing that had energized him as he worked every day to be the best soldier he could be. She and her dad might not think there was worth in being a grunt. So Andre had decided to be the best grunt he could be. The best soldier, the best brother to his friends.

Now he had to be the best number two Zander ever had. Something he would never say out loud, as the guys would bust up laughing. But he'd never had a better boss, team leader, or commander.

"So what do we do about Burgess?" Andre figured they needed to find out what the guy was planning. The setup had been solid at the compound, but still there'd been an air of planning and preparation going around. Lucia had confirmed that. "Isaac gave us a flash drive, right?"

Ted nodded. "I'm working on cracking the password. In the meantime, there are feds at the hospital where we dropped those women who escaped. I got authorization to view the digital recordings of the interviews, so I'm waiting for those to come through."

"They say anything about Lucia?"

Ted shook his head. "They didn't ask, so I didn't tell. When she wants to make contact is up to her."

So many parts and pieces. Still, at the core of it remained the fact Burgess had to be taken down.

Stopped.

A guy like Burgess wasn't going to be organizing anything good. He was likely going for mass-scale destruction, or some other kind of huge statement no one would be able to ignore. The last thing America needed was another catastrophe as a result of a terrorist attack. Because Burgess was a domestic terrorist—or he would be, when he enacted his plan.

Andre just hoped they wouldn't be too late to stop it.

16

———————

Nora stepped into the main living space first. Lucia stayed right behind her, though she stopped at the mouth of the hall and leaned against the wall so she could watch.

"We weren't allowed to talk to each other." A woman's voice emerged from the speakers of a laptop on the table.

Andre sat in a chair, leaned precariously back on two legs while he held onto the table with his fingers. The dark-haired man who'd given Andre the scanner sat in front of the laptop.

Zander was in the kitchen with the other guys, including the one who always wore a mask. He wasn't wearing one now. Just like he hadn't been in the hallway at the last house. Though, as soon as Zander spotted her, he tapped the man on the outside of his arm.

The two men shared a look, and the man whose face she had recognized from the FBI's Most Wanted List moved away from her without turning—without ever showing her his face. He disappeared out the door on the far side of the living area.

The woman on the screen of the laptop continued. Lucia wondered if it was a video call, but no one here spoke as she said, "They treated us worse than the dogs."

Lucia recalled the cafeteria, and what had happened there

with the animal and the woman. She must have made a sound in her throat, because Andre snapped his chair legs to the floor and turned. She didn't want him getting up, so she waved him off. It was her problem to deal with, not any of theirs.

He twisted in his chair to look at Zander. The team leader shrugged and went back to mixing whatever was in the big bowl.

Nora lifted up to speak in Zander's ear. He stopped what he was doing to listen, then leaned down and touched his lips to hers.

Lucia couldn't help but think again about the difference between her and this woman. Nora had class, and all Lucia had was a preference for shotguns and a gaming addiction. One of them had a husband and a loving relationship. The other—her —lived in an empty apartment wherever she was assigned and hadn't spoken to her husband in years.

A man off camera spoke, the sound coming through the laptop speakers. "How long had you been there?"

The woman brushed a shaky hand under her eye, and Lucia realized she was in a hospital gown. She must have been one of the women the helicopter flew away with. "About three weeks? I don't exactly know. It might have been longer."

Probably not long enough to have learned what Burgess was up to. Lucia wanted him brought down in a serious way. Enough she could push aside her attraction to Andre, and the fact they should sit down and have an entire conversation. Actually resolve what was between them. Instead, she was determined to focus on this investigation and everything that had gone wrong. If Campbell truly had been linked to Burgess, either as some kind of plant in the bureau or compromised to some degree, there would be a microscope turned on any remaining members of the team.

She still needed to call in, but none of these guys—or Nora —seemed inclined to hand over a phone so she could do that. Nor had anyone said a word about her going home. What if she had a pet? She'd need to call someone to feed the poor neglected animal.

It was like they didn't think she had a life aside from the mission. Either that was the way they lived, or none of them had a high opinion about her living a full life of her own. The alternative was that they'd already hacked her entire life and drawn their own conclusions. Andre had said as much.

What did he think of what he'd found?

Ted clicked a button on the mousepad. "Not much there."

Lucia spoke before anyone else could. "Because she's a victim. They're putting together a picture of what happened to her. They didn't even get to Burgess yet." She pushed off the wall to try to shake the mental images she'd seen at the compound. The woman still on the screen had seen even more than her, considering she'd been there for weeks.

Lucia continued, "What we need is someone who was there even longer than her. They'll have had the chance to maybe overhear something that could be useful."

They all stared at her.

"Like the pregnant woman who got on the helicopter."

Andre shot her a look. "The one who stabbed me?"

She blinked.

"That was after she killed a puma, or whatever it was."

Judah strode out from behind the kitchen counter. "You saw a pregnant woman kill a puma? And you didn't tell me?"

"She's not your soul mate, bro." Badger tossed an orange at the British man's head.

Judah caught it and bit down into the skin, before peeling it away and sucking out the juice.

Nora snuggled up to Zander's side, a smile on her face. He put his arm around her shoulder, and they watched the team's antics together. Only Andre didn't seem amused by it.

Andre shook his head. "You can't go talk to her, Lucia. You're in protective custody."

As if she was going to let that stop her. "You're injured. I'm a fully trained federal agent. Which one of us has the jurisdiction and the ability to go after Burgess right now?" Lucia folded her arms.

He had to know she wasn't going to back down. Had she ever? They might not have a consensus on what was between them right now, but they could agree on the facts at least. But he only flashed her a Cheshire grin. The same one that had won her over so many times when she'd had second thoughts about his plans.

Was he going to share with her now?

Maybe Lucia didn't even want to know what his idea was.

To prove it to him, she turned to Zander. "The pregnant woman is at the hospital with the others, right?"

"She'll be interviewed by the cops, just like that one." Zander motioned to the laptop.

"Actually," Ted began, "only a couple of the women were willing to talk to the feds when they showed up. The pregnant woman wasn't one of them."

"She'll talk to me." Lucia was sure.

"Yeah?" The challenge was clear in Andre's tone.

She told Zander, "I was there. She'll talk to me."

None of these men knew DEA Special Agent Lucia DeSoto. She wasn't about to brag over her achievements. They could believe her or not, that was up to them. She knew how good she was—because the job had been her focus since she'd graduated college.

Lucia wondered if Andre would say the same about his career. The way he'd carried himself that night in the wild area of the compound, she figured he at least understood his skills. She knew her limitations as much as her strengths and worked to balance both, the same way she knew this moment would be a turning point between her and the men of this team.

Mercenaries. Private contractors. They might work with the feds so that they had access to the witness footage—at least she hoped they'd obtained it legally—but they certainly weren't cops.

"What's your stake in this?"

Zander studied her before answering her question. "I don't like men who victimize women."

"It's more than that with Burgess." She would also argue that, in a way, it was how the world worked. How deals were made, and favors exchanged hands.

Sometimes fighting the tide of evil sucked her down in the undertow.

Only by remembering there was more than enough good in the world to overcome the evil could she manage to lift her head. Keep going. Keep fighting.

Zander nodded, conceding her point at least. "We need to know what he has planned."

"That's why we're watching these." Andre waved at the computer.

"I'm going to the hospital." Not only could she try to talk with the pregnant woman, but she could also speak to the feds there. That would be better than just calling. Face-to-face was always her preference.

Andre actually snorted. "How are you going to get there, cupcake?"

Ugh. They were back to that. She spun to him. "On my two working legs, considering I didn't get shot."

His eyes narrowed. She thought she'd scored a hit until he said, "It's a hospital. Get me a wheelchair, I'll blend right in."

"You guys can't carry a gun into a hospital. I can."

"You don't have your badge," Andre said. "Do you?"

Lucia pressed her lips together.

"We're rolling out." Zander kissed Nora on the cheek. "Let's move."

Everyone in the room except Lucia and Andre immediately headed out.

Zander walked Nora toward her. "Fifteen minutes."

Lucia nodded. "Thank you." She knew he was doing her a favor.

He gave her a nod, which she took to mean, *Don't mess this up.* He then left with Nora, who squeezed her shoulder.

Which meant Lucia was alone with Andre again. So she stayed by the hall, because the last time they'd been alone and in close proximity, he'd kissed her. She'd shoved him away.

There didn't need to be a repeat of that.

"Happy now?" He lifted his chin.

There were several things she could've said. Lucia settled on, "I need to do my job. I know firsthand how bad these guys are. If Burgess has a plan in the works, which I believe he does, then it's up to us to stop it."

"Yeah?" He moved so the couch wasn't between them but stopped four feet away, not giving away one ounce of the pain he must've been in from the gunshot. "Us?"

"This is my job."

HE WAS ONLY HERE because he'd been contacted as the next of kin.

That was the thought that stuck with Andre during the plane ride to the hospital. Lucia was right, this was her job.

He had the chance now to see her in her element, watch her work as a federal agent.

As they approached the front doors of the hospital—everyone except Eas, who remained in the car out of sight—Zander said, "The feds are gonna meet us in the lobby."

"At least Burgess isn't gunning for us the way Gladstone and Patchuli did." Badger pushed the door open first, holding it so they could all go through.

"Don't remind me," Andre told him.

"What happened with Nora's father?" Lucia asked. "I read

in the paper that she used her foundation as a front. But then it was her father who was arrested."

"She didn't do a thing." Zander's clean-shaven jaw flexed. "Her dad set her up, and in the process dragged us into it." He blew out a breath, his gaze on Lucia. "That was a lot of paperwork to sort out."

Andre saw the smile she gave his boss. It was one he'd considered his favorite in high school. And she was giving it to another man, now? Sure, it was his boss. She wasn't flirting. But seriously? "After that whole implicated-by-association thing, I'm not too hot to repeat it anytime soon if Burgess decides that's going to be his tactic."

She glanced at him. "I can't believe that was you."

As long as she didn't bring up the fact they'd been contracted to take out Patchuli and he'd failed. Andre didn't need to be reminded. "We're freelance, but we take government contracts. Or we did until it was discovered Gladstone used his position to make illegal money."

"And you saved Nora in the process." Lucia's lips curled up, as though she was proud of what they'd done.

"Zander did that." His boss had gone in single-handedly and rescued her from her dad's head of security, a man who'd been obsessed with her.

"Kind of like you walked into that compound with no backup and no weapons…and saved me?"

He didn't know how to answer that. Was it even a question?

"Nora told me you risked everything."

Now she was going to be sweet, in a hospital lobby surrounded by his team. Andre would've rolled his eyes, but he had to watch his step because walking *hurt*, and he didn't need to stumble. The human body might be capable of taking a serious amount of punishment, but that didn't mean he wanted to make it any worse for himself by falling on his leg—or bracing a fall with his injured arm.

"We can talk about it later." Andre wanted to tug her to his side and walk with his good arm across her shoulders, the way they'd done so many times. Right now it would be about her helping hold him up.

Zander strode to where two agents waited for them. Lucia went after him, striding with that confident cop walk so many of them had. She shook hands after his team leader did.

Badger showed Judah something on his phone that made both of them laugh. He was about to tell them to knock it off, even if Badger engaging with anyone was a good thing, when a crackle sounded in his earpiece.

"Um…hello?"

Andre figured Zander couldn't respond, so he turned away from anyone able to see him and said, "Nora? What are you doing on comms?"

Even Lucia had an earpiece in. Judah had made a big deal about helping her seat the thing in her ear, so it was barely visible. Andre had been about to punch him when Zander interrupted and asked Lucia a hundred questions about procedure—everything they needed to know about what she'd do, just in case something went awry.

Considering that happened a lot the last time they'd thrown a woman in the mix, Andre figured it was a good idea.

"Andre," the voice in his ear said, "where's Zander?"

"Talking to the feds. What happened to Ted?"

"Oh well, he had to run out. He was late for premarital counseling, and he forgot it was today until his phone alerted him. He said if he was late again that Jess would kill him."

Judah snickered.

Badger didn't react at all. In fact, his expression blanked, and he looked…cold to everything going on in their lives.

"They'll be fine." Andre studied Badger as he reassured Nora. He wasn't certain this was a woman problem. It seemed like what was wrong with Badger was more than just heartbreak. Andre missed his joke-around friend, even if it was only him playing a part.

"Anyway," Nora said, "Ted left me a whole handbook, which is titled *The Complete Noob's Guide to Chevalier Protection Services*, and I'll be having a word with him about that."

Andre spotted Zander shift and look at his feet for a second.

"But I should be able to do…some of what he does. He already got into hospital surveillance because they back everything up onto the cloud, so I'm ready to go."

"Anything we should know about?" Andre watched Zander and Lucia head to the elevators with the feds. The rest of the team followed, all crowding in the tiny box as they ascended to the floor where the women were being treated.

Zander asked the feds how they liked the local FBI office and found they'd flown in from Salt Lake City to conduct the interviews. Andre figured that at least gave them a shot at these guys not being anywhere near Campbell and whatever corruption had poisoned his career—and his ethics.

Nora continued, "Ted opened a program that does facial recognition, such as it is with grainy photos from terrible surveillance that should be far better quality. Telling me all that was why he was late. There was ranting."

Andre scratched the stubble on his chin to hide the grin on his face. He'd have interrupted her, but the feds would realize they were on comms.

"Any…way." Nora spoke slowly. "I'm clicking…and dragging. The instructions say Control and Function, plus the *V*… oh, there it is. And Enter." She sighed. "Okay, it's searching for their faces. The two FBI guys who are there with you. We do *not* need another repeat of the whole Campbell thing, okay? One bad guy is plenty, cause this one has a whole army of men. I don't think I want to meet him."

Zander got his phone out and tapped the screen.

A second later, Nora said, "I love you, too." Humor laced her tone. "And I'm being quiet now."

The elevator doors opened, and the feds walked out with Zander and Lucia. She might not have her badge, but he figured they'd recognize one like them—and call in to confirm her identity.

Andre, Judah, and Badger hung back in the hallway.

They were backup, there to provide support in case anything went wrong. Andre had the guys stand at opposite ends of the hall. Their presence there, with the cops, was accepted by the staff. One nurse even asked if they wanted coffee, something that didn't happen often in his experience. Usually people were too wrapped up in their own thing to be inconvenienced by someone, even if that person was actively hunting a domestic terrorist.

"Um, Andre?" In the background of the connection, he could hear angry tones from the computer.

He replied on comms, "Yeah, Nora?" He figured she'd pressed a wrong button, but it wasn't as if he could help her.

"Let me see if I can send it to your phone."

"Tell me what it is while you do that." Maybe one of the feds wasn't who they said they were. It might even be Lucia for all he knew. Andre wasn't going to let himself be surprised by something like that.

"It's Isaac. According to the angry beeping...he's in the parking lot."

"Probably something else. He's not here, Nora."

"He is." She said, "Look on your phone."

Andre swiped the screen. His brows rose. "Isaac."

At the end of the hall, Badger pushed through the door to the stairwell at a run.

17

____

"We appreciate you letting us do this," Lucia told the feds. She even took a step toward the hospital room door, so that their attention followed her. Rather than it being on Zander, currently quietly fuming about what was going on over comms. Not the part where Nora was valiantly attempting to fill Ted's shoes, but the part where Badger had run off and Andre was now limping after him.

Lucia carried on the conversation with the feds while Judah said in his clipped accent, "I'll stay in the hall."

Zander looked at his shoes for a second, then back up.

Lucia headed for the door.

One of the feds caught her before she could open it, saying, "You were really there, in the compound?"

She glanced back at him. "Only for a few hours. The task force operation went wrong, and I wound up dragged back there by one of Burgess's guys."

She figured they'd know she was telling the truth because she looked like she'd been in a place like that, beat up and rumpled, though she had taken that shower at the first house and Nora had found her some clean clothes. They didn't exactly fit great, but they were better than what she'd been wearing before.

She wasn't sure why she was so worried about her appearance. But when the right people started asking questions about Campbell and his betrayal of the oath he had taken, these two in front of her would provide an account that should play in her favor. Because it was the truth.

The fed who hadn't asked that question winced. Because they knew what the captives went through? The other one looked entirely too interested in what she might tell them. "I can give you a statement, after I talk to this woman."

"There's something else at play here?"

She nodded. "We have intel that suggests Burgess is up to something. We just have no idea where he's gone."

Zander stepped close to their huddle. "Has anyone said anything here that gave you an indication of where he might be?"

One of the feds shook his head. "Mostly we've just been getting the lay of the land about what the compound was like."

Lucia would have done the same, coming into a situation like this with little idea what it was about. They'd have read the investigation file, hopefully. But with Campbell working for Burgess on the side, exactly how much had been written down in that file? He could have augmented the reports. Hidden details of the operation. Left out key information that would've described the threat.

Now Burgess was out there. And thanks to Campbell, it was possible no one would know exactly how serious this threat was. Her former task force supervisor could have done whatever he wanted.

She'd had no idea.

Great. That was just hitting her now? With everything that had gone on, she hardly had time to process Campbell's betrayal. Or how thoroughly she had failed not realizing he was on the take. Not to mention potentially other members of the task force, as well.

She'd messed up in a big way.

Lucia pushed all that aside. "The pregnant woman was there a lot longer than the others, so we're thinking she might have some information about what Campbell is doing now."

One fed nodded. The other one looked like he was about to speak.

Zander motioned to the door. "I guess we'll find out."

As they walked to the door, Nora's voice came over the earpiece she'd been given. "Isaac is with someone in a wheelchair. It looks like a woman, but only because they have long hair. I can't really see enough to know for sure."

"Copy that." Judah was the one who had replied, the only one not occupied like Badger and Andre were, or within earshot of someone who would realize they were wearing comms.

How was Andre even going after his teammate when he'd been grazed in the leg by a bullet? His ability to power through an injury impressed her. Even as she wondered exactly how hard he would crash when he pushed himself too far and his body didn't appreciate it. He said they needed to get him a wheelchair so he could blend in. But had he done it? No.

He'd always been stubborn like that.

Lucia pushed open the door.

"Oh," Nora said, "I think the person in the wheelchair is pregnant."

The bed in the hospital room was empty. Lucia's stomach clenched. "We need to talk to that woman."

The feds appeared in the doorway behind them. "She's gone?" As though that wasn't a completely obvious statement.

Lucia was about to respond to it when Nora spoke again. "Ted's program thingy finished with the feds' faces. I have their personnel files, but there's nothing on here about internal investigations. Nothing about disciplinary action. In fact, one of them has a commendation. They look solid."

Lucia paced away down the hall, as though moving so she could think through the situation. When she was out of earshot of them, she spoke low in her comms. "Andre, we need him stopped. We need to talk to that woman."

"And Isaac," Judah said. "Because I, for one, don't think he should get away with this. It's time for a reckoning."

Eas came on. "You want me to head around to the parking lot and cut him off?"

"I'll let you know," Andre replied. "Badger, you need to lock him down. And don't let the woman get away." He sounded like he was worried what Badger would do.

Lucia didn't know this team well, but she was getting the lay of the land on their dynamics. The depth of their feelings for each other was clear in the way they supported and challenged one another. Something her team had never done.

She'd met Isaac at the compound. He'd been nice to her, almost guarding her when Burgess and his men had wanted to continue hurting her. Isaac was the one who'd carried her back to her room and made sure she didn't suffer more than she had.

These guys seemed to think he was a threat. Or at least involved somehow.

Even with them being on different pages about Isaac, she loved this interplay. Being on comms and part of an operation made everything inside her reverberate in harmony. Rather than the last few days where she'd felt at odds, or dissonant. She hardly knew how to explain what it felt like to have Andre in her orbit again. Or maybe she was in his, considering this was his world.

She let out a long breath and spotted Judah at the end of the hall. He motioned to her with a flick of his fingers.

Lucia headed for him, and Zander fell into step beside her. She didn't want to get used to being part of the team. Soon enough it would be over and she would be back in her own life. But for now, she felt a whole lot better being part of something even if it wasn't official. Even if she didn't have her badge and gun.

"What is it?" Zander asked the British man.

Judah said, "Two doors down on the left."

Lucia hung back. She figured if it was somebody from the compound, they might recognize her. It would be better if Zander was the one who appeared nonchalant.

He glanced in the room and then made his way back. "Take a look, Lucia. He's unconscious."

She did as he asked, making her way far enough she could peer into the room. The man in the hospital bed had his eyes closed. She recognized him from the compound. One of Burgess's men who had beat on her in the arena.

A flicker of worry moved through her stomach as she made her way back to them.

Zander said, "The code on the door means he suffered a gunshot wound. The police might have already come and talked to him, or the doctor is waiting for him to wake up. Because the hospital staff would have alerted the cops to his injuries. It has to be reported and investigated."

They walked back to the door. Lucia stepped into the room. If he was waking up soon, then she was definitely going to speak to him.

Zander said, "Nora, mute me and Lucia. Judah can knock if you need us." Then he shut the door behind him.

It took a minute, but the man in the bed opened his eyes. She saw the second he recognized her. "You smell like a cop."

But he hadn't noticed it when she was in the compound, which Lucia considered a good thing.

Zander stepped up to the end of the bed. "What do I smell like?"

The man's eyes flickered with fear.

Zander said, "Let's talk."

ANDRE JABBED at the elevator button until the door slid open. He stepped inside, and the older guy in a white doctor's coat said, "Going down?"

Andre figured that was obvious given he'd stepped onto the elevator that was descending floors. But he didn't say that. He simply said, "Parking lot, please."

That was where Isaac was, pushing a wheelchair with the pregnant woman in it. That's what this had to be. He was helping her get out for some reason.

Badger had raced down the stairs much faster than Andre could with his gunshot wound. So Andre had pushed out onto the hall two floors down from where he started and found the elevators. He wasn't going to be able to cut off Badger, but hopefully he could get there quick enough to mitigate the damage his friend was going to do.

He leaned against the inside of the elevator, ignoring the man's study of him. His leg hurt even though he'd descended the stairs with one hand on the rail, only landing on his good leg and letting the other trail behind. His arm, he didn't want to think about.

Later, he could sit down and rest.

On the third floor, the doors opened and the doctor exited, which left Andre alone in the elevator. All he could do was wait for it to get to the bottom floor, the parking lot. Then he was going to have to run again, which meant he needed to conserve his strength.

Nora had muted Zander and Lucia, and Judah had told them all the two of them were interviewing someone they thought was one of Burgess's men. Neither would be able to hear him.

Andre closed his eyes. "You need to listen to me, Ry."

He had no idea if this was even going to work. Let alone actually slow down his friend. But he had to try.

"I get you." Andre gripped the rail that ran around the elevator at hip height, taking some of the weight off his leg. "I hate that we trusted him and he betrayed us. We put our hearts and souls into this team, and Isaac just walks away? No. That's not cool at all."

Frustration burned in his gut.

Was Badger even going to listen to him? Andre had been just as angry. He simply dealt with it differently. Badger had said he'd kill Isaac if he saw him, or so Zander said. Andre hadn't been there at the time. In the heat of things with Nora's father, Andre had been on an airplane with Isaac. The man had been injured and barely said anything at all, except to try to explain to the former president and his wife on board that there was a serious threat in play.

Isaac had spoken with an authority Andre had never seen before.

But he hadn't been willing to talk at all about the team, except to whine about how he'd had no choice. Nothing about the fact he'd turned Zander over to the police and walked away like it was nothing. Given he'd revealed Hanna's identity to them, Isaac probably thought he'd offered consolation in the process. As if anyone would believe that made up for the betrayal.

"I want answers as much as you do. I want to know why he did this, and who he actually works for." Andre pushed out a breath. "I want to know why he lied to us and if any of it was even real. You want an explanation, I get that. Living without one twists you up. It keeps you awake at night wondering what you could've done differently. Instead of being able to move on, you're always back there in that moment when you discovered the truth wasn't what you thought it was."

But instead of remembering those moments with Isaac, all he could think about was Lucia and the way she'd yelled at him that it was over. He knew her father had died after he left for boot camp. But she was supposed to have moved into his apartment, and instead he'd gone home to find her stuff gone. She'd never even tried.

Months after their wedding, Lucia had been enrolled in college two states away from their home. It had been as though she erased her entire life in California and started over in Washington. Like everything they had mattered nothing to her.

He opened his eyes to a blurry elevator, feeling the burn of frustration behind his gaze.

This wasn't about her. This is about Isaac, and the things Andre could control in the present. Goals, and his ability to achieve them. Lucia had always been an impossibility. She'd shot him down fifteen years ago and given him absolutely no way to figure out a way forward. Eventually he'd had to move past the whole thing and accept the fact he could never resolve it. Only now he realized he might not have been as "moved on" as he'd thought.

Andre shook off the idea as the elevator doors opened.

To anyone observing he would appear like the next of kin of a person admitted to the hospital. Turning over the emotions of having a loved one in intensive care, or with a horrible diagnosis. Too bad for him this was just his normal life.

When he got his hands on Isaac, he was going to punch the guy. At least he would if Badger had left anything for him to do.

Andre scanned the parking lot. He spotted Badger running down an aisle to his right, headed in that direction.

Isaac waited beside a car. He ducked out of sight and then rounded the rear of the compact. As Badger approached him, Isaac pushed an empty wheelchair at Badger with enough force to knock the guy aside.

Badger hit the ground and rolled, planted his foot, and launched back up.

Isaac was ready for him.

The two had trained together extensively, both using weapons and in hand-to-hand combat. They knew each other's strengths and weaknesses in a way that made for an explosive fight.

Badger slammed into Isaac. They grappled with each other

for a second before he grabbed Isaac and spun him. Isaac's back banged against the car trunk. Badger pulled his hand back and slammed his fist into Isaac's face.

"Hey!" Andre raced over as fast as he could while his leg screamed with every step. He gritted his teeth and fought his body's need to collapse to the ground. "That's enough!"

Badger didn't listen. He punched Isaac again, while the former spy rummaged in his pockets. He brought out a hand-held device, no bigger than a phone. Andre heard the crackle a second before Isaac pressed it against Badger's side.

Badger hissed and backed up. They'd trained extensively with stun guns as well. Badger shook off the sensation, both fists raised in front of him.

Isaac raised both hands. "I don't wanna fight you. If I do, you won't like what happens."

Badger looked ready to launch himself at the other man again. "You don't go near her."

Isaac's expression shifted as Andre approached, saying, "What's going on?"

Neither of them paid him any attention.

Badger said to Isaac, "Hannah doesn't want to hear from you."

Isaac lifted his chin. "That's Hannah's choice."

Badger exploded at Isaac again. Their former teammate braced, knowing it was coming even before Andre grasped Badger around the waist and pulled him back.

Andre tried to shove Badger away from Isaac. "Don't. That's enough."

They weren't ever going to get answers as to who Isaac really was, and why he'd walked away from the team, if Badger didn't back down.

"Can we go?" The pregnant woman stood beside the open passenger door, an impatient expression on her face. "I have to pee."

"There are people upstairs who want to talk to you," Andre told her.

Her impatient expression shifted as she shrugged. "And I'm supposed to care about that?" She glanced at Isaac. "We have somewhere to be."

Isaac pushed off the car and straightened. "I'm leaving now."

"And we're supposed to just let you go?" Now Andre was getting as annoyed as Badger, although considering this was also about Hannah—and not just Isaac's betrayal of the team—maybe that wasn't true.

"Doesn't matter." Isaac shrugged. He glanced at Badger. "You said what you came here to say. Now I'm done."

Badger pulled a gun from under his jacket. He pointed the barrel at Isaac. "I don't think so."

Andre spun to him. "Are you seriously going to shoot him when there are surveillance cameras everywhere?"

"He deserves it."

"You're gonna have to explain that to me, Ry."

Badger pressed his lips together and shook his head. "I'm just gonna kill him first."

"You kill him, we never find out why he's doing this," Andre pointed out.

"That's what this is about?" Isaac shook his head. "What if there's no good answer, at least not one that's going to satisfy you?"

"That's easy," Badger said. "I just kill you."

Over Hannah? Andre definitely didn't have all the information about what was going on here. "Isaac—"

Before he could finish, the pregnant woman tossed something at them.

There was no time to even yell a warning.

The flash bang hit the ground, and the world exploded in a wash of blinding light and a deafening pop.

18

———————

Lucia stared out the window. The moment the crackle exploded through the open comms channel, she tensed, forcing her body not to turn to where Zander spoke with the man on the bed.

Nora hadn't muted the comms. At least not on their end. Even if the others hadn't been able to hear her and Zander, they could hear everything. And after Andre's heartfelt speech to Badger, she'd hardly been able to focus on them. Instead, her mind had filled with memories.

Andre had almost sounded like he was talking to her while he reassured Badger that they needed answers and not to go off half-cocked. Still, that was what Badger seemed to have done. Even going so far as pulling a gun on Isaac.

Then the channel had shut off somehow.

All she could think of were Andre's words about being hurt. Betrayed. She pushed aside the thoughts when she heard Judah say, "Nora, what was that?"

Lucia glanced back over her shoulder at Zander, who stood at the end of the bed, looking down on the man lying there. If he was aware at all of what was going on over the comms line—

which she figured he probably was—he gave nothing away in his body language.

Nora replied to Judah's question. "Hang on. Give me a second to figure out what it was."

Lucia turned from the window to face Zander and the man. Her body just couldn't handle remaining still any longer. She wanted to head out the door and burn some of this energy by going downstairs and finding out what'd happened to Andre and Badger. There had to be a reason why the feed suddenly cut off.

A voice spoke in accented English over comms, "I'll go check what happened."

Zander glanced over and gave her a tight shake of his head. He didn't want her going. And on top of that, she realized he could tell how she felt not even having been looking at her.

It was both good and bad that he could do that, as a team leader. He would know exactly how Andre felt about her, and likely how she felt about him.

Zander spoke to the injured man. "We know he has something in the works. If you tell me what it is, I can get you into federal protective custody." Before the man could object, Zander said, "Burgess will never find you."

The man's jaw flexed as he clenched and unclenched his teeth.

Lucia didn't know if he would actually tell them anything worth sticking around for, but just on the chance he might they had to stay here and find out. If there was something going on with Andre and Badger, Judah could always go down there as well. Once Nora got the surveillance running.

When they were all back at the house, or wherever they would go next, Lucia needed to have a conversation with Andre.

She'd broken things off between them and never explained the truth, because she'd been far too ashamed of what had happened. It was entirely her fault. Lucia wasn't the kind of person who deserved to be happy after that.

But she could explain it to Andre now. After all this time, she owed him the truth. They needed that between them, and not this confusing détente that had them dancing around each other and the feelings that were so clearly still there between them.

"You think federal protective custody is going to keep me alive?" The man on the bed scoffed. "Burgess will find me, and he'll kill me."

Lucia said, "Maybe so. But if you tell us what he's up to, and we stop it, then you've at least done something right with your life for once."

He turned to her. "You don't know anything about me and the things I've done."

She gave him a look, considering she'd been in that arena with him. She knew very well some of what he'd done. She also personally knew that trying for years to right a wrong and make up for being a terrible person didn't do much to alleviate the guilt.

One big sacrificial action? That might be a better idea, especially for a guy like this.

And such were some of you. The truth was, she was no better than this guy. That was why Lucia had specialized in her career as a fed.

Sure, she hadn't victimized anyone—least of all an innocent. But she had killed a man, something she would have to live with for the rest of her life. Thinking she was somehow above this man here would only lead to pride.

What she needed was the opposite. Now that she knew exactly how deep she'd hurt Andre, she could maybe give him some peace and help to heal the wound.

Then she would go back to her life and try to fix her own heart.

If that was even possible.

"There's an alternative." Zander shrugged one shoulder. "We can leave you here, and everyone will know you were the one who spoke to the cops. The guy who talked."

"Not if I never said anything."

"Do you think Burgess will take that risk?"

Lucia figured Zander was right. Burgess had shot Lydell for deviating from the plan and bringing her into the compound without telling anyone first. Even though his men could do whatever they wanted, she still figured they were ruled with an iron fist as it were. Burgess didn't seem to suffer fools. He'd probably used this opportunity to pare down his army.

Which meant if this guy was here, and not back with the group, then he was expendable. Otherwise, Burgess would have rounded him up, even injured.

"I don't think you know anything." Lucia wandered to the door. "If you were worth anything to Burgess, he'd have come here to get you."

Kind of like the way Isaac had shown up to retrieve the pregnant woman—before they could talk to her.

Which begged the question, had Isaac taken her because she meant something to him or whoever he worked for, or had he taken her first so Zander and his team couldn't speak with her?

She didn't think he was working with Burgess. It was more likely that he was there at the compound to undermine the man's operation.

But did he know the woman, or was he simply trying to get her out of the way so Zander and the men of his team couldn't find out what they needed to know?

Which meant she was valuable at least in some way, if not for her knowledge of the operation.

The man in the hospital bed lifted his chin. "You think I mean nothing to him?"

Lucia shrugged, positioned behind Zander now. He didn't seem to care that she was at his back. That meant he trusted her not to do anything he wouldn't see coming.

Zander said, "When he finds out you betrayed him, what will he do then?"

"So I'm supposed to just tell you everything?" The man

scoffed again. "Why don't you send the real cops in here, and they can talk to me about a deal."

"The deal is this," Zander said, "you tell me, or I kill you."

The man paled. Clearly he believed what Zander said, as he stammered out, "Okay, okay. Calm down."

She figured Zander could look threatening when he needed to, and she was glad she couldn't see his expression, although she was curious.

"Talk." She figured he needed a nudge.

"He tried to get his hands on a bomb, a big one. But it didn't work because someone else stole it." The man sighed, shifting on the bed. He winced and continued, "The convention is coming up in a few days."

Lucia felt her eyes widen. Burgess was going to use a bomb on a convention? "Where?"

"Some big city." The man glanced to the side.

Zander said, "So, Vegas then."

"I never said that."

Zander shrugged.

"How do you know that?"

Lucia would have grinned at any other time. "Talk to the feds outside and tell them the rest of what you know."

Zander took a step back. "Talk deal with them. Get yourself protected."

Evidently Zander wasn't worried the man would tell the feds Zander had threatened to kill him in a hospital bed. They could get the transcript of the interview later. Right now she figured Zander was as eager as she was to find out what had happened to Andre and Badger.

"Let's go."

Lucia didn't need Zander to tell her they were headed out, but she was glad for his decisive nature. He was a good team leader, and this experience was helping her see the way Andre lived. And how a team could be when it functioned effectively. When everyone cared about everyone else.

"How did you know it was Vegas?" she asked.

Zander shrugged. "Burgess wants splashy, right?"

Judah joined them at the elevator lobby. She hit the button to go down when the accented voice came back on comms. "Isaac is gone, and both of them are down. Looks like a flash-bang went off."

Lucia turned away from the elevator and headed for the stairs at a run.

ANDRE GROANED AND ROLLED OVER.

A few feet away he heard Badger say, "Get off me."

Andre blinked and saw Badger shove Lucia. She stumbled back in her crouch and fell on her behind. Andre sat up. Everything swayed, and someone touched his shoulder.

It was Zander. "Easy." He squeezed Andre's shoulder. "What happened?"

Before Andre could say anything, Judah helped Lucia to her feet. He watched them, trying to ascertain if Lucia was unharmed. They both stared down at Badger.

"That was not cool, dude." Judah seemed about as impressed with Badger's behavior as Zander.

As for Andre, he reserved the right to be even more irritated given the guy had just sent Lucia to her bottom on the dirty ground. What was his friend's problem? Andre could understand being angry at Isaac. The guy had allowed them to be incapacitated, so he could escape with his woman friend.

Whatever that was about.

They needed to discover if the baby belonged to Isaac. That would explain a few things. But Andre wasn't sure if whatever he had going on with that woman was business, or if it was personal.

"Need a hand?" Zander straightened his legs and held out one hand.

Andre figured he could've probably got up on his own, but didn't know how his leg was going to react to standing. He clasped Zander's wrist with his good arm and let his friend pull him to his feet. Walking was not a happy endeavor at all. But he made his way to Lucia and stood between her and Badger who was still on the concrete.

He mostly managed to hide how much pain he was in.

Until he realized Zander was staring at him. Then he figured maybe not *mostly*, but at least some.

Before Andre could use a word he wasn't supposed to say to ask Badger what was going on, Zander said, "Care to explain what that was?" The team leader folded his arms across his chest.

"Isaac got away." Badger didn't look at any of them. "What does it matter?"

"What matters," Andre said, "is that this wasn't about Isaac's betrayal. It was about Hannah."

Lucia, Judah, and Zander all turned to Andre. He realized then what'd happened. They had no idea. "You tossed your earpiece, so no one heard you confront him."

Badger pulled it from his pocket and stuck it back in his ear.

Lucia spoke quietly. "The same Hannah who is Nora's half sister?"

He glanced over and gave her a tiny nod. Then to Badger, he said, "Okay, so you pulled it out."

Andre didn't exactly care either way. The point was that no one had heard him talk when he'd approached Isaac, so they also didn't know he'd held a gun on their former teammate. Probably, at least. Andre had been too far away for Badger's words to be transmitted through the open comms channel, so he reiterated now. "You told Isaac to leave Hannah alone."

Zander said, "What did you mean by that?"

They all waited for Badger to explain what had been going on with him the last few weeks. He only looked to the side, still sat on the floor. The expression on his face was more akin to grief than heartbreak, though maybe they weren't too dissimilar. He looked younger than he was. But still, with all the things he had seen there was an edge of danger that would always be in Badger's expressions.

The last thing they needed was for their friend, with his usually sunny demeanor, to turn into an angry loose cannon.

The fact it was similar to how Andre had been behaving gave him pause. They all played off each other, which meant he could easily have been encouraging Badger to reach this point. Even without words.

He should have realized he had that effect on his friend. But he hadn't, because Andre had been entirely too wrapped up in his own situation.

"Start talking." Andre was done waiting around.

Badger glanced at Lucia, then at him. "This is team business only. She's not one of us."

Lucia flinched, just a tiny movement that may have gone unnoticed. Andre wanted to reach out and take her hand, tug her close to his side if not hug her altogether. "You get that we're married, right?"

"Yeah, that's why we all knew she even existed."

"I knew," Zander said.

"I told you as well." Andre had shared with Badger. "But it was a long time ago."

Badger shrugged, unable to hide a wince. "When she never showed up, I figured you were making it up. I didn't know it was true."

"So, not only am I not someone you trust, but I'm also a liar? Is that it?" Andre figured he wasn't entirely wrong about Lucia not being one of the team. But it wasn't like any of this was sensitive information. She could probably help them with the whole Isaac situation.

"You're not a liar."

"Yeah," Andre said. "I know that."

Lucia shifted a tiny bit, moving closer to him. A way for her to show she would take his back if necessary. Andre didn't want to divide the team like that. They didn't need to be fractured any more than they already were after Isaac's betrayal. But the fact she was willing to stand by him even with everything that had happened was at least reassuring. Maybe she was content to meet him halfway in this.

"Isaac has been harassing Hannah." Badger let out a long breath, as though he'd been holding that in for far too long. "She doesn't know who he is, and she won't let me take care of it because she's a cop. And then she tried to push back, but Isaac is somehow untouchable. She's having a hard time at work. As if it's her fault that she's his target."

Lucia inhaled through her nose.

Andre looked down at the expression on her face. "No." He turned fully to face her, tugging her around to face him. "You don't get in the middle of this."

One sob story, and she wanted to wade in like a warrior?

"I don't know what you're talking about." She tried to look innocent, but it wasn't like she'd ever been able to fool him before. Until she did a complete one-eighty, then nothing had made sense to him at all.

Zander said, "Badger, do you need help with Hannah?"

"No, I do not." He got up off the floor with Judah's help.

Andre looked around to see if they'd drawn any attention, but it seemed like the area around them was clear. Despite the fact a flash-bang had erupted, they didn't seem to have ruffled any feathers here. Maybe the security guard was on his lunch break.

A van eased through the parking lot.

Andre said, "Our friend is here for pickup."

Eas wasn't one to sit idle in the parking lot, waiting for them to come out. Not when he could show up and help.

It was a good thing he had. Because Andre wasn't sure he could walk any farther.

"Time to go," Zander told them all.

Lucia ducked under Andre's arm and held his hand so it lay across the back of her shoulders. As they walked, he heard a voice behind them. "She's not part of the team?"

It was Judah, who seemed inclined to push any situation just to get a reaction out of whoever he was with. Andre figured this probably wasn't the time.

He heard Badger reply, "Shut up."

Instead, Judah said, "I knew this was about Hannah. Woman troubles always make a guy moody."

Lucia chuckled under his shoulder. As they approached the van, she stopped and looked up at him. "I'm glad you guys are okay, but Burgess is going to set off a bomb at a convention."

She stayed quiet and let those words sink in. He couldn't exactly decipher the look on her face. But he knew what she was most worried about. "He's going to kill a lot of people."

She nodded.

"I think he was looking for the same bomb we were looking for." Zander shot him a look.

That was news to Andre. A plan to kill a bunch of people wasn't something he would put past the guy like Burgess, so long as he could make a statement when he did it. Make the world sit up and take notice. He was just that kind of radical domestic terrorist. And they already knew how vicious he could be.

But the same bomb they'd been looking for?

"We still need to find that thing." Andre didn't like that a warhead was still out there. At least Isaac didn't have it.

Zander nodded. "We need to figure out who got to it before we did."

"And then we can put a stop to Burgess and his plan once and for all."

"I like the idea of doing that." Lucia looked up at him, a soft expression on her face. "He needs to be brought to justice."

Andre didn't know if she was talking about her brand of justice.

Or his.

19

The van rumbled along the city street, headed wherever they were planning on going. No one had told Lucia where it was. Given everything that'd happened, she was content to sit quietly in the back of the van with her knees pulled up.

Andre was doing the same, but she knew he was in a lot of pain.

"Is that doctor of yours going to be there, whenever we get where we're going?"

He glanced at her, sat on the floor of the back just like her. "Was that supposed to have made sense?"

She grinned, but the humor was short-lived. "After you see the doctor, can we have a conversation?" Maybe he wasn't going to like it, but she did want to settle things between them. "I want to tell you what happened after you left. Fifteen years ago."

It wasn't about to change things between them. But the idea he was torn up inside, or tangled in knots and unable to move on from her didn't sit well. She'd tried to move on. The fact she hadn't wasn't the problem. It was the issue of him not moving on either. Maybe it was just that neither of them had been willing to break their marriage vows. But they also hadn't asked the other for a divorce—until recently.

He hadn't moved on, because of her.

Because she hadn't been willing to explain things, and let him go. Lucia had trapped him for years and kept him connected to her life.

Andre studied her face. How much was he able to read her expression?

It could simply be that he didn't want to say too much in the car with the other guys in hearing range. Badger had tried to remind them all that she wasn't part of the team. As if Lucia didn't know that.

She might want to be, but she knew what the reality was.

This was only a glimpse of Andre's life. It wasn't her life, and it wouldn't ever be. She was a DEA agent who needed to get back to her life.

"Can I borrow your phone?"

He said, "Later. When you can make your call in privacy."

She didn't much care about privacy, but she wasn't about to argue with him when they were all listening. Judah would probably think it was hilarious, but then again he seemed to think everything was hilarious.

Zander twisted around in the front seat. "Nora has footage of Isaac leaving the parking lot with the woman in his car. She got the license plate, and she's going to have Ted figure out who the car belongs to and where they went as soon as he gets home."

"Where are we going?" Lucia needed to be brought up to speed here. Maybe the rest of them either didn't ask, or already knew, but nobody had said what the plan was. "We need to find Burgess and put a stop to him, right?"

Judah was driving. He called back over his shoulder, "So we need to figure out which convention he's going to hit. And if it really is Vegas like Z thinks."

"That means splitting up," Zander said.

"Lucia is with me."

She turned to Andre, wondering what those words meant. It wasn't like she should read into them too much. He might have kissed her, but that didn't mean he would trust her after what she had to tell him.

He probably wouldn't even want to keep her around.

"Heads up." Judah jerked the wheel hard to the right for a second, then straightened.

Zander twisted to him. "What is it?" He looked out the mirror on his side. "Oh, I see."

"Are we being followed?"

Zander nodded, not taking his gaze from the view he had of whoever was behind them. "Two trucks. Multiple guys."

Lucia tried to look out the back window, but it was frosted over. The guy on the team that she'd seen in the hallway, the one she knew for a fact was on the FBI's Most Wanted List, sat by the back doors wearing a mask over his face. In fact, she had only seen him unmasked in private. Now she knew why. Andre hadn't even wanted her to say his name out loud. Let alone ask what on earth he was doing with them.

At the other corner of the back of the van, Badger had his eyes closed. His head rested against the side wall. Was he seriously asleep at a time like this?

Lucia glanced around. "What do we do?"

Andre patted her knee. "You don't need to jump in right away. Calm down for a second."

Everyone in the van reacted, shifting in their seats. Even the guys she thought were asleep. Judah hissed a breath between clenched teeth. "Bro, did you seriously just tell a woman to calm down?"

Lucia shot Andre a look. Because Judah was exactly right.

She wasn't being overly emotional—she was displaying the correct amount of anxiety for the situation they were in.

"I guess I don't know as well as you do how to deal with women. *Bro.*" Andre's gaze shot daggers at his teammate's back.

Lucia said, "I just want to be ready, in case we have to move quickly." There was nothing wrong with her being prepared. That was what had kept her alive until now.

"Andre, give her a gun."

He moved as soon as Zander gave the order, reaching over to a duffel bag and digging inside.

She winced. "Be careful of your leg."

Andre sat back, handing over a pistol. The expression on his face stated clearly that he didn't exactly agree with her feeling that he needed to be careful. She left that alone.

The gun wasn't the same brand she used for a service weapon, but she had this model at home in her gun safe. A home she hadn't been to in days. So long she barely remembered it. And there was probably mail piling up in her mailbox, about to explode all over the foyer of the apartment building.

"If I'm gone from home much longer, I should probably put a hold on my mail."

"Where do you live?"

"This is what you want to talk about?" She stared at him. "Someone is behind us. Two trucks, that's what Zander said."

She had to stop, just to take a breath. But there was more to be said. "Are we going to chat about my inability to raise houseplants? Or possibly how I never have time to go grocery shopping so there's nothing in my fridge except moldy takeout in a Styrofoam box. Because it's hardly the time for that right now." She could see why he chose to live with his team. That certainly made it so none of them had to cook meals all the time, and they could share the chores.

Andre twisted his upper body, and she spotted a frown on his face.

"What—"

He touched her face, his hands to her cheeks. His palms

warm. She could smell concrete from the parking lot where he'd fallen. "Oh."

"Oh, what?" She shook her head. Or tried to, considering her face was between his hands.

"It doesn't matter if that's Burgess back there. He isn't going to get his hands on you. There's nothing to worry about, Lucia. Ambush, or not, we won't let him take you again."

A shiver moved through her entire body. She realized then that she *had* been worried about exactly that. But she'd also pushed it down, shoving it deep inside her so she didn't have to deal with the fear.

The way she always dealt with it. Denial. Evasion.

Focus instead on the mission. On the goal in front of her, and how she was going to achieve it. Her feelings shouldn't factor. Most of the time she could even get to the point she actually believed that.

Somehow, with Andre, there was nothing she could do to combat the feeling. He went right in and dug it out, exposed it to the light, and allowed the glare of his warmth to eliminate that cold she lived with.

"But what if—"

He cut her off. "You have to trust us, Lucia. You know what we can do. You've seen it for yourself." Andre motioned with his head. "Everyone in here is going to make sure you're safe."

"He's right." Those words from Zander allowed her to take in a long breath and push it out slowly.

The breath shuddered as she exhaled.

Andre leaned in and kissed her forehead.

She closed her eyes, and he left his lips there. Touching her skin. At the same time the best feeling in the world, and the worst. He saw her weaknesses and tried to give her his strength. But she couldn't accept it. Lucia had to stand on her own.

She had to find strength so she could do this, even without him. After all, it was inevitable that sooner or later she would be alone again.

Judah muttered under his breath.

A second later something slammed into the back of the van.

ANDRE TWISTED AROUND. Now that he knew what Lucia was actually worried about, he could focus on making sure Burgess never got his hands on her again.

He didn't know how he'd figured out the root fear, under the surface. But something in him just told him what was going on, and it turned out he was right. For all her strength and independence, Lucia had the same fear everyone did—at least, that was what he figured. She didn't want to be powerless again in the face of the superior force. Especially one that had overcome her once, and left her suffering.

Eas moved to the sliding van door and pulled the handle. The door rolled back, and wind blew in from the road. The rush of air that came with moving fast down the street.

"You said two trucks?" Andre needed to get his head on straight. He had to focus, or they would risk more than they needed to, and open up the possibility things here could go wrong.

Zander pulled his gun. "Correct."

"Badger?" Andre needed the man to get with the program.

The youngest member of the team rolled his eyes. "You want me to open the back door so we can all get shot?"

Andre said, "Bust out the window."

Badger shot back, "You bust out the window."

Zander said, "No one is busting out the window."

Lucia sat stiff beside him, but she wasn't overcome by fear. He knew she was holding back simply to get the lay of the land as to how the team would take care of a situation like this. As soon as someone gave her an instruction, or an assignment, he knew she would jump into action.

"Here they come." Eas's voice was muffled behind his mask.

If he hit a button, they would all be able to hear his voice, but it would be disguised electronically.

Zander said, "One on my side, one on yours."

Whoever he was referring to, Andre figured the two trucks were trying to flank them. The question was whether they would force the van to stop or simply destroy it. They could either be here to kill everyone inside, or they would try to take Lucia. Which he'd told her would never happen.

"Copy that," Andre said. "Eas?"

His teammate pulled the mask away from the lower half of his mouth. "You want me to make him mad?"

Badger chuckled. "I do."

His teammate pulled a gun with his left hand, used his right to hold onto the rail they had fitted to the ceiling and hung his body out the open door.

From the front seat Judah said, "What, no knives?"

Badger pulled out his phone. "I'll see if Ted is back from his appointment. We could use a set of eyes in the sky. Or some backup."

Lucia nodded beside him. "Backup would be good. I'm all for pitching in in a pinch, but I figure 'the more, the merrier' applies in this case."

Andre squeezed her knee. She covered his hand with hers and returned the gesture. This was the solidarity he'd wanted with her fifteen years ago. Not that he'd bring her on missions if she wasn't a displaced DEA agent, but why couldn't he have fallen for a woman who stuck around long enough to be part of the life he loved?

Eas squeezed off two shots, then ducked back inside. The side of the van was peppered with gunshots. One of the trucks slammed into them again, this time on the back left quarter panel.

The whole van lurched, and everyone shifted. Eas nearly fell out the door, but caught himself in a way that probably wrenched his shoulder. At least it was his good arm and not the injured one. Andre knew they weren't supposed to be aware of the wound he'd received before joining the team. But they worked together closely enough it was hard to hide something like that.

Which was why he'd been surprised the whole Isaac thing was something else entirely with Badger. He'd never said one word about Hannah.

Zander leaned out the window, facing the back of the van as he squeezed off two shots of his own. There was a pop outside the van, followed by a bump. One of the trucks slammed into the back of the van again. "I got a tire. But he's not slowing down."

"Are they trying to box us in?" Andre figured there were a limited number of scenarios in play here. "Maybe they're herding us somewhere they can force us to stop." It would probably be a spot there was little chance of anyone seeing and calling the police.

"Hold on." Judah's shouted command came from the driver's seat. He sped up, and the van responded with a screaming engine.

Wind buffeted them, until Lucia leaned close to him. Allowing him to protect her again. This time with his body between her and the wind.

"Take it," Zander ordered from the front seat.

Judah yanked the steering wheel hard to the right. The van went up on two wheels, and they turned the corner.

Lucia huddled closer to him, hanging on to his arm the way he wanted to hang onto her.

The van straightened, and the two wheels slammed back on the ground. Eas knocked his head on the inside of the door frame.

Andre braced his good foot and got up in time to grab his teammate and pull him back into the van before he fell out. He laid Eas down into a slump on the floor of the van and heard him mutter, "Should have worn a helmet."

Andre figured the guy was probably right as he used his own gun, in his offhand, to defend himself as he leaned out the open door the way Eas had done. The knife wound stung. "One vehicle is hobbled. The other is right behind us."

Both were still chasing them. Which made them very real threats at getting to Lucia.

Had Burgess done all this just so he could get his hands on her? It made no sense that he would do it for one woman. But if he also knew she was a federal agent, then he might have wanted a bargaining chip like her.

Andre wasn't going to let that happen. He ducked back inside. "Give me my backpack."

Badger tossed it to him. Andre rummaged inside, found what he was looking for, and assembled a small explosive device. The blast wouldn't be any bigger than a grenade, but it would do the trick.

"What are you—is that another bomb?" Lucia gasped.

"I call this one the Andre special." He grinned, glad she was getting to see him in his element again.

Andre pressed the button and armed the device, then leaned out of the van again. He tossed it horizontally toward the underside of the van and watched it hit the ground.

Then he ducked back inside the van. "Just like skipping rocks."

The bomb detonated. Their vehicle was shoved forward as the truck behind flipped upside down.

It was the first time he'd seen Badger smile in weeks. "Sure, if your rocks are the exploding kind."

Andre said, "The best ones always are." He thought it was funny. But when he saw the expression on Lucia's face, she was only blinking at him.

"You gonna make another one of those and take out the

other truck?" Judah seemed eager to see that. Andre saw his grin flash before he looked back at the road in front of them.

"The hobbled one is still coming?" Andre didn't want to lean out the open door again, or he would likely get his head shot off.

Judah said, "Coming up behind us fast."

"Copy that." Andre quickly assembled a second device, forcing his brain to think through the process so he didn't miss a step or get anything mixed up.

"This is what you do?"

He glanced at her, recalling something her father had said to him once. "Turns out I'm not just a dumb grunt."

She flinched. "I never said you were."

Andre finished the bomb. Just before he could press the button and toss it out the door, Zander said, "Hold up."

"What is it?" He didn't bother lifting up to look between the front seats when that would hurt his leg. And he was having too much fun tossing bombs out right now. It was exactly what the team needed, even if Eas was struggling to sit up and probably didn't care about explosions right now.

He helped his friend to straighten, and Eas pulled off his mask. Blood ran down the side of his face.

Lucia gasped. "Where's the first-aid kit?"

She didn't say anything about who Eas was. She only jumped in to help an injured man. That boded well for what would happen when things were wrapped up with Burgess. Maybe she wouldn't turn Eas into her agency.

"There's no time for bandages." Zander's voice was low and controlled. "We've got two more trucks ahead of us blocking the way out."

"What are we going to do?" Badger's voice held a quiver of nerves Andre didn't like one bit.

This whole situation was one he didn't like at all. The only bright spot was having Lucia here.

And now she'd seen what he could do.

In fact…

"I can build a bigger bomb." He figured it was a pretty good suggestion. A bigger one, and Lucia would be even more impressed.

"We might need more than one." Zander didn't sound happy at all. "We're being ambushed."

20

———————

Lucia could hardly believe this was happening. They'd been forced to stop. Trucks had surrounded them, and men were climbing out now. She could see them through the front windshield. More were at the back, beyond the closed doors of the rear of the van.

Soon enough men would approach the side door.

She checked the weapon in her hands and did her best not to reveal exactly how scared she was. Andre had—fortunately or unfortunately, depending on how she wound up looking at it—pinpointed exactly the problem. She didn't want to go back to Burgess. Ever.

Lucia hadn't even been aware she was worried about that, and yet he'd seen it in her anyway. That innate ability he had to break through her defenses as though they weren't even there. No one else had ever been able to do that.

And she was just supposed to let him put his life on the line for her? Lucia had never done him any favors, beyond their wedding vows. Maybe he counted that as a good thing. But what she'd done to him afterward, ending things the way she had, likely severed anything good that he held onto from it.

"Focus up." Zander's voice cut through her musings. She

had to wonder if he was talking to her specifically, or all the guys in general. "I don't want any slippery trigger fingers. This could turn nasty fast."

"Aren't they just here to kill us all?" That was Badger, who still had the disgruntled look on his face he'd been wearing since she first met him. It seemed as though the guys were surprised and irritated he was acting like this. Which meant there was another Badger, one she hadn't seen yet.

"They're after revenge, no doubt." Zander shifted and she spotted him assessing the situation out the front windshield. "Climb in the back, Judah."

The British man nodded. "You go first. I'll be right behind you."

Judah covered Zander while the team leader climbed over the center console and into the rear of the van. He hunkered down beside the open door. Behind the passenger seat, where he was ready to look out.

It completely exposed him. As though his intention was to get hit by whatever came at them first, before anyone else in the team—something that surprised her. Though, at this point she didn't know why it did. She already knew Andre's team was different than any she'd worked with.

Judah climbed in the back as well. Lucia had to shift out of the way, and made sure to move closer to the door so she could get a better view. "What are we waiting for?" She figured it was okay to ask, since Zander wasn't her "Don't ask me stupid questions" boss. The one she now knew had been feeding information back to Burgess. Maybe more.

"I'd like them to make the first move. If they're just planning on killing you and Andre, we'll know their intentions and we can punch back." The measured way Zander spoke reassured her.

But still, the fear was there underneath everything. Now it wasn't just Andre putting his life on the line for her after he got involved and made himself a target of Burgess. Now it was his entire team, and one of them had already said something about being implicated in the whole business with Director Gladstone. The last thing she needed was for them to be swept up in a plan to bomb a convention.

They needed to be going after Burgess, finding out exactly what he was going to do.

Lucia considered that. "If we can capture one of them, we can interrogate him and find out where Burgess is really going to set off that bomb."

Zander nodded. "Now you're getting it."

Lucia grinned, then saw men approach out of the corner of her eye. "Incoming."

It seemed like even the one in the mask was ready. He should probably be resting, benched from whatever was about to happen. She figured he probably planned to dive in just like the rest of them.

"Exit the vehicle." A tall man with dark brows that met in the middle stopped six feet away and held a gun loosely pointed in their direction.

"So not just a massacre."

She heard the words muttered from the back of the van and figured it was Badger, but couldn't be sure.

If they slid the door shut, Lucia wondered if the van would be bulletproof. They seemed like the kind of people who would put those safeguards in place ahead of time.

"Andre?"

An object flew between Zander and Lucia and out the van. She just managed to clap her hands over her ears and close her eyes before it hit the ground outside and exploded in a boom and a flash brighter than several million candles.

She hissed out a breath. Zander was already out the door.

He hit the first man on the side of the head with the butt of his gun. Nonlethal force? That surprised her, given how they had been ambushed and the likelihood that these men were here to kill some of them. If not all of them.

Andre scooted to the edge, past her. She climbed out as well not wanting to be left behind. A man approached from the right, his finger on the trigger of his gun.

She shot first and he collapsed to one knee, bringing his gun up one more time. She put another bullet in his head.

More men approached from around them, and her hearing became a wash of grunts, screams, and gunfire. She felt the displacement of air as a bullet whizzed past her face but couldn't make out the sound she should've been able to hear.

Everything dissolved into chaos.

When her awareness coalesced, she realized the men of Zander's team surrounded her. Between Lucia and the approaching force, there was a man with his back to her in every direction.

She angled her gun down so she didn't accidentally discharge and hit one of them.

"Are you guys serious?"

She didn't even know if her voice was audible. With all the chaos going on, she couldn't hear it in the ocean of noise.

Lucia scanned in every direction. She spotted a man about to shoot Badger while he grappled with another. She took him out, everything in her humming with a resonance that seemed to be in harmony with what was going on. As though each move was choreographed between her and the team. They were in sync, moving as though they knew where the others were at all times.

Lucia felt like a part of it, after not feeling like part of anything since she forced Andre to cut himself off from her.

Judah's body jerked, and he went down. One knee hit the floor, and he planted both hands on the ground. Lucia moved up behind him, covering him with her gun.

"Ack." The British man grunted. "That's going to leave a bruise."

That was when she spotted the man in the truck. The one who had been promoted when Lydell was killed for bringing her to the compound. The new second-in-command, the one who would know everything Burgess had planned.

Lucia strode around Judah, ignoring the eruption of yells. Probably the team trying to get her to stop. But she was going to do her job regardless. That was why she had come here, why she'd stayed with them. Not for some overblown sense of hope that she could rekindle things with Andre. She was here to do her job, and nothing else.

Lucia aimed at the windshield with her pistol and approached the vehicle. He was just sitting there, watching everything unfold. Allowing his men to be killed while he stayed safe in the vehicle? That wasn't leadership.

As she approached, she saw his lips curl into a grin and the white of his teeth flashed. He thought she was amusing?

This was going to be fun.

"Get out of the car now." She rounded the front corner to the door and held her gun pointed at the window while the chaos continued behind her. In a way, she had to thank the team for making it so she could do her job while they took care of everything else. Lucia knew that. She could put it in her report that Zander's team of private security agents had assisted in a federal investigation.

They might even get recognition for it.

He cracked the door and pushed it open but didn't get out.

"You're under arrest."

* * *

ANDRE DOWNED A GUY. There weren't many left, though not all on the ground were dead. Plenty had been incapacitated in various ways. He took a second and cataloged the situation.

He spotted Zander doing the same thing.

"Lucia?"

Zander pointed.

Andre found her over beside a vehicle, her gun out and pointed at a man sitting in the front seat. "Let's go."

"Badger, with Andre." Zander motioned to Judah. "I'll cover him."

Andre and Badger moved.

As they approached her, the man in the car shoved the door open fast enough she had to take a quick step back. But she'd been far enough away the door didn't hit her.

She kept her composure, all that training she'd had now dictating her stance in the way she held her gun. The words she spoke. This was the woman she had become, and he was proud of her as much as it frustrated him that she'd cut him off from her life. He'd never even had the chance to know this woman.

"More coming from the rear." At Zander's call, Andre looked back over his shoulder.

Judah seemed to be good, though he hadn't moved. Andre had no idea where Eas currently was. A gunshot had him turn back around. The man Lucia had been trying to arrest fell to the ground.

She spun to Badger. "I needed him alive."

Andre's teammate motioned to the man. "He's not dead. Yet."

She flipped the man to his front and patted him down, securing his hands behind his back. "I need some kind of cuffs." She sounded exasperated and Andre didn't blame her.

"Badger, go help Zander. More men are coming."

Lucia glanced over at him, worry on her face.

Andre said, "We'll take care of it, just like we took care of this."

"I need to question this guy."

Andre nodded. He knew she wanted to get on with her job and get them a lead on Burgess, but they had to resolve the situation before she could do that. Still, the fact they were working together at all and had gained a victory meant he felt that surge in him. The one that came when everything in his life was right, and he realized it. It was as though pieces fit together, like in a puzzle.

The way things should be.

Until everything broke apart again.

Lucia knelt on the man's back, holding his hands. Andre turned and scanned around them so he could cover her, making sure no one else approached.

A second later there was a rustle of clothing, and she said, "Derek Severn. Any outstanding warrants I should know about?"

Andre twisted back to her. "What did you say?"

"His name." She held up the man's wallet. "Derek Severn."

He moved to see the man's face and discovered it was the guy he'd known years ago. "Severn. It's been a while."

"You know him?" Her tone was incredulous, as though she couldn't believe he might be acquainted with a man who was now their enemy.

"Don't worry about my honor. This guy was skirting the edge when I knew him, dipping a toe over the line anytime he could. Just to see what would happen." Andre could remember a few specific instances where he'd had to pull Derek back from the edge. Then Zander had gotten involved, and Derek had no choice but to follow his sergeant's orders. "It doesn't surprise me one bit he's working for Burgess now."

"I guess we'll find out how that all happened soon enough." Her confidence shone through her tone, and her expression. Until she frowned. "Why are you looking at me like that?"

"Like what?" He scanned around them and spotted Zander in a standoff with several men.

Badger stood beside him as the team leader pointed his gun at the guys trying to kill them. Burgess's guys did the same, but they seemed to be disinclined to kill right now. Probably because they were all realizing exactly the level of fight they would be in for if they proceeded with this. Half their guys were dead or unconscious.

The smart move would be to back down and break off.

"Let's put this guy in the van." Andre helped Lucia haul the guy to his feet, and they walked him back to the van, mostly just so they'd be within earshot of whatever Zander was saying.

"Not gonna happen." The man facing off with Zander shifted his stance, keeping his legs loose so they didn't lock. It was a tactic that they all used. No one wanted to be stiff when they had to move quickly at any moment. The guy continued, "Give us the bomb maker, and we'll be on our way."

Everybody shifted.

Andre straightened out of the van and blindly handed Lucia the ties to secure Derek.

Badger scoffed. "Say what?"

"That's all we want. The bomb maker goes with us, and we leave. No one else has to die."

"I'm not giving you one of my people." Zander's tone was firm. Andre also detected a thread of anger running under it, which if he was honest felt pretty good. "Leave, and no one else has to die."

His intention was clear. If they tried to take Andre, blood would be shed.

Andre didn't want anyone to die because of him. Unless it was one of these guys.

The man shifted, taking a half step toward them.

Andre only registered the aggression in his body language a split second before a knife slammed into the man's shoulder.

He grunted but didn't go down. Surprise washed over his face, and he grabbed the handle of the knife.

Andre didn't grin, even though he wanted to. Did Eas ever miss with his knives? Plus Andre knew exactly how that felt. His shoulder still stung.

A second later, the guy pulled the blade from his shoulder. "Fine." He spoke through gritted teeth. "I accept your terms."

As if he had any choice. Zander probably wanted to grin, but figured that would be unsportsmanlike. Wherever Eas was, he'd clocked this man's intentions before anyone else and taken care of it with a show of force that had more finesse than anything the rest of them would've come up with.

"But we take that guy with us." He motioned to the guy Lucia had captured.

"Loyalty," Zander said. "I wouldn't have thought that of you guys."

"You of all people should understand." The man facing Zander lifted his chin. "Sergeant O'Connell."

"You guys did your homework," Badger quipped. "So what? Except that means you should have known better than trying this."

"Should we?" There was something in his tone Andre couldn't quite get a fix on.

A tone that had been there when he said, *You of all people should understand.* As though continuing the banter to cover something unspoken.

He realized Zander clocked it as well when he said, "These guys aren't yours?" He motioned at the men around them on the ground. "But you want the leader?"

"I have not been provided authorization to read you in on this."

Who were these guys? Andre wasn't sure he believed they weren't Burgess's men. And yet they'd known to show up here, and they were asking for Andre? They wanted the leader now, and they'd come for him. At least they didn't want to take Lucia with them. That wasn't something he would allow.

"What I can tell you," the man said, "is that we aren't your enemy."

Andre believed that about as much as he trusted this guy—which wasn't at all since they didn't even know him. Unlike Burgess's man, who Andre knew from the army and knew for sure he didn't trust. This guy was even more unknown. A new player they had yet to sus out.

"And what do we get in exchange for giving this man to you?" Zander used his diplomatic tone.

The man's expression shifted, his eyebrows lifted, and Andre read the lack of surprise on his face. He'd expected this—which meant he knew enough about Zander to see a compromise coming. "Fair warning. Burgess wants your man here." He motioned toward Andre.

Lucia made a noise in her throat.

Zander said, "Thought that was you."

"We'd put him in protective custody." The man shrugged. "Make sure Burgess didn't get him."

"No thanks." Andre folded his arms.

"Mitigating the risk is never a bad idea."

Still, Andre said, "A warning would suffice." Even if it was unnecessary, considering the fact they were constantly on alert for any threat like that. It was why they lived the way they did. Always under the radar.

Lucia said, "Why does Burgess want Andre?"

"So he can replace the bomb that was stolen from them." Something in the man's gaze said they were the ones who'd stolen it.

Though, Andre didn't know more than that, and it was only a guess.

"It didn't happen to be a nuke, did it?" Zander asked, his tone cautious. They'd been chasing a warhead recently, but the device had slipped through their fingers.

The man's expression blanked. "Only a small one." As though that meant it was hardly anything to worry about.

Lucia whispered, "Did he say 'nuke'?"

The man looked at his watch. "Time to go." He motioned to Burgess's man. "He comes with me."

Zander shook his head. "Not today."

21

"I can't prevent what happens if you don't hand him over."

Lucia wanted to roll her eyes. She might not know half of what these guys were talking about, but she knew one thing. "We can handle the consequences."

Zander shifted, and she realized she'd gone around him and tromped on whatever he'd been about to do.

She stood by it, nonetheless.

The man shrugged. "Not my funeral." He made a circle in the air with his finger. "Let's go."

They dispersed quickly, and if she'd closed her eyes for a second, they would have been gone by the time she opened them again. Moments later, two cars pulled around the end of the alley.

"More gunmen?" Her adrenaline levels were sky-high right now. Lucia was having trouble keeping her hands from shaking. But she had the man secure, sitting on the ground and leaning against the wheel of the van. She kept him in sight as she watched yet more people approach.

Zander listened for a second, and she realized he had his attention on comms. She'd put hers in her pocket. No wonder she hadn't heard the rest of them during that whole altercation.

"The cops were called," Zander said. "This looks like federal agents, but the locals are on their way as well."

Lucia exhaled a long breath, not realizing she'd been holding it in for a while now.

Andre glanced at her with an expression she couldn't decipher.

She studied him. "You okay?"

He'd just found out he was the target. Burgess might not even want her, or even know who she was. He'd been trying to take Andre. The bomb maker.

He just shrugged.

She wanted the chance to talk to him, preferably when they were alone. But now feds were making their way over. The two guys from the hospital, and several other agents. No one she recognized from her task force team. Local cops in uniform, along with a sergeant also approached.

Zander took point, and they each told the agents what had happened—all except their friend who always wore a mask, who had somehow completely disappeared again when she wasn't watching. He probably had to do that often. The sergeant took control of the man she'd arrested, and she thanked him for helping.

"I'd also like to listen when you question him." She wasn't sure how much the guy knew about Burgess, and what was going on. But if he had any intel, then the team needed to know about it. She needed to know so she could relay the information back to the task force—or what was left of it.

Cops walked the scene. Andre and Zander spoke with the special agents. Lucia spotted two special agents from her task force at the end of the street, speaking with a uniformed police officer.

She lifted her hand and waved at them.

They waved back, motioning for her to go to them. It was such a relief to know that someone from her team was alive. She headed over, the weapon at the small of her back a comforting sensation. As she went to meet up with Special Agents Brinton and Gage, Lucia drew the earpiece from her pocket and stuck it in her ear canal, as if untucking hair from behind her ear.

So many crazy things had happened—even just in the last few hours. She could hardly keep it all straight.

But she was going to do what she could to keep herself safe.

"How are you guys doing?" She smiled.

They both nodded. Brinton said, "We were worried about you. But it seems like you came out of that compound unscathed." He glanced down at her shoes and then back up.

Lucia had ditched the sling but wore the bandage on her wrist. "I wouldn't exactly put it like that." Still, Simon and Bill had lost their lives. What she'd been through wasn't worse than their families having to live without them.

Gage watched her carefully.

Brinton said, "We thought you'd have called in by now."

"I know. That's on me." The task force had been decimated. "What about Campbell?" She was about to comment on the fact he was dead when Brinton cut her off.

"No one has seen him. He hasn't checked in, so the nearest we can figure is something isn't right."

She'd been wondering since Lydell killed two of her teammates in front of her if there wasn't more going on. Was it only Campbell and the men who'd shown up with him, or had there been more corruption in the task force than that? "The situation definitely seems strange."

"Everyone's running around freaking out about Burgess." Gage shook his head, his expression almost amused.

Speaking of strange. "We have one of his guys here." She motioned to the group back by the van. "The local police are going to interrogate him. We should be able to get intel from that."

"Sounds good." Brinton nodded. "All's well that ends well, I guess."

"It's far from done. Burgess has a plot in place." One that

apparently was supposed to have involved a nuke. Even a small one could do epic amounts of damage, especially if it was deployed in an urban environment. "We need to stop him."

Then she would talk to Zander about what he knew of this warhead. It was the first she'd heard of it, but it seemed as though no one around her was surprised when the subject came up. Lucia didn't like feeling as though everyone knew something except her. It wasn't a comfortable spot to be in, even if she could simply ask and be briefed.

"That's what we've been doing." Gage shrugged. "And you helped, getting everyone out of the compound and breaking up the entire thing."

"Not without serious cost."

Neither man reacted. It was almost as though they weren't bothered at all by the deaths of their colleagues. She needed to push a little and test the waters.

"I've heard some disturbing things since I managed to escape." She wasn't about to mention Andre to these two.

"Let me guess," Brinton said. "It was about Campbell supposedly being linked to Burgess? That was just a smoke-screen." He shook his head.

"Then it wasn't true?"

Gage chuckled. "As if it's that clean-cut. This whole thing turned into a mess we're going to have to wade through. But not before we get the rest of the team together and figure out how we're going to lay this out."

That sounded akin to getting their stories straight. "I think it's more important to take down Burgess."

"Not if we all get dragged through the mud in the process," Gage said.

Brinton glanced between them, studying her and then Gage in turn. "I'm sure you understand." He shrugged. "If we all have different stories things could get complicated, and that's the last thing we need right now."

Lucia had to tread very carefully here. Gage seemed more

inclined to give himself away, but Brinton's assessment meant he wasn't sure if she could be trusted. "I'll go with you. No one needs me here, and we can get this all figured out. After that, our priorities should be Burgess and finding the bomb he was planning on using. If it's out there, then it needs to be back in official hands."

Gage shifted, and she saw something in his expression.

"Don't tell me you guys have it." She tried to look excited, even as the dissipating adrenaline left her fatigued. Her body wanted to remind her of her injuries. "Seriously? You found the nuke?"

"It's only a small one." Brinton assessed her. "A suitcase nuke."

"Still, they can do a serious amount of damage. Are you turning it back over to—who are we supposed to give a nuke to?"

Gage shrugged. "Doesn't matter. It just matters that Burgess didn't get his hands on it. That's why we had to let Lydell take you. We were waiting for word that it'd been retrieved, which only came in after you were gone."

"You stole it from Burgess?" A sick feeling moved in her stomach.

The whole situation had been even more of a setup than she'd imagined.

Brinton frowned. "If you didn't know that, then we have a serious problem."

"Campbell didn't tell me much." She needed a way to convince them she was on their side, but she couldn't fake knowing things she had no clue about. "I thought after we started sleeping together, he'd tell me more. He said he would, but that was only a couple of days before the operation." She shrugged. "I thought we were nabbing Lydell so we could flip him for Burgess."

"He was our point person." Burgess shook his head. "We just didn't know he was obsessed with you enough to double-cross us and take you with him. Guess he didn't care too much for hearing you were involved with Campbell. Or he didn't care."

Lucia had been a bargaining chip. Someone they could wave in front of the target and use as a distraction to get what they wanted behind everyone's back.

"We should head out." Gage watched the group, over her shoulder. "Before we are forced to interview witnesses or help secure the scene."

As though doing their actual jobs was an inconvenience. "What's the plan?"

Were they all dirty? She didn't know how many players in the task force had been as well. The two that had died weren't, considering they'd been taken out.

Now it would be Lucia who was expendable.

***

ANDRE LOCKED GAZES WITH ZANDER. His friend held the phone to his ear. "Got it." Zander moved the phone away from his mouth. "It's still live, but she's muted. She can't hear us. It's only us who can hear her."

Andre glanced over at the two men still talking to Lucia. If there was anything to overhear, the cop wasn't close enough to do so.

However, he and the rest of the team had heard the whole thing after Ted—back from his appointment—turned comms back on.

Andre owed him for being on top of things enough to realize something was going on between Lucia and the man she was talking to. He'd given them the heads-up that the guys were dirty after listening in himself. The agents had all but admitted they were the ones who had the missing warhead everyone seemed to be looking for.

There were so many players within this situation he hardly

knew how to organize it all in his head. First it was Burgess, and more recently this other organization—one he wondered if Isaac was part of. That made the most sense, considering they'd clearly followed either Zander's team or Burgess's people. Someone was under surveillance. They'd rolled up as soon as the coast was clear. Not the kind of people who would wade into a dangerous situation in order to assist, or even get the upper hand over their enemy. No, they'd waited until the dust settled and then approached.

Now two federal agents had effectively done the same.

Ted had clocked them as members of Lucia's team, all of whom they had run background checks on as soon as they heard she'd been captured. These two hadn't been implicated the way Campbell was, but the team as a whole was marred by their association with Campbell so that even Lucia had been under suspicion at one point.

Ted had turned on the channel again so they could all hear her conversation with those two guys. Now they thought they were gonna take her with them?

"I'm gonna go get her." Not that he needed Zander's permission, but it was important that he let his boss know given the situation.

He started to walk away but Zander said, "What if we let them take her?"

Andre spun back. "Say what?"

It wasn't bad enough that Burgess was after Andre. The *bomb maker*. Now Zander was going to allow Lucia to be taken by dirty members of her task force? It was looking like it would turn out that she was the only honorable one among them except maybe the two that had died when she was taken.

"They're the ones who have the warhead." Zander stared him down. "If we follow her, they could lead us all the way to where they're keeping it."

"That's a long shot, and you know it." It grated Andre that Zander was going to risk a woman Andre cared about losing her life. For the sake of a warhead, he could see how the greater good came into play. But this was Lucia. "We could blow the chance to get our hands on it if it's not there. We'll tip our hands, and they'll be twice as careful. Plus, it could put Lucia's life in danger."

"Her life is already in danger." Zander moved closer, speaking low so the cops talking to Badger and Judah didn't overhear their conversation. "As are all of ours. And you think they aren't heavily guarding a nuke?"

Andre figured he was right.

Zander said, "Isn't it at least worth a shot to get that thing out of the wrong hands?"

"Fine. But at least this time she'll be taken knowing we're right behind her." The last thing Andre wanted was for Lucia to believe she was alone. She'd been so scared at the idea of being taken by Burgess again. These were her task force colleagues, people she was supposed to be able to trust. It turned out they were all working in complete opposition to everything they had taken an oath to uphold.

Andre walked away before Zander could ask how he was going to achieve that. Mostly because he had no answer for the inevitable question. He figured he'd make it up as he went along, or have a divinely inspired epiphany on the way there.

They started to walk away with her.

Andre called out, "Special Agent DeSoto." He picked up his pace to a jog even though it hurt his leg even more than it already ached. "Hold up a second."

He figured she hadn't told her colleagues she was married, the same way he hadn't told his team all that much about his past. He wasn't about to reveal their personal connection if he had to. Unless they already knew.

She raised one eyebrow. "Yes, Mr. Martinez?"

He held out his hand as he came to a stop. "I just wanted to say it's been a pleasure collaborating with you the last couple of days. I'm glad we could get you out of there safely." He assessed the two agents out the corner of his eye, but given there was a whole task force, two men out of the group weren't going to be consequential.

He wondered briefly who was in charge now that Campbell was gone.

No wonder they hadn't shown up for several days. The whole team was likely in disarray after what happened. They'd sacrificed members of their team—and made a play for the bomb by the sound of it.

Which meant, the night he'd been under that truck on intel, the nuke had been somewhere else entirely. Someone had fed that information to their informant falsely.

They'd been played.

More than one group was currently after the nuke. And these guys had it?

Andre wanted to know how long they'd been in the illegal weapons sales business. And what else they were up to.

She smiled. "Thank you again for your help."

He squeezed her hand. "Anytime."

Lucia gave him a short nod and turned away. He watched her leave, following those two men in a way that made his guts churn. He wanted to run up behind them, tackle one and then the other. Snatch her back, as though she were a favorite toy someone had stolen from him to play with. No, obviously it was more than that. His actions might appear like that on the surface, but the truth was that his feelings for her ran deep, even if on the outside he acted like an immature youth.

Now that he had her back in his life, he wasn't about to let her go again. Not if he could help it.

As soon as they were out of sight, he jogged back to Zander.

"You need to be careful on that leg."

"We have bigger problems right now." Andre whistled to the others. "Let's get moving."

"Badger can drive." Zander got in the back of the van,

helping Judah to sit. He'd been hit in the vest, leaving a huge bruise that wouldn't feel good at all.

Andre got in the front passenger seat.

Zander said, "Ted is following her on surveillance."

Andre figured that meant they'd be far enough back so as not to be seen, but Ted would know where she was at all times. It probably should've been reassuring, but not having his own eyes on her made him more nervous than he would care to admit.

Badger pulled out, immediately hitting the gas. The van was in rough shape but still worked. The cops on scene could finish processing everything. The team had done all they could, and it was time to go and rescue one of their own.

"I have to say," Judah began, "up until now I kind of didn't believe there even was a nuke out there. Maybe I won't truly believe it until I see the thing with my own eyes."

Zander said, "Even if it's small, it can still do a serious amount of damage."

"How small is a good question." Andre was glad for the distraction. "If you're inclined to pray, ask that we find it wherever they're taking Lucia. Otherwise, we'll have no leads again, and this situation is already complicated enough."

Things had changed so fast his head still spun. Now Lucia was gone, and he'd been the one who let her go. If anything happened to her, it would be his fault.

"Who were those guys who showed up, Z?" Badger's question was surprising. He'd been so surly of late, and now he seemed to be invested in this situation. "You think they have something to do with Isaac?"

Zander's phone rang before anyone could speak their real feelings about that. "What is it?" He paused for a second. "What do you mean you lost her?"

Andre grabbed the phone from him and held it to his ear. "Ted, you better get her back right now."

22

Lucia touched her back to the tiled wall and slid down until her behind touch the floor. She was exhausted enough to not care this was a dirty bathroom and anything more than that she wasn't going to think about. Like how long she would be here, or what they were inevitably going to do with her.

She closed her eyes and tried to picture Andre's face. The way he squeezed her hand. She'd listened more to the tone of his voice and what his body language said than any words that came out of his mouth.

That was what she was going to trust. Because out of all the people in the world, Andre was the only one in whose hands she would put her life. He wouldn't let her down.

She knew that the same way she knew she had loved him even when she pushed him away.

Lucia was the one with the problem. Now, and back then. She was the one who was toxic in their relationship, knowing that if she stayed with him then she would inevitably cause his death the way she had caused her father's.

Even now so many years later she could see him in her mind. The way he'd clutched his chest. She'd told him about her hasty marriage to Andre in Vegas. It hadn't felt hasty to her, but that was what he'd said when he told her it would turn out to be the biggest mistake of her life.

A second before he'd clutched his chest and collapsed to the floor.

Her happiness. Her marriage to Andre. It had cost her father his life, and there was no way she could have carried on then with the relationship knowing that. She'd spent weeks alone while he was in basic training. Weeks that turned into months.

She'd buried her father. Moved out of her house. Gone to college. By the time he'd returned from basic training and come to see her, to ask why she wasn't living in their apartment and waiting for him, she had told him she never wanted to see him again. She'd made up her mind and torn out his heart, the way hers was already torn. Shredded by the consequences of their childish actions.

Now she held one of the most dangerous jobs in the country. There was no way she could have a relationship at this point, given what she faced every day even standing behind the badge. Supposedly backed up by her colleagues. Or behind a gun, and all the training she'd received.

None of it had kept her from getting hurt. Eventually she would live her last day. Eat her last meal.

Breathe her last breath.

The last thing she wanted was for Andre to be anywhere near her when that happened.

She was glad he'd let her go now. Back to her life, which led her to being locked in a bathroom while they called the rest of the team in to discuss what they were going to do with her.

A boom rattled the whole building. An abandoned office, closed when the company went bankrupt.

Lucia opened her eyes as dust rained down from the ceiling, but she didn't move. Nor did she allow the idea to creep in—the hope—that Andre was coming for her.

She heard them enter the building. A distant door slammed

shut. Boots could be heard on the tile floor. A swarm, upstairs and all around her.

More boots than there were men on Zander's team. It must have been echoes. Some gift she didn't deserve, the reassurance that a veritable army was on its way to save her.

Thank You.

It was a grace she'd never measured up to. Even her father had known she wasn't worth giving gifts to, not when she couldn't even achieve the standard he set for her.

And then she'd killed him.

Andre had been another gift she hadn't deserved. Lucia barely recognized it back then. When she'd been a high school kid who thought the world revolved around her. Now she knew everyone believed that when they were young. Life had taught her the truth.

Or maybe it was still revealing itself to her. She hadn't thought rescue would come, and yet here it was. Something surprising. Unexpected.

The door flung open, hit the wall, and bounced back.

Several people in black fatigues entered, armed with more than one weapon each. She recognized the man who'd come up to them after the ambush. The one who talked to Zander and tried to take Andre into protective custody. As if Zander would trust a stranger to protect his friend.

The first into the bathroom was that very same man. "Well, well, well," he said, as surprised to see her as she was to see him.

Lucia said nothing.

A woman pushed past him and looked at her. She was older, her hair pulled back into a severe ponytail. A warrior who had risen to the top of her business. She exuded confidence, and Lucia would have guessed that there was nothing gentle about her. It was in the line of her jaw, and the way she stood. The way she held that weapon. "The one Lydell had a thing for?"

The man said, "She doesn't know anything."

"I'm guessing she's about to put it together here pretty

soon." She seemed sure of herself, and not in a way Lucia would consider foolish bravado.

Anything Lucia said, they would jump on it and draw conclusions about her usefulness. If she turned out to be anything but an asset to this woman, she would probably find herself on the receiving end of a bullet.

And yet, there was no energy in her to try to play this game. To convince them to keep her around.

The task force she'd been a part of was dirty, and they'd stolen a warhead from a known criminal. Even if they'd effectively prevented Burgess from carrying out his plan, it wasn't as though they'd turned around and surrendered it to the government for safekeeping. No, they'd been talking in the car about who they would sell it to. Some foreign organization, or a terrorist group. The list grew worse and worse the longer it went on.

Until she'd had to tune it out, sickened by their complete lack of care for human life.

She'd gone into this task force job with one assignment. Now it was so much worse, because she knew the full extent of the poison that had infected the people she worked with. People who should've been striving for justice in this country.

She figured that if she died today, at least she'd seen Andre before that happened. He knew she'd never found anyone else the way she knew the same about him. Sure, there were plenty of regrets in her past. Plenty of guilt and shame she didn't know what to do with, but at least she could say she'd tried to do the right thing.

She would always love him.

"It's not here." A man she knew strode past the crowd of people and came to the woman's side. "And neither is half the team." Isaac didn't look happy. He seemed kind of irritated actually.

"Not having a good day?" As soon as she said the words,

Lucia bit her lips closed. The last thing she needed to do was antagonize them.

Isaac shot her glance, then said, "We should have waited."

Lucia pressed her lips closed. If she said anything, she was only going to end up aggravating them until they killed her. She wanted to at least go down fighting. Otherwise, she might as well just lie still and give up completely.

She wasn't going to waste time wondering if she would ever see Andre again. She would accept her fate, because she was going to do everything she could to see tomorrow. To not give up. To try to make her life something good, instead of what it had been.

The woman tapped the first man on the shoulder, turned to Isaac, and said, "Put a bullet in her and let's go."

Lucia's stomach lurched.

They hadn't found what they'd come here for. The task force still had the weapon, and Burgess wanted to take out whatever convention he was targeting.

If Lucia died here today, who would put a stop to it? She knew her task force better than anyone. She might be at a disadvantage right now, but she had been planning on spinning that in her favor ever since she joined them.

As soon as she was alone with Isaac in the room, Lucia said, "You thought the warhead would be here?"

"That's not exactly what it is."

"An explosive device?" The payload might not be nuclear, but that was what everybody kept calling it. She wanted to get a look at the thing.

He shrugged one shoulder and lifted his gun.

Lucia braced herself.

"Tell Zander I had no choice." Isaac pointed his gun at the wall and pulled the trigger.

IT TOOK FAR TOO long to find the building where Lucia had been taken. The second they breached, Andre spotted a dead man on the floor. "I've got one, already cold."

He scanned with his gun pointed everywhere his gaze went. Keeping his focus moving around all sides so he never got caught off guard. One single small charge on the door. Not much, after he'd been throwing homemade grenades out the door of the van. Now it looked as though someone had done their job for him.

Over the communications channel Zander said, "Me too. Two on my side."

Judah remained in the car, where Zander had argued Andre should have been. For a second anyway, until he realized it was pointless to try to convince him to stay out of this.

Eas moved right behind him, completely silent so that if Andre didn't have his friend in his field of vision intermittently, he could almost believe the guy wasn't even there. A ghost.

Zander kept Badger with him, making sure the man was at least contained. Until they figured out how to get him to work through all of his feelings over Hannah and Isaac.

Andre pushed through the door. "One more." He wasn't sure how they were going to find Lucia in this maze. They would end up searching every room and every hallway. Every stairwell and open space. If she was alive, she might call for him.

There was nothing but silence, and the echo of his footsteps as he climbed to the second floor. Zander and Badger were going to clear the first. They were supposed to head up.

At the door to the second floor, Eas patted him on the shoulder. "I head upstairs." He motioned to the third floor above them.

Andre nodded.

Over the comms Zander said, "Copy that."

Frustration burned in Andre's gut as he pushed out the door into the second-floor hallway and tried to ignore the pain in his leg. This whole situation was a total mess. He was the one who was supposed to be the target, and Burgess was probably still looking for him as the bomb maker. Meanwhile, Lucia was the one who was taken. By the very people who were supposed to have her back as a special agent.

Andre would've liked to have been the one to put bullets in them, but whoever had beaten them to it seemed to have done a pretty good job.

"Any sign of her?" Andre kept moving down the hallway, opening each door as he came to it and scanning the rooms. Even going so far as to look under desks he found, and in closets.

The last door was a bathroom, and the slight odor hit him before the sight of Lucia huddled against the wall.

She whimpered.

Andre moved to her, wanting to crouch but knowing that if he did, he would just collapse on top of her. Instead, he held out his hand, "I don't suppose you're available for rescue?"

One corner of her mouth curled up. "I think I could squeeze that in. Although, my calendar seems to be pretty busy these days."

Andre lifted her to her feet, and she didn't stop moving toward him. She wound her arms around his middle, and he placed his chin on the top of her head. He gave her a long hug, wanting more, but knowing it wasn't the time.

"Thank you." She pulled back and lifted her chin to meet his gaze. "I want to say more than that, but I need to tell you that Isaac was here with his people. The man from after the ambush, and a woman."

"You can describe her?" Andre tried to reiterate what Ted had told them. "Something about this building means we can't see inside. If she showed her face anywhere indoors, we probably won't be able to get an image of her, unless it was outside in full view of the neighboring building's surveillance. Or a street camera or ATM."

There were literally no banks anywhere near here. So that last one was an impossibility.

"I'll figure out who she is," Lucia said. "I have access to federal databases, so I can search for parameters and sift through the results to find out what her name is."

Through his earpiece, Zander said, "Tell her we appreciate that. But you should also both know we have vehicles on approach."

Lucia said, "Comms?"

Andre nodded.

"They took mine." Her face paled, and she held her wrist against her stomach.

"Hurts?" He touched her cheek.

She nodded, and he pressed his lips to hers far more briefly than he wanted to.

"We need to go." Andre took her hand and led her from the room.

"What is it?"

Instead of answering her, he said, "Zander?" Andre needed all the information he could get before he reiterated it to her. But he walked her to the front of the building where they could look out the windows. "I'm guessing that is the rest of the task force?" He lifted his chin and motioned to two cars on approach. They pulled up to the front, and seven people climbed out.

He glanced at her.

Lucia nodded. "They only left a couple of guys here with me, maybe four. One of the two who brought me here, Gage, went to go get the rest of them." She blew out a breath. "Which turned out to be a good thing." She leaned close to him, and he realized she was trying to speak near his ear enough for the microphone to pick up her voice. "Isaac and his boss, and the rest of their group didn't find the warhead here. Maybe these guys have it?"

Andre said, "If they do, why are they coming back here to get you?"

Judah started yelling over comms about how to speak to a woman.

"I only mean," Andre said, "that it seems as though using or selling a nuke might be more important than one person."

"Unless they need me to do that," Lucia said. "Probably so they can implicate me in the process. Get evidence they can present to the US attorney that proves I was the one working with Campbell. They'll sell it anyway, then pocket the money while they pin the whole thing on me."

Andre nodded. "That makes sense."

In his ear, most of them agreed. There was a reason the task force was keeping Lucia around. She was a liability who could cause serious problems for them, and if they were worried about that then they would have killed her already. Unless they had another plan.

Zander said, "They're all coming in the front door."

"Idiots. Do they know that's a bottleneck?" He could hear the excitement in Badger's voice.

"On the lobby," Zander ordered.

They moved to the stairs, and Lucia said, "I want a gun."

Knowing she needed to feel able to defend herself, Andre handed her his backup weapon from the ankle holster in his boot. He saw her check it as they descended the stairs. The fact it made her more attractive to him wasn't something he was going to dwell on. They had enough problems without him developing new ones.

Gunfire erupted in the lobby before they even reached it.

Lucia and Andre both waded into the fray, but he made sure to keep her behind him. He took out two guys, then ducked and pulled her down behind a couch. It pinned them between the wall and the piece of furniture but gave him enough cover to change his clip for a full one and pop back up. He shot once more but missed. Someone fired at him and hit the wall behind his head.

Eas rushed one man from the side, slamming into him a second before he could shoot at Zander. They tumbled to the floor and rolled.

Badger took out a man, which left the one remaining guy as the one Eas fought with.

Andre got up, but had Lucia stay behind the couch just in case the man had a gun and it went off. She wasn't completely protected. Though, he figured it was better than nothing.

"Come on, bro." Badger huffed. Probably mad he wasn't the one who got to fight this guy hand to hand. "You're just dragging it out. End the guy, already."

They grappled more, and the man got the mask off Eas's face.

He took one look at Eas and gasped.

Before anyone could react, the man was on his feet and outside. The door slammed the walls so hard the glass panel shattered. It crunched under Andre's boots as he raced after the man.

No one could know that Eas was on US soil. He couldn't let this guy get away.

The man tried the door handle of a car, realized Andre was right behind him, and started to run again. Andre was just about to jump at him in a tackle when a truck pulled around the corner ahead of them. It swung toward the man he was chasing, and the window rolled down.

Someone fired. The barbs of a stun gun slammed into Andre's chest. One hit his neck.

Electric current, more than he'd ever felt before from one of these things, coursed through him.

Andre hit the ground, and the world went black.

23

Lucia pushed out the door before two men grabbed Andre, hauled him off the ground, and dragged him into their truck. The engine revved, and the truck sped away.

She pumped her arms and legs, the gun Andre had given her still in her hand. She forced her legs to stop, planted her feet, and squeezed off two shots. They pinged against the back of the truck but did nothing to slow it. Let alone make it so she could get Andre back.

They'd kidnapped him.

Zander stopped beside her and put a hand on her shoulder. He gave her a squeeze, then turned to the man on the ground while Lucia sucked in heaving breaths.

Special Agent Gage. That was who Andre had been chasing. Lucia walked over and kicked his shoulder so he rolled onto his back. He hadn't been hit by the stun gun the way Andre had, but he still didn't look good.

Abrasions on his hands and face were visible as he lifted his palms to face her. "Don't kill me."

"Give me one good reason why I shouldn't."

She was mad enough to do it. That much couldn't be denied. And yet in this situation she was the only one who had remained true to the oath they'd taken. Gage was a liar and a criminal posing as the good guy.

"You make me sick." She stared down at him lying on the ground. "You're no better than Burgess."

Gage glanced aside, his jaw flexing. She didn't see an ounce of guilt on his face. Only the disappointment that had come from being caught.

It didn't matter what she said to him, or how she tried to reason with him over the things he'd done. There was nothing that would break through the hard shell where his conscience should've been. He was so far past empathy he would never understand the wrong he'd done. All because he was selfish and wanted to make money or have whatever he wanted. She didn't know the reason, and she didn't much care.

Zander moved beside her, standing shoulder to shoulder as though offering her solidarity. "Tell me everything about the truck. You saw it."

"Why would I do that?" Gage looked around, avoiding eye contact. "You're harboring a fugitive. You think that's not as bad as what I've done? Wait until I report it to my superior. We'll see who winds up in prison…and who gets a commendation for finding one of the FBI's Most Wanted Fugitives."

Lucia hissed out a breath. He was going to hand over Andre's teammate, someone they were protecting, just to get himself out of trouble. "Scumbag."

Gage huffed out a breath. "It's good you finally noticed."

Lucia didn't like the sting of those words. She'd been blind to the fact it was apparently the entire team who was dirty, rather than just one person. And she hadn't even noticed Campbell was the one who headed up the whole thing. She'd been surrounded by dirty agents, with no clue it was happening.

She wanted to kick herself, if that was even anatomically possible. Burgess was a serious threat, but she could even argue that her team being dirty had much wider implications. Maybe not, if the domestic terrorist murdered a lot of people in the next few days. But her team could operate under the radar for years.

Maybe they'd already been doing that.

At least long enough for her superiors to figure out there was something wrong and send her in.

"It wasn't just me that noticed. Someone slipped up, because otherwise why would I be sent in to root out whoever was dirty?" She shrugged. "Looks like I figured it out. I wonder what they'll give me after they arrest *all of you*?"

"You're an informant?"

She let the pleasure show on her face, enough to watch him realize she was telling the truth. "Where's the warhead? I'm guessing you're going to need the bargaining chip over the next few months." Lucia folded her arms, holding the gun down by her side. "Tell us where it is, and we'll put in a good word for you. I'll tell everyone I work with in the Inspection Division that you cooperated."

He swore at her, then glanced at Zander.

Lucia realized Badger was on her other side, a few feet back so he could protect her. Andre's teammates were keeping her safe. And they were as intent on getting him back as she was.

The warhead had to be a high priority. But she could admit, at least to herself, that her personal priority was Andre.

She figured it was Burgess who had taken him, but the reality was, she had no idea. It could've been those men Isaac seemed affiliated with. They might have come back and decided to take Andre with them. For whatever reason Burgess also wanted the "bomb maker" brought to him.

She shuddered at the idea of facing Burgess again. For Andre, she could tamp down the fear and face the worst nightmare she'd suffered in a long time.

No matter that she could cause his death the way she had caused her father's, Lucia knew she didn't want a world where there wasn't at least a possibility that Andre could be in her life.

After all, there had never been anyone else for either of them.

Zander crouched and touched the barrel of his pistol to Gage's thigh. "You might not have been the one who shot my friend in the leg. But I'll return every injury he has back on you until you tell me what I want to know."

The obvious threat in his voice brought a shiver down her spine. Badger took a half step closer to her, probably realizing she was scared. Or maybe he wanted to offer the solidarity of being near to her at a time like this.

Lucia figured she was thinking about all this stuff because she didn't want to face the fact Zander was doing something so out of the realm of her professional conduct that she didn't quite know how to process it. Was he really going to shoot this guy in the leg?

She had seen a lot, and done a lot. But when good guys did bad things, it never sat right with her. That was why she was an agent for the DEA branch that was like Internal Affairs within a police department, their Inspection Division.

She'd been called a lot of things, but at the end of the day she could sleep well at night knowing she held people accountable to always do the right thing. To uphold the oaths they had made. Even if she hadn't done that in her life, with her marriage. She'd broken her promise. The way these men had done.

Everyone in the world had broken a promise at some time in their life.

Gage huffed out a long breath. "Fine. Don't shoot me. It's in the back of the car."

Badger turned away, and she glanced over to see him picking at the lock of the trunk. All she could think about was the fact that, in a way, she was no different than any of the people she worked with who broke the law. Or bent the rules, even if it was for the sake of justice.

She owed Andre a serious apology.

When they got him back, which they would. Lucia was going to make sure of that.

"It's here," Badger yelled. "Big hard-sided storage case. But there's a biometric lock on the case."

Lucia stared down at Gage. "Who can open it?"

He shook his head. "We don't know. That's the problem."

Zander hauled Gage to his feet and held onto his elbow. "I'll call in the police and feds. You and Badger, go with the others. Call Ted and find Andre."

Lucia nodded. "We will."

Another promise. Was she going to break this one, as well?

Gage sneered at her as Zander walked him to the car. He didn't need to do that. She already felt bad enough about the mess she'd made of her life, she hardly required him to add to it. Lucia hung her head for a second and closed her eyes.

I'm sorry, Dad.

She didn't think he could hear her. Not anymore. But it gave her a semblance of peace to say the words, even only in her mind.

Then she opened her eyes and saw Badger in front of her.

He studied her. "Ready?" He already had his phone out.

They set off toward the van. "Is Ted going to be able to find him?"

"He found you, didn't he?"

He was right. But the problem was, someone else had found her first.

ANDRE'S HEAD SWAM. He rolled slightly with the motion of the vehicle he was in. He tried to get his thoughts to coalesce into one thing, but it was like swimming in an ocean of them. Trying to catch one in a cup and drink it.

Or he was on a boat, and that was why his mind was doing this.

But when he managed to open his eyes, the blurry vision in front of him seemed to be the back seat of a truck. The bench behind the two front seats inside the cab.

He was lying on the hard seat. Outside the windows he saw only the dark of the night sky.

How long had they been driving?

The road under them was smooth, maybe a freeway. It didn't sound like any city. More like the open road.

Andre shifted his hands and used the texture of the fabric covering it to anchor himself in reality. He blinked again.

The man in the passenger seat turned to look at him. "He's awake again." The guy let out a frustrated sound and brought his arm back toward Andre.

There was a burning sting in his arm. Andre tried to argue with them, or say anything. All he could do was moan before black descended again.

When he woke next, Andre couldn't move his arms.

He tried to shift one foot and heard a shuffle around him.

He brought up his head but couldn't see anything. A bandage covered his eyes.

Given the way his body was bent, and the thing under him, Andre was in a chair. Tied to a chair.

It wasn't like that'd never happened before. But it never felt entirely comfortable, not knowing what would happen next. If the blindfold remained on, he might never know the identity of his captor. They'd played it like that in Delta Force training. Putting him through high-stress situations along with the other candidates. He had survived that. He would survive this.

If whoever took him wanted him dead, they'd have killed him already.

That thought should anchor him.

Every moment he was alive was another moment he had to figure out how to get away from these people. After he found out who they were, and what they wanted. Answers came first. Then escape. That was the way it always was. Never mind the fear, or anything else that was going on. Andre needed to focus his thoughts with laser precision and put everything he had toward survival.

Andre didn't need to think of his team. Or Lucia being back in his life.

Tied to a chair, everything governed by the person holding him captive, he couldn't only think about himself, or he would make decisions based on emotion.

Zander wouldn't let him remain here for long. The whole team and Lucia would be looking for him. In the meantime, Andre had to work on an escape of his own.

Shoes clipped on the tile floor, loafers with hard soles.

The blindfold was torn off.

Andre blinked. He leaned his head to one side and then the other to stretch out his neck. He didn't want to appear completely apathetic, but the truth was that this man had no understanding of his training and the lengths his superiors had gone to in order to make sure he would never lose his cool even under extreme stress. At least as much as a person could control.

Everyone had their breaking point. The difference was, Burgess had no idea where Andre's was.

Or how far he would have to go to find it.

Andre lifted his chin and blinked again to clear his vision. It took a minute to shake off the aftereffects of being blindfolded. He didn't like being at a disadvantage, tied to the chair. But considering he couldn't change it without escaping the bindings, there was no point dwelling on it, or complaining.

He stared at Burgess, waiting for the man to speak first.

Burgess stared down at him. In Andre's peripheral he could see at least three men, all armed. There were probably more out of sight. The room was an open plan kitchen, living and dining area. The floor was white tile. Ceiling fans. Outside the window the patio light was on, revealing palm trees at the end of the yard. The house next door had a terra-cotta roof.

Arizona, or Southern California. Maybe even the Nevada

desert, somewhere close to the plan Burgess wanted to carry out.

"They say you are the best. That is what I need right now."

Andre still said nothing. The more he knew about what Burgess wanted, the better position he would be in. Burgess needed a bomb maker. Andre could provide that service, or he could refuse. Regardless of the leverage Burgess planned on employing, it was still up to Andre whether or not he did this.

That meant he had the power, and the leverage to make demands.

Burgess wouldn't like it. But it was the truth that even tied to a chair Andre was the one in control.

"They say you can make a bomb."

"I was well trained."

"Yes, by the US Army." Burgess put his hands in the pockets of his linen pants. This wasn't a man anything like the one who had been at the compound. That guy had dressed like a domestic terrorist, ready to go to war against the government at any moment. This man was sophisticated. He lived off other people's money and did whatever he wanted.

"So you read my file." Andre tried to shrug, but it was difficult when his hands were tied to the legs of the chair. Still, he figured his demeanor came across as he needed it to. "Doesn't mean I'm in the business anymore."

Isaac could've told Burgess any number of things. Derek, who'd been working for Burgess, could have recognized Andre at the compound and handed over information in exchange for a higher position.

Either way, Andre had been sold out.

"I think, for tonight, that you are back in business." Burgess walked to a liquor cabinet in the corner of the room and poured himself a drink.

"And if I refuse?" Andre didn't exactly want to know what the answer was, but all the information he could gather would aid him.

Burgess glanced over at someone behind Andre and nodded. This wasn't going to be good.

He figured he would be beaten from behind. Or thrown to the ground and stomped on. His thigh already hurt from being tossed in the truck and dragged here. More injuries weren't going to feel good.

"I need my hands. Like a surgeon." If they broke his fingers, he wouldn't be able to do anything. Burgess needed to realize that he could shoot himself in the foot by mistreating Andre.

"So you will make me a bomb?"

Andre pressed his lips together.

Burgess glanced over Andre's shoulder.

Someone approached him from behind. Andre would have spun and attacked had he not been tied up. As it was, he had no recourse when another needle was stuck in the outside of his arm and the plunger pressed.

Fire burned through his bicep. Across his chest. To every nerve ending in his body. The inferno raced like a wildfire down a valley, incinerating everything in its wake.

His spine snapped straight. He tried to blink around his burning vision but could see only the ceiling. It was like having his fingers stuck in an electric outlet as lightning whipped through his body, contorting him.

He shook in the chair, straining against the bonds. Unable to think of anything there was so much pain. Andre tasted blood in his mouth.

He tried to breathe through the sensation, and it dissipated. Probably within minutes, but it felt like half an hour.

Sweat rolled down his face.

He gasped in a breath and blew it out slowly, then repeated that several times. Enough his thoughts could reboot and enable him to control himself once again.

"Now you understand." Burgess took measured steps toward him and sipped on his drink. "That was just a single drop in saline. Imagine if I administered a tablespoon. Or more."

Andre's body shuddered. He was unable to control the reaction, even as more sweat rolled down his face.

"I can keep you alive in unimaginable pain for as long as I like."

Andre gritted his teeth. His tongue was swollen, and the drug had caused him to lose control of his bladder. Not the worst situation he'd ever been in, but it was pretty high up there. What he needed now was for Burgess to believe he had the upper hand.

Andre sniffed, as though fighting back emotion. "What do you want me to build?"

24

"This is the one?" Lucia stared out the front window, her gaze angled up at the scale of the building.

Badger pulled under the alcove in front of a huge Vegas hotel. The glitz and sparkle of this place wasn't enough to outshine the darkness under the surface. She'd never understood why people enjoyed coming here. Indulging had never been her thing, as there was hardly time for it when she had a demanding job that was more of a mission to her.

The few vacations she'd taken were to the West Coast, small towns in Oregon where the beach was windy and on the off season, barely inhabited.

Badger put the rental car in park. "Ted says this is where the convention is being held."

"How do we know it's this one?" She glanced out the back window and spotted Judah and their normally masked teammate pull up behind them.

But in the seat was a man she didn't recognize.

"Huh."

Badger checked his mirror. "Oh. That's a disguise."

Given this was Vegas, she figured no one would've questioned a man wearing a full-face mask to hide his identity. Plenty of people here stood out from the crowd, though usually because they wanted to and not because they were trying to hide.

This was a place to be whoever you wanted, even if that was nothing like the person you were in your real life.

A disguise? That was a good idea, if it was done well.

Meanwhile Lucia just wanted to be the DEA agent she knew how to be. Someone who was going to stop a domestic terror attack and get her husband back.

"This hotel is the only one hosting a convention this week," Badger said. "At least the one that Burgess would be interested in destroying."

"I'd like to say this situation is unreal, that the idea of bombing a hotel and causing so much destruction is unimaginable? But the truth is, no matter what he wants to tell the world by doing this, he will just be tomorrow's news, and as soon as it blows over, no one will even remember his ideology."

"Maybe he just wants to be famous."

Lucia glanced over at him. "You seem like you don't think that's a good idea."

"In our line of work, living under the radar is the best course of action," Badger said. "If we draw too much attention to ourselves, then we can never work covert operations again. We're too exposed. Our pictures get out there, and our enemies target us. But I heard about a company that is like a witness protection for people who that happens to."

"Like you would testify against your enemies?" She knew they needed to get out of the car. But the fact he was opening up, even if it was only to her, would mean something to the whole team.

Badger shook his head. "It's about getting a new identity. So you can live a life of peace, after giving everything in service. Even your name, and everything about yourself." Then he pushed the car door open.

Judah and their disguised teammate caught up to them as they approached the front doors.

Lucia glanced over. "I kind of need a name for you. If you don't mind."

Badger glanced at the guy, then at her. "You can call him Eas."

"Is that okay?" She asked him. His Asian features were barely visible. He had long hair tied back. A string tie. His ears and nose were different. He could've been a wealthy Native American. Complete with gold designs on black cowboy boots.

Eas only gave her a small nod. She figured that was enough.

Inside the lobby she spotted the head of security, dressed in an expensive tailored suit. An older man with graying hair and several rings on his right hand. He spoke with two suited men and a woman—federal agents. Probably FBI, but maybe they were DEA like her.

The group spotted them approach, and everyone introduced themselves. The two men were FBI, and the woman DEA.

Badger told the group, "We're freelance. But we have a previous working relationship with the FBI. So I can provide credentials if you need them."

Lucia had to say, "I don't have my badge with me." It wasn't good. She could get in serious trouble, operating as a federal agent without her ID.

"That's why I brought this." The female agent reached in and pulled a folded wallet from her purse.

Lucia opened the wallet containing a copy of her DEA identification, along with her photo. "Thank you. I appreciate it."

The woman nodded. "Your assistant director filled me in on the task force, and your role in all this. He said to give you whatever support you need."

She nodded, in lieu of saying thank you yet again. They needed to move this along swiftly. "As we already informed the hotel, we have reason to believe that Burgess will attempt to bomb this hotel during the convention."

The head of security said, "It's due to start first thing tomorrow morning, but most of the attendees arrived today, and they're gathering in the banquet hall tonight for an informal get-together."

Lucia looked at her watch. It was just after eight in the evening. Andre had been taken earlier today, and even now hours later they had no idea where he was. Ted hadn't been able to locate the truck. Or figure out where they had gone.

Burgess was completely dark.

Even though she was working the situation here to ensure Burgess couldn't carry out his plan, all her thoughts were with Andre and what was happening to him. She wanted desperately to turn and run out the door. Do everything she could to find him, if that meant going door to door across the whole city trying to get him back. It would never work, but the desperation inside her meant she needed to do something.

"Serious planning went into this." Lucia needed them to understand what she did about Burgess. "This man has no regard for the lives of the people here. All he wants is for the world to be the way he believes it should be."

One of the FBI agents nodded. "Don't worry. We'll get everything in place, and no one will be able to bring anything in."

In her line of work, Lucia was trained to root out agents who might be subverting the cause of justice, for whatever reason. It led to her having a healthy suspicion of every agent she met. These ones weren't necessarily dirty, even though the last several she'd met—and everyone she worked with on the task force—turned out to be.

All she had was worry for Andre. She didn't need to let that skew her opinion of perfectly good people. Even if they didn't do things the way she thought they should.

Lucia said, "Shouldn't we cancel the convention altogether?"

The security guard sniffed. "I hardly think that is necessary. Between you all things should be squared away fairly quickly."

She figured he was trying to use flattery to get them to rise to the occasion and not disrupt hotel operations. It wasn't going to work with her. "We cannot assume everything will be fine. This is a serious threat, and the hotel needs to act accordingly."

"Of course we will do that. However, in the event that this man is stopped and the bomb never arrives at the hotel? I'm sure in that case no one needs to be bothered over a potential threat."

Lucia hissed out a breath between clenched teeth. She heard Judah stifle a chuckle behind him. She was glad someone thought this was amusing, because this situation needed the cooperation of hotel security.

Burgess was a very real threat. He might not have the warhead, as Zander was now in possession of it. However, with Andre she figured he could pull something together that would cause a serious amount of destruction.

The female DEA agent didn't look impressed by the security guard. However, the two FBI agents didn't seem too bothered by the security guard's lack of concern for the seriousness of this threat.

One of them said, "Let's find a conference room and plan this out. If we can ascertain how he will get a bomb into the conference, and where the vulnerabilities are, we'll have a better chance of stopping it."

She figured that was as good of a shot as they were gonna get.

All their other chances of this being nothing—no disaster, no tragic event? All of it was down to Andre.

She wanted to pray for him, that he would be able to hold out. But she had no right to speak on his behalf. Not when she was no better than the dirty agents she had worked with. Even if her father's death hadn't been preventable, it still happened by her hand. Because of her words, and the stress she had caused him.

She prayed anyway, because she needed to so desperately. Whether God heard her or not, she asked for Andre to not be another victim of her existence.

They started to walk away. Judah squeezed her shoulder. "Okay?"

Lucia nodded. She had no right to make this about her when it wasn't. "Let's go."

ANDRE SNIFFED. He shook his whole body to try to get rid of the feeling under his skin. Flicked out his hands. Rolled his shoulders. Everything itched, and when he closed his eyes, it felt like needles were stabbing his eyeballs.

It had to be the aftereffects of whatever Burgess had given him.

He shifted on the chair, and the wheels moved to one side an inch and then the other. Andre rolled his shoulders again and looked at the worktable in front of him. At least they had untied his hands, or this would be very difficult.

They had walked him to what should probably be the pool house. Two men remained with him, but Burgess had delivered his threat and then left.

Make a bomb, or be killed.

Andre figured they were going to kill him after he was finished anyway.

He stared at the schematic diagram that had been unrolled on the table, alongside a ton of hardware and a case containing two vials of liquid. If this was a movie, one vile would have been blue and the other red. When mixed together, they would create a violent purple color that preceded a devastating explosion. Sadly, both liquids were clear, though someone had labeled the vials so he would know which was which.

Andre rubbed his hands down his face and squeezed his eyes shut for a second. He was in no condition to be doing this, but what choice did he have?

He grabbed the two ends of wires he had stripped and twisted them together. Then he went back and double-checked everything he'd done so far on this mechanism. If something went wrong, he was going to be the one missing a finger. Or his whole head. He could only hope that if an accident happened, he could have the gift of a grace that meant he took the whole house with him.

Unless there were any innocents here.

If Andre could be sure he took Burgess along with him, he would probably be tempted to do it. Build a bomb—without the two vials—and blow the whole house, killing himself in the process. But he couldn't be certain he would get the man responsible.

Andre leaned over and stared at the schematic, as though contemplating the wiring on that side of the device. Every bomb maker had a signature. This seemed relatively generic, which made him wonder if it was the work of the government scientist who had been murdered a few weeks ago.

Stuart Edwards had taken proprietary technology and deconstructed it for the government, providing them with plans to build it themselves. Didn't matter what it was. Computer systems, devices, or weapons. He had been kidnapped, forced to construct a targeting system that had destroyed an airplane minutes after Andre descended the stairs.

Plenty of people had died that day. Now Edwards's legacy would live on after his death.

Andre wanted nothing to do with it. He would rather have torn up the schematics, tossed the vials at the nearest wall, and made a run for it. If he wouldn't end up with a bullet in the back of his head.

According to the schematics, the two solutions mixed together would create an explosion that released toxic gas into the air. Right now they were in a storage container that could withstand the blast of a volcano eruption, but he had looked inside to see what he was dealing with.

Burgess wanted to stage a chemical attack in a hotel? No way was Andre going to allow that to happen. Whether or not he lived through it.

Sure, he wanted to have one last conversation with Lucia where he got to tell her how he felt. Still, even now.

Maybe he was the biggest idiot for not moving on. But he had always thought that some people only had one person who was their everything, their whole world.

He didn't want her to live the rest of her life alone, but Andre had always thought he was one of those people.

And so he got on with the rest of the bomb he was constructing, praying that if he died she would find someone else. He didn't want her to be alone anymore. He wanted her to be happy, and loved.

"Ugh." One of the gunmen groaned. "This is literally taking all night."

Andre glanced at the clock on the wall. "It's barely midnight. Or is that past your bedtime?"

He heard the man tromp over to him. The guy squeezed the back of Andre's neck and leaned close, his pizza breath wafting across Andre's face. "Why don't you just get on with what you're doing."

It occurred to him he could grab one of the vials and smash it in the man's face. Too bad one of the toxic chemicals alone would kill both of them—even after just breathing in a handful of the molecules.

Andre had no plan to be writhing on the floor, choking on his own blood. At least not anytime soon. He would very much like to speak with Lucia before that happened.

He gritted his teeth and waited for the man to move away. "If you want it to be done quicker, then maybe you shouldn't interrupt me. Yeah?"

Andre soldered a circuit board to the mechanism. He didn't hook it up, and it had no functional purpose. But it made the thing look very official—maybe even deadly. He'd found C4 among the supplies. Probably it wasn't for this device, as it didn't actually require the use of plastic explosives. The mechanism only needed the two liquids to mix together. That alone was enough to cause an explosion. However, it was the answer to a small prayer he had whispered while tied to that chair.

Andre pushed back from the table. "I have to go to the bathroom."

The man looked down, then back to Andre's face. "Hold it like a big boy."

"Are you sure you want to smell that, when I can't hold it anymore?" Maybe he should have said, "I've been holding it all this time." His brain wasn't actually firing on all cylinders. Burgess had probably made a misstep bringing him here and then shooting him up with whatever had been in that syringe. It could prove deadly if Andre made a mistake, but there was little time to sit and wonder about that.

The man stood up. The gunman by the door rolled his eyes. "Fine. We don't need another mess." He reached for the handle. "But make it quick."

Andre shrugged one shoulder. "I always thought it just takes as long as it takes. I mean, can you really make it go faster?" He slipped out of the room, and the man watched him limp down the hall to the bathroom.

Two rooms down on the other side of the hallway, he opened the door and stepped inside. The bathroom was fancy but also completely filthy. He felt bad for the homeowner. It was going to be expensive to recoup their losses after this.

He had just flushed the toilet when a boom shook the building.

He'd honestly thought it would be faster than that, but apparently he'd misjudged the timing.

Andre cracked the door and peered out. When he saw no

one, he crept out and headed for the room he had just exploded. Half the exterior wall was gone, along with the man who had been standing on that side. The guy he'd just spoken with was on his side on the floor, looking a little charred.

Andre rummaged in his pockets for a phone and used the man's thumb to unlock it. He dialed Ted's number, excitement buzzing through him.

His thumb went to the green button to connect the call.

A heavy object slammed the side of his head. Pain erupted in his skull.

He dropped the phone, not knowing if the call went through or not. He heard it shatter and turned, but not fast enough to evade the baseball bat now slicing through the air to hit his upper arm.

He absorbed the hit. Ducking would have made it slam his head again, and if that happened, he would be unconscious now. He tried to move, then stumbled and slammed against the wall. He couldn't shake off what happened. He couldn't think what to do.

The phone. No, that was on the floor.

Someone was coming at him again.

He realized he was on his hands and knees. He'd fallen.

He had to get up now.

The baseball bat slammed between Andre's shoulder blades, and his face smashed the tile.

From a distance, he heard Burgess say, "Make a call. It seems like our friend needs some additional incentive."

25

———————

Lucia followed the security guard down a quiet hallway behind the casino floor. She could hear the echo of people and the whir and ding of slot machines, along with the music pumping through speakers overhead. "We appreciate your help with this."

She didn't need to remind him that no one wanted a tragedy and figured the guy would agree considering the target was his hotel. As the head of security, it would fall on his shoulders to react to a threat such as this. Either by doing everything he could to prevent it or, if that wasn't possible, attempting to minimize as much of the damage.

The security guard nodded, glancing back over his shoulder at her.

Badger, Judah, and Eas had been antsy to say the least. Roaming the casino floor. Waiting for a call back from Ted, or communication from Zander that would confirm the warhead was now in official hands—ones that would safeguard its capabilities. Maybe even destroy it.

They'd told her the device came in a small hard-sided storage case. None of them had seen it, but the container had been considerably smaller than Badger thought it should've been—even for a suitcase nuke. The government probably wanted to take it apart to see how it worked. Eas had a slightly more cynical viewpoint, one that had the US Government retrofitting versions of it for small targeted strikes.

Lucia didn't love everything the American government did, but she agreed with the principles of freedom and being a force for good in the world. Those weren't the things she had a problem with. It was usually when people got a hold of them that everything was messed up in implementation. Selfishness crept in, and deception. People had their own agendas, and that superseded any goodwill they may have had going into it.

Then people like Burgess rose against them, attempting to cleanse the landscape. To prove their point by any means necessary, drawing everyone's attention back to the right things—even if their methods were misguided. It was a cycle that seemed to repeat itself over and over.

Lucia just wished it didn't involve so much death. And if it wasn't so often financed by the sale of drugs, she wouldn't even have a job.

The head of security had an office bigger than her living room and kitchen combined. Considering she lived in an apartment, that wasn't saying much. Everything about it was high end, from the lights and fixtures to the furniture. Even the tile on the floor and the rug under the desk. The interior decorating alone probably cost more than her annual salary.

She wandered to the hutch on one side, aware she was dirty and mussed. Although she'd managed to clean up a bit and run a hairbrush through her hair before she secured it in a ponytail. Beside the hutch was a print of a Hawaii beach, making her think of Nora and the elopement with Zander. She studied the picture while the security guard got a phone call, thinking Zander and Nora's relationship wasn't too different than her and Andre's in the beginning.

They had known each other longer than Nora and Zander. However, they also had married quickly on the spur of the moment. Lucia hoped for their sakes that the relationship lasted longer than Andre and Lucia's had.

On the hutch was a picture of the head of security with a woman and two children—a girl and a boy. The photo beside it had the boy in a football uniform, red-faced with damp hair, his arms above his head in celebration. Beside that, the young girl sat with her mother on a towel, both dressed in swimwear.

"That's my daughter. My wife is with her at the hospital right now, as she is suffering badly with her diabetes this week."

She glanced aside at him. Her phone rang in her pocket, but she couldn't answer it right now. "I'm sorry to hear that. Having to deal with this threat is probably the last thing you need, but I'm grateful you can provide assistance for us."

She pulled the phone out. The ringing had stopped.

Before she could look at who had called, he said, "You seem to be thinking of something else as well, are you not?"

"He's not in the hospital." She didn't know where he was, or what was happening to him. "But he's someone I care about deeply."

He nodded slowly. "I think you do not need to be worried. You will see him soon."

She started to turn as he brought his hand up. Her palm thrust before she even registered that he held a needle in his hand. Lucia grabbed his wrist and held it fast.

He thought he was going to stick her with that needle?

The security guard used his free hand to punch her diaphragm.

Lucia bent forward and coughed. There was barely enough space between them to do so, and she wound up brushing his shirt buttons with her hair.

But she didn't let go of his wrist.

He dragged her two steps, moving back as he attempted to pull his wrist free of her hand. She stumbled against him. He tore his arm free and came at her again.

Her back hit the hutch. Something toppled over and shattered inside.

Lucia reached for her gun. He knocked it out of her hand far too quickly, in a way that shot fear through her. It wasn't supposed to end like this.

His forearm held her against the hutch. Her phone started to vibrate across the tile, and while she struggled, he stuck the needle in her neck and pressed the plunger.

He stepped back, and she had to force herself to remain upright. They stared at each other. It took only seconds for her to realize the burn of the needle hadn't stopped. And now it grew, moving through her. Spreading like a wildfire that licked at her skin, shooting lightning to her nerve endings.

Lucia gasped. Her legs gave out, and she slammed to the floor. She braced her weight with both hands as pain shot up her injured wrist. She screamed, but there was no strength to combat the sensation.

Her face slammed against the tile, and everything went black.

The first thing she became aware of was that someone was touching her face. Lucia lifted her good hand and tried to push whoever it was away.

"Ouch. Okay, it's okay."

She knew that low rumble, a voice she liked to listen to far too much. Lucia blinked and opened her eyes. Andre's face swam in front of her. He smiled, but the expression didn't reach the darkness in his eyes. It didn't overcome it.

"There you are." Relief softened his expression. "I was getting worried you weren't going to wake up after they carried you in here and dumped you on the floor."

She glanced around. "Are we in a storage unit?"

"They had to relocate me." Amusement flickered in his eyes. "There was a minor mishap with some C4. Which they now know I don't need, so they took it all away. Unfortunately."

"Andre?"

He shook his head. "Don't try to sit up. You look about as good as I feel."

Well, that wasn't entirely flattering. Apparently he didn't think much of the way she looked right now, and how could she help that? She could barely even move her fingers.

Andre exhaled, leaned down, and kissed her forehead. "You're beautiful. Don't look so worried, I will always think you're beautiful. No matter what."

She figured of all things, that likely wasn't the problem that held them back from each other. But it also wasn't something they needed to get into right now. "Did Burgess kidnap me?"

She didn't know if it was for the second time, or if technically only the first. She'd lost track of everything that'd happened since before Andre walked into the compound to save her.

But she was glad he had.

He touched her cheek with his thumb, stroking the skin there for a second. "They think I need more incentive to do what they asked. Burgess probably figures if we talk to each other, we'll get all emotional. Then when he threatens to kill you if I don't make the bomb, I'll react based on emotion and comply to save your life."

"Why does it sound like you're not planning on doing that?" Maybe he had already concluded that losing her would be for the greater good. That he couldn't build the bomb, no matter what the stakes were.

Lucia frowned, wondering if that was the man he had become since she'd broken his heart. Something new she was just now discovering, when she'd believed she had figured it all out.

Maybe she'd done even more damage than she thought.

"You're right." She didn't look at him. He would probably only try to say something that softened the blow. "We can't let anyone die."

ANDRE STARED. "I'm not going to let Burgess kill you."

He wanted to shake her, but she already looked a little worse for wear. He probably did as well since they'd dosed him again with that drug. Now he was even shakier than he had been before.

"Lucia, I'm just saying we need a plan, because I'm not going to make the bomb, but I'm also not going to let him murder you. All we have to do is figure out how to get that done."

He wasn't sure he even made sense. The words didn't exactly come out in the right way. Did she even understand what he was saying?

She shifted on the floor and used one hand to push herself away from him, then sat up. "What difference does it make? You're going to build the bomb, so he'll kill me probably."

"Then he'll kill me, too, because I'm not going to let that happen. Then he'll have to find someone else to make the bomb, and people will still die anyway." Andre willed her to understand. "That's why we need to take him down. Once and for all."

She blew out a breath, looking exhausted.

Andre held out one hand and said, "Come here."

Tears filled her eyes.

Andre shifted closer to her and tugged her against him.

Lucia set her head on his shoulder, her face against his neck.

He heard her exhale and felt it as he wound his arms around her. "We will figure this out. It's going to be hard, because they already know I'll put up a fight. That's why you're here." He kissed her forehead. "Something I am unbelievably glad about."

She sniffed.

"I love you," he told her. "I didn't want to be alone, so I'm glad you're here with me now."

Even if it was for the wrong reason, it was still true. Burgess might have brought her here, but there was nothing Andre wanted more. Even if it would be used against him as leverage. Burgess would threaten to kill her, and Andre was supposed to be scared enough of losing her that he would comply.

She shifted and leaned back, tilting her head to look up at him. "You don't mean that. You can't, not when I destroyed it."

"Maybe love doesn't make any sense. Maybe it's infuriating. And confusing and wonderful all at the same time."

"Until you realize I can't be the person you love, because you'll lose everything in the end."

Andre wanted to say something smart and funny. The words died on the tip of his tongue. He scanned her face, trying to figure her out. Was it the drugs or something else? "Tell me."

"I killed my father." Her gaze slid to the side, as though she couldn't bring herself to face him. "When I told him that we got married that weekend in Vegas, he was so upset he had a heart attack. He lived long enough to make it to the hospital before he had another massive heart attack and died. There was nothing they could do." As though maybe there had been something she could've done. It was there in her words, that she believed herself responsible.

Andre said, "If he had a heart attack, then there was nothing you could have done to prevent it." Sometimes hearts were simply ticking time bombs.

His thoughts about her father were entirely separate. He hadn't known the man well, but what he'd seen of him Andre had put together why Lucia demanded so much of herself. The man had been exacting and set a high standard.

Hearing she had married the boy he hated, the dumb jock and wannabe army grunt—her father's words—had no doubt stressed the man. But to the extent he had a heart attack? That was something Andre hadn't expected.

No wonder she had retreated into herself and erected walls no one had been able to break through. She'd sent him packing.

"You should have told me."

She shook her head, tears in her eyes. "You would have convinced me to try. I couldn't do that, not when I...I killed him."

"I knew I didn't deserve you. I worked through it, and we came out stronger. I had to teach myself to believe I was good enough for you even when everyone said I wasn't. That we could have something good." And yet, she'd pushed him away.

He had to admit, at least to himself, that hurt him. He'd found himself fighting those same feelings of inadequacy all over again. Rather than allowing him to help her deal with her grief, by the time he'd shown back up in her life—the first chance he got after basic training—she'd had enough time to convince herself that separating was for the best.

"It wasn't your fault, Luce." He laid his forehead against hers. "No one blames you. Your father was in control of his own health. You were only trying to live your life and make your own choices. You couldn't have known that'd happen."

"He..." Her face scrunched up, and she ducked it back against his shirt, crying while he held her.

"I'm sorry you had to see that." Her father had died in front of her. It might've happened while he was in the hospital, but it began while she watched. In a way that made her believe she was responsible. "I'm sorry you lost him when I was gone." He could have helped her through it right away, but they hadn't been in contact through those weeks.

She cried for a few more minutes, then finally lifted her head after his hip had gone numb. "I'm sorry I screamed at you."

"Don't be. You were grieving."

"Did you really want a divorce, at the house, when you said you did?" She bit her lip.

"I thought that would fix what was torn up in me. But it won't." He knew what would, but didn't know how she'd feel about it. "Do you wish you'd ended it?"

She hadn't filed for divorce, or even an annulment. Either of them could have done so at any time. But they didn't.

Now they were still married.

"I didn't want to."

He didn't know what to say.

"I wanted you with me." She sniffed, looking nervous still. "Even though I knew you never could be, because I killed it."

In a way, she had. But he knew what she meant. "It wouldn't only be your fault. I could have fought harder. Come back again, and dug to find out what happened."

"You had to go back to the army. I knew that, and I used it to force your hand." A tear slipped from the corner of her eye. "I'm sorry."

"Maybe we should start fresh." Andre held her hand. "I don't have a ring, but…will you marry me again?"

Amusement tugged at her lips, much better than the grief still shadowed there. "Yes. Of course."

"Of course," he repeated.

She touched his cheeks this time, tugged his face toward hers, and they kissed. He felt her sigh against him. The kiss lasted until she leaned back, and he remembered the situation they were in.

"Burgess."

She nodded.

Andre groaned. "To be continued?"

"I hope so."

She looked so cute Andre touched his lips to hers one more time.

"I see no progress has been made."

Burgess. Andre didn't look at him. He held Lucia's gaze instead. "I wouldn't say that."

She smiled.

One of Burgess's men grabbed her arm and hauled her from his arms, took three steps back, and pulled her to her feet at the same time.

"Easy." Andre stood, though it was difficult because it hurt *a lot* to stand. He exhaled. "Is this the part where you threaten her so I comply?" He should've been figuring out the plan with her, but getting their relationship on the right footing hadn't been a bad thing by any means.

"Construct the device." Burgess motioned to the storage container on the table with a fresh set of components and new schematics. The container had burn marks from his bomb but remained intact—as did the chemicals inside.

Andre waited for the threat.

Lucia let out a surprised noise. He spun around to see her convulse. She dropped to the floor leaving her captor standing there with a needle in his hand.

"Two drops," Burgess said, his tone void of emotion. "This time. She will continue to suffer while you complete the task. If you take too long, eventually her heart will simply"—he spread his hands—"give out."

26

Lucia pushed out a breath. She'd been dragged from the storage unit Andre was in to a bigger one, opposite it but offset so the garage style doors didn't face one another. Why she was obsessing over the doors lining up, she didn't know. Maybe it was just better than thinking about what was happening. Or that it represented the fact nothing about this lined up.

The security guard had been in on it.

Her entire task force had been dirty.

She and Andre had never divorced one another, and the spark was still there. He wanted to be married to her.

It was enough to make her head spin. Until Burgess crouched beside the cot she lay on. Then everything coalesced, and she could do nothing but watch him stare at her. Of course this had to be weird.

She didn't want to give away the fact she was more scared than she'd ever been in her life, but wasn't sure she'd be able to hide it. Not with her skin humming as though a million ants crawled under the surface. Her fingers and toes, even the top of her head. All of it felt as though she'd been electrocuted.

That was twice now she'd been stuck with a needle. This time had been worse than the first, when it should have been easier to manage after she already knew what to expect. But it hadn't been. And he'd said something about two drops instead of one.

She couldn't even imagine what kind of chemical did that.

Lucia moved her gaze from his, not wanting to participate even one second longer in the existence of a man like this. She wanted nothing to do with him.

Across the room were a card table and single folding chair. None of Burgess's men were in this unit with them. He could do whatever he wanted, and no one would be here to see. But no doubt Andre would hear her scream from across the hallway.

Lucia couldn't hold back the shiver that ran through her.

On the table was a laptop, and the screen displayed an image of Andre. One of Burgess's men was in view. He must have set up a surveillance camera so Burgess could watch the progress.

Because Andre had set off a bomb the last time? Maybe. She knew now that he had watched their entire exchange, and maybe even listened given the headphones on the table.

"I admit, I can recognize what he sees in you."

"Is that supposed to be flattering?" She could barely voice the words, but got enough out he understood.

Burgess's lips curled up.

"You probably think my feelings are irrelevant. I doubt you even register the fact you have any of your own."

"Why would I not?" He still studied her with those green eyes. "If I had no feelings, how would I be able to experience pleasure seeing the look on your face…or hearing you scream?"

Lucia bit the inside of her lip, the pain helping her focus her thoughts. She didn't want to give him anything. Especially when he would be amused by it—or worse. "Is that why you're blowing up the convention? To hear people scream?"

"You tell me. Who is this convention hosting?"

She had seen the posters, and the feds had received a list of the registered attendees from the head of security. The one she now knew had been either paid off by Burgess or leaned on by him. "A number of pharmaceutical companies." The guest of honor. "And the Secretary of Health and Human Services."

She couldn't help thinking of the head of security and his daughter with diabetes. A little girl was suffering in the hospital, and her father supporting a cause that pushed back against the companies who controlled the distribution of drugs that would help her. Doing it in the worst way.

Burgess made a humming sound in his throat. "And why might I want to destroy a gathering of those people?"

She shrugged, only because it would infuriate him. Cooperation wasn't the goal here. "Because you hate America, or whatever. What does it matter?"

His gaze narrowed. "You think it doesn't?"

"Blah, blah. Manifesto." She shrugged, wrinkling her nose. "It's all just crazy ramblings, as if anything will change." She was definitely at a disadvantage, laid out on a cot while he leaned over her. He could do whatever he wanted, and she would be making him mad.

She was, if the look on his face was truthful. He wasn't trying to convince her around to his way of thinking. At least, he should know that wasn't possible. But still, he thought he was the one in control because it was the way he lived. Never mind what she wanted, or the things she still needed to do in her life.

She'd have thought he would reach out and wrap his hand around her throat, attempt to squeeze the life from her as he tried to convince her he was right.

Instead he simply said, "Change only comes after blood has been shed. We all know that by now."

"What about when there is blood, but no change? What's the point in fighting when things remain the same?"

And yet, even as she said it aloud, Lucia knew that part of her held onto Andre all these years because she wanted to fight for him. She never wanted to completely sever the connection they had. Neither had he.

She glanced at the computer now, taking a second to watch him work.

Burgess would know. He'd see her, but with the camera he already knew. Why else would she be here? He'd known since she escaped his compound with Andre that there was a connection between them. Maybe not how deep it ran, but they cared for one another enough Burgess used her as leverage to get Andre to build a bomb that would destroy a hotel.

"My intention is not to change your mind." Out the corner of her eye she could see him watching her, even while she kept her focus on Andre. He was her anchor. Her lifeline while the world spun around them. He always had been, and she knew now that he always would be.

No matter that she had tried to push him away.

Andre was her family, the only family she had left. After years of striving to do the right thing, her life amounted to little substance. The things that meant something? She had kept those from her own life on purpose. Living behind a wall she put up to keep her heart safe from feeling any more guilt or grief. Instead, she had kept herself from love and happiness.

From Andre.

Burgess said, "It is to simply inform you of the war you will be a casualty of."

So he *was* going to kill her.

No matter what Andre did, Burgess intended to end her life and probably Andre's too. As soon as he didn't need them anymore, he would kill them.

It was a small comfort knowing they'd shared their true feelings with each other at least. Each knew where the other stood, and he had put her wedding ring back on her finger. They were connected again, even if only in that small way.

"Most people die meaningless deaths after living meaningless lives." He stroked a finger down her arm. "Yours will count for something."

Yes, it would. But not in the way he thought.

If she had any strength at all she would get up from this cot and fight Burgess. Do her job, bring justice even if that was by taking his life. But she had no weapon and couldn't even move her arm out from under his finger.

His hand moved, and his finger traced the hem of her shirt. He moved it away from her pants, sliding the material up to reveal her waist.

His fingers stroked the skin there while she screamed inside her mind. Unable to voice it aloud, even if she could. She wasn't going to do it because Andre would hear. She couldn't let the sound out because she knew how much it would torture her to hear him suffer. There was no way Lucia was going to let that happen when he had already endured so much pain because of her.

Andre.

A radio crackled. It was on the table. "He's done."

Burgess's hand stilled. "Shame." Then he leaned down and bit the skin over her hip. Hard.

Her whole body clenched, and the cry rent from her lips anyway. She moved so fast her back slammed the wall. Burgess straightened, laughing as he went to the laptop.

Across the hall she heard Andre cry out, then a crash.

THE STOOL he'd been sitting on skittered across the floor. There wasn't far to go, so it hit the wall. The gunman he'd tossed it at flinched and lost his grip on the weapon he held.

Andre rushed him, shoved the guy against the wall and grabbed the gun from him. He squeezed off a round, the gun pointed at the man's throat. The bullet exited the back of his head, and the man fell to the ground. Not exactly the plan, but it at least served to alleviate some of the frustration he'd felt hearing Lucia scream.

He had no idea what Burgess was doing to her. But he was going to find out.

Andre shoved the dead guy out of the way and twisted the door handle. Burgess stood in the hall. Lucia in front of him.

A syringe to her throat.

He didn't meet her gaze, recalling that moment at the train station when he had found their enemy with a knife to Nora's throat. She had been an ordinary citizen, innocent of everything she'd been accused of. Lucia was a trained federal agent. But in the moment, with a syringe to her throat, who knew what muscle memory she would fall back on.

Neither of them was going to risk her life.

Andre pointed the gun at Burgess, tempted—so tempted—to squeeze off a shot and end all this. But if he did that, there was a chance Burgess might press the plunger as his muscles contracted. The moment the bullet hit him he could end Lucia's life.

The cost of taking him down would be everything Andre had ever wanted.

He wasn't going to risk it.

"Let her go." Andre gritted his teeth. He forced his body to stay where it was, every instinct in him screaming to rush the guy.

Take the shot.

He couldn't though, because he wasn't willing to watch her die. "Let her go, now."

Burgess took a step back, down the hall. He dragged Lucia with him.

Andre could see a drop of blood bead where Burgess held the syringe. He could so easily cause serious damage, not even pressing the plunger. Andre shook, his body practically vibrating with the need to drag her from that man and save her.

"I said, let her go."

"You are in no place to bargain."

"I finished the weapon." Andre stared down the barrel of

his gun at a man he very much wanted to shoot. "So let's make a trade. You give her to me, and I give you what you really want."

Burgess grinned a sick smile. "I think I'll take both. After you put the gun down."

Andre's stomach lurched. He took another step toward them, pain shooting through his injured leg. He pushed aside the sensation and moved anyway. One step. Another. "I will shoot you."

"And I will kill her. Then what will you have?"

"Still more than you." Andre could tell him about the team. But what did Burgess care about friends who were more like family? The man knew nothing of good or even healthy relationships. They were the beginning and end of everything good that people could make for themselves—that need to connect in positive ways was fundamental to human existence.

Lucia whimpered.

Burgess took another step, the needle still poking her skin.

Andre moved with them. Even in all the time they were estranged, she had still been part of his life. That wasn't ever going to change, whether she was here.

Or if he lost her.

Andre met her gaze with his. He put everything he was feeling into his expression, not wanting to say it aloud so Burgess would hear. So that he would cheapen a moment of genuine affection.

She nodded, the faintest of movements. Then she lifted two fingers and swiped down at an angle.

Then she raised four. Counted down one by one. Whimpering, pleading with Burgess to let her go.

Andre readied himself to take the shot.

Lucia lowered the second to last finger, leaving one remaining. Then her eyes widened.

Andre heard a shuffle behind him. He was about to turn when someone slammed into his back.

Andre fell to the ground. The gun skittered away.

Blows rained down on him. Punches. Kicks. He reached for the person, came up with a baggy pant leg, then pulled it up and bit the man's shin. He ignored the taste and aimed to draw blood.

The man screamed, leaned down, and slammed Andre's injured leg with the butt of a gun. "Please let me kill this guy."

"Not yet," Burgess said. "We need him to plant the weapon and arm it. After all, it isn't any of us who are going to end up on hotel surveillance." Burgess sounded entirely too pleased with himself. Everything in his plan was coming to fruition. All of it would be in place soon enough, and Andre would be fingered as the one responsible.

After all, he had built the bomb, so his fingerprints were all over the components. Not only that, but as a disgruntled former army grunt, he would be pegged as a hero who turned to the dark side. Someone who wanted to get back at the very people who had failed him.

Only his team and Lucia would know the truth. Everyone else would paint him with the same brush, but it only mattered that they believed him.

If it came to that. "I'm not going to do whatever you want."

"He'll probably screw it up." The man who'd tackled him kicked Andre then, with the leg Andre had bitten. He called him a foul name and said, "You need someone with half a brain to do this right. And the boys want to hunt."

He was volunteering?

Burgess didn't agree, or disagree. He simply said, "Pack it up. Let's get moving." He nodded toward Andre's weapon. "Give me his gun and take her."

The guy seemed happy to comply. He swiped the gun from the ground and handed it to Burgess in exchange for Lucia. He held her against him, and Andre realized why he was so pleased.

Andre stared up at the man from the floor while Burgess returned to the needle and pocketed it.

"Quit messing around, Peters. There will be time for that later," Burgess said. "We're on a deadline. This needs to be done by morning."

Peters dragged Lucia to the room where Andre had been working. Burgess held the gun on him. "Get up. You make one move I don't like, and I shoot you in the head. You've cost me far too much already."

"Only followers." Andre rolled over and pushed off the floor to stand. "I'm sure you can get plenty more of those when your campaign goes viral." He leaned against the wall, trying to look nonchalant. The reality was, he barely had the strength to stand.

Burgess motioned with the gun. "Let's go."

Andre moved ahead of him down the hall. Peters pushed Lucia out of the room so that she ran right into Andre. They held each other up as Peters carried the crate with the bomb in it.

Peters went first. Burgess shoved Andre with the barrel of the gun while Lucia held onto him, and he slid his arm around her. More so they could hold each other up than for any other reason.

Andre moved his mouth close to her ear and whispered, "I love you." He squeezed her shoulder, and she returned the gesture, her hand on his forearm. Three squeezes in a row.

Love you, too.

Memory rushed back. She'd done that years ago, a silent communication in the days they'd had to keep the truth of their feelings for each other low-key. Now he hardly cared who knew how he felt about her.

But for the man behind them carrying a gun.

The man ahead of them carrying a bomb Andre had made.

The men who appeared at the end of the hall. Behind them. Around them. More than he thought Burgess had brought to the storage unit.

They loaded into a passenger van, Andre and Lucia in the

middle row. Loaded weapons pointed at them from almost every side.

They drove three hours, headed northwest according to the rearview mirror with the tiny letters in the corner. *NW.* Until Burgess ordered the van to pull over on the side of the highway in the middle of nowhere.

In the middle of the desert with an ocean of stars overhead.

Burgess twisted in the passenger seat and faced them. "Last stop."

One of the men slid the door open. "This is where you get out."

Lucia shifted to the door, Andre moving with her.

Burgess pressed the button on the side of his radio. "You give them a ten-minute head start, and then you go hunting."

Andre's stomach sank toward the desert floor. He nudged Lucia. "Go. Run."

27

———————

"Where?" She looked around, but there was nothing except desert. In the dark she couldn't see anything. No buildings or even shrubs, just the road and two vehicles. The one they'd been in, and the one that had followed behind them, where Peters had the weapon.

Andre nudged her forward. "Just go. We have to run."

She set off, her gait stiff from all her injuries. And yet she wasn't the one with the gunshot wound in her thigh. Andre would be in so much more pain than her. She could hardly complain, even if she was flat out exhausted, in serious pain, and it was the middle of the night. She wanted to be curled up, back in that twin bed where they'd slept beside each other. Was that really just a day or two ago?

Lucia and her husband—it felt so strange to think of him that way, even if it was true—had faced death so many times since then. Now it seemed they would do it once more.

She stumbled in the dark. Andre took her hand and hastened their pace. Running slightly in front of her so that he tugged her along. Not too fast or she would fall.

Lucia glanced back at the van and the SUV behind it. The men inside stared at them, watching as they ran away. "They're going to hunt us, aren't they?" She had no doubt her voice carried in the night. There was nothing out here to absorb the sound. But still, she had to ask the question. Andre knew something she didn't about what was happening.

"Don't stop running."

She picked up her pace a little to come alongside him rather than drag behind. She could hear the desperation in his voice, and even that was enough to get her to comply. Let alone the group of men with guns.

"Burgess is taking the bomb to the hotel. But one of his guys, or maybe more than one, are going to hunt us." Andre huffed out a breath, sucking in a long inhale. "That's why we have to run."

"We're not animals." It wasn't as though Andre didn't agree with her. But apparently Burgess thought they were little better than mindless beasts who should be put down. A little sport, and he could guarantee they were murdered. Out here where there were no houses or buildings. No emergency services or even power. Probably no cell signal either, though they didn't have a phone between them. Or a weapon.

No one would find them. Once whatever animals were out here took care of their remains there wouldn't be anything left at the end to be found.

Lucia sucked in a breath, the end of that burning in her lungs. "Where are we going?"

A skilled hunter could pick them off from hundreds of yards away. Let alone someone trained as a sniper in the military. They would be easy pickings, not much sport.

If they could find somewhere to take cover. A weapon. Somewhere they could hide, or call for help. But out here in the dark in the middle of the Nevada desert, there was nothing. Just them, and someone with a loaded gun trying to kill them.

"Don't stop running."

She huffed out a breath, ready to retort. Then she realized he might need to tell himself that. Maybe as much as he felt he should tell her. To remind them both there was nothing for them if they stopped. But if they kept going—and going…and going —they still had a chance. With every step they took, they still had a chance.

"We're headed to that hill." He motioned with their joined hands.

Lucia hadn't even realized there was anything over there. In the dark, it simply looked like the absence of stars rising in the night sky. Like a void. Now her eyes began to adjust, and she could see it was an elevation in the terrain. A hill they could climb, or go around.

"There might be something behind it. It's our only shot." He sounded as though he didn't exactly believe what he was saying. But he was being reassuring for her, and she loved him for it.

Lucia wasn't the kind of person to live in denial, but sometimes she required a healthy amount of hope. How else did anyone live life, always overwhelmed with the reality of whatever situation they were in? She knew exactly how bad things could get. She saw the worst of what humans did to one another on a daily basis.

Friends.

Family.

Women.

Children. Those cases were the worst.

And when agents betrayed their oath, she could hardly even believe a person could be so selfish. But it was true. People acted in their own interests all the time, regardless of the ways they hurt others.

The next breath escaped as a whimper, and Andre squeezed her hand.

There was no time for him to say more, but Lucia had something she wanted to say. "I'm sorry. You know that, and I know I said it already. But I do love you. And I really am sorry."

He groaned, and they kept running. Pushing one foot in front of the other.

Until her leg muscles burned as much as her lungs.

"Come on." It was a command, encouragement, and reassurance all in one go.

She wasn't alone.

They were out here together. The way they should have been all along, before life got in the way.

Lucia's foot tangled in a bush, and she stumbled. Andre dragged her out of it, tugging her along practically still running. She winced as her foot angled in the wrong direction.

"Luce—"

"Just go." She tugged on his hand this time, pulled him around the hill on the decline so that she had to angle herself against the slope of the hill. They disconnected for a few minutes. Each stumbling, one hand to the earth. Pounding through the desert sand.

Andre let out a noise, half groan and half triumph.

"What is it?" She had barely finished the question before she spotted a structure in the desert. Hidden by the hill, they hadn't seen it. A trailer.

"Come on."

Everything in her wanted to run away from the structure. She could hardly believe it was even there, and her entire body rebelled against the idea of going toward it. What if there was more danger there? What kind of person would live out here in the middle of nowhere? Surely not someone who would be helpful to a stranger. Or lend a hand to someone in need.

But what did she know?

This was no oasis in the desert. It was someone who didn't want to be found.

Andre dragged her toward it. She knew he could overpower anyone he chose to, but he was exhausted and injured. More than she was. But still he proved he was stronger than anyone she had ever met.

He was her home. And her lifeline.

Being without him for years, she'd been barely alive, living essentially as a shadow. Moving in the world but not really alive. Now that she was back among the living, with him, it wasn't an entirely comfortable place to be. Lucia didn't like feeling this fear. She didn't like worrying about Andre, or wondering if they were going to live through this.

She stumbled, not paying attention. He hauled her up, and they kept going once more when her legs barely wanted to work. She commanded her body to go anyway. "Move."

Andre let go of her and pounded up the porch steps—three rickety wooden stairs and a rail that would have broken had he pushed against it with more force than he did. He pounded on the door, turned the handle, and stood still on the porch while the door swung in.

"Hello? We need help. Do you have a phone?" He kept his voice low, only audible to whoever might be inside.

But no one answered.

She wanted to scream that they needed help, but whoever was chasing them would round that hill with their gun and shoot before she and Andre had even found something to fight back with. Or a place to hide.

"I don't think there's anyone here." He held out his hand to her. "Come on."

Lucia stumbled up the steps and fell against him. She steadied herself, he wound his arm around her back, and they headed inside.

The interior of the trailer smelled like death.

ANDRE TRIED A LIGHT SWITCH. He really shouldn't, given the sudden illumination would destroy their night vision. Plus it would alert whoever was out there to their presence here.

Thankfully, the light didn't come on. The smell was enough.

Someone inside here was dead. He'd smelled that odor before, when a body remained closed up in one place long enough for the scents of decomposition to permeate the air.

He didn't want to look at whoever it was.

Lucia clutched the back of his shirt and peered around him.

"Look for a gun," he told her. Andre headed down the hall, his shoes clipping a couple of things on the floor as he passed. But he didn't feel anything move. There were no animals in here. Or living people.

He prayed they found a gun, or something else he could use to defend them with.

The smell was strongest in the bedroom. He ignored the bathroom, and a pile of whatever it was that had been dumped or stacked in the tiny tub. This place wasn't bigger than a travel trailer.

Flashlights illuminated the outside.

"Lucia, get down." It wasn't far to call to her, so he kept his voice quiet.

She crouched. He ducked beside her, reveling in the feeling of having her with him. Lucia hadn't been taken away. She also hadn't sent him away. No, she was with him, and even though he'd initially been taken alone, they had been reunited—even in a situation like this. It might have been Burgess's doing, but they were together.

Finally.

If he'd been alone, Andre would have lost his cool. He'd have gone off the deep end way before now as he wanted to do in this minute. But that wouldn't protect her.

He loved it that she was here with him. He didn't want to be anywhere else but with her.

For better or worse.

The lights flashed through the curtains in the windows. He spotted the man on the bed, a distended belly higher than the rest of him. Sprawled out, breathing his last here. Whether by natural or unnatural means Andre didn't know, but there was a glass bottle in one hand.

"Sorry, friend." Andre took the bottle, and the lighter from the ashtray on the side table, and went back to the kitchen where Lucia pulled open cupboards. "Find anything?"

"Just a knife." She held it in one hand.

He loved her and wanted to tell her. The way she had while they'd been running here.

Her words had been the sweetest thing he'd ever heard. Still, Andre wanted her to get to the place where she didn't feel like she needed to apologize to him, and there was only the love they had for each other.

"A knife is good." She offered it to him, but he said, "Keep it."

He set the bottle on the counter in a bowl that was crusty, but empty. Then he grabbed the table, which thankfully wasn't bolted down, and upended it against the door. It wasn't much of a defense, but it might stop someone from shooting them through the thin walls.

From the sound of it, there was more than one man outside. They were probably congratulating themselves, thinking they had Andre and Lucia pinned down. Andre grabbed a dish towel from the rail in front of the oven and tucked it in the end of the bottle. Thankfully there was enough liquid.

He could hear the man outside coming up the stairs.

Andre used the lighter to set the rag on fire, praying there were no fumes inside the trailer that might ignite as well and send the whole place sky-high. He was taking a risk, but at this point there wasn't much else that would be of use to defend them.

He twisted the handle of the front door fast, tossed the bottle outside, and slammed the door shut.

He grabbed Lucia. "Down."

Andre heard the whoosh as the bottle broke and the liquid

ignited. Someone screamed outside. He covered her head with his arms, protecting her with his body.

Gunfire shattered the kitchen window, spraying glass all too quickly across the interior of the trailer.

"What are we going to do?" she whispered. "They'll come in here."

Hopefully not both of the men outside.

Andre watched flashlights swipe across the room from outside, illuminating the walls while someone outside screamed and writhed on the ground.

Another man yelled. The light flashed again, someone waving their arm around. Frantically trying to put out the fire he had caused.

The light was enough he spotted a long black object on the wall—one he knew well.

Andre jumped to his feet, praying all the while he set one foot on the cushioned seat and grabbed the gun off the wall.

He ducked back down just as quickly as he had popped up. No one shot at him, but the men outside seemed to have resolved the fire situation.

"Get in the bathroom." He checked the gun but couldn't see bullets. He then felt with his fingers. There were no shells in this shotgun. He hissed out a breath through clenched teeth.

"Now, Lucia." There wouldn't be long before someone came in.

Andre kicked out the window above the table, already broken from gunshots.

He jumped off the seat and outside, bent his knees, and rolled along the ground. Pain ricocheted everywhere. He couldn't pinpoint one spot. His body washed with fire, and he came up in front of a man. Andre slammed the gun at him, clipped the man's weapon, and sent him sprawling.

He smashed the shotgun down on the man's head, dropped it, and pulled the man's rifle into his own hands. It was satisfying, but not the answer to the situation they were in. There had to be more than one person.

The feel of a loaded weapon in his hands rolled through him. But there was no time to revel in the satisfaction, not when someone could be inside the trailer hurting Lucia at exactly this moment.

Andre raced around the trailer and saw the front door was open.

Was someone inside?

Two men stood at the bottom of the stairs. Andre shot them both, then ran over to the spot where they had fallen. He rummaged in jackets for a cell phone and came up with one.

How many had come after them?

Lucia screamed.

Andre dropped the phone and grabbed a flashlight. His shoulder smarted but he ignored it. He raced up the trailer steps into the hall, shining the light in time to see Lucia slash out with the knife.

A man cried out.

Before he could retaliate, Andre aimed the gun at the man's chest and squeezed the trigger.

Lucia screamed again.

Andre turned the flashlight to illuminate his face but saw hers crumple just before it was shadowed. "I was going to kill him." He turned the flashlight back to her. "Maybe we could talk about that while we get out of here."

"How are we going to do that?" She sounded exasperated, at the end of her rope and about to lose her cool.

"Let's go outside and figure it out."

She nodded and stepped over the dead man, took his hand, and followed him outside.

The night air held a chill that cooled the sweat on his forehead as he led her away from the dead men, but not before he grabbed the phone from the ground.

He handed it to her. "See if you can make a call."

He kept his attention on the terrain around them, just in case anyone else was going to be coming after them. The man inside the trailer had been burned. The one hit with the fire when he'd thrown the bottle outside. So were there only four, or did Burgess send more than that after them?

The fear rolled through him like a sudden rush of icy wind.

She looked up. "There's no signal."

He turned to her, hugging her for a second before he said, "There's a truck around back. Let's go check it for keys."

She glanced around. "Shouldn't one of your people be showing up with a helicopter right about now?"

He hugged her again and laid a kiss on her forehead. "We're going to have to drive to civilization. Then we can call for help. Come on. Let's get to it."

"Why does that sound like an invitation I don't want to accept?"

He chuckled. "Because you know me."

"You always were up to something." She sighed. "But we're not through the worst of this, are we?"

"No, we aren't. Burgess still has the bomb I built, and he's headed for Vegas."

And while Andre had built in a safeguard or two, the bomb was still very much capable of detonating. Burgess could kill a lot of people if they didn't warn the rest of his team.

"Come on." He squeezed her hand. "There's no time to lose."

28

Lucia climbed out of the passenger seat of the dead guy's truck, then turned back to see if Andre needed a hand. Despite the fact hospital staff ran from the doors at the far end of the pick-up lane, she still wanted to be the one to help him.

He put his good foot down, then hopped to settle his weight until he could remain upright.

The hospital staff pushed two wheelchairs toward them.

"I'm good, I can walk." Lucia didn't want to be pushed. She wanted to get back to work, not be stuck in a hospital for hours waiting on a busy doctor. "I feel fine."

The first nurse, or doctor, whoever it was shot her look. "This isn't up for discussion." She pointed at the seat. "Get in the chair."

Andre chuckled beside her. "I guess they got the memo about us."

The nurse said, "Someone named Zander O'Connell called ahead of time and informed me."

"He's here?" Andre asked.

"Inside. So look sharp, soldier. Otherwise, the boss will see you disobeying orders." The nurse grinned, watching while they sat in the wheelchairs.

A couple of orderlies pushed them to the door and inside. Lucia tried not to sink too much in the chair. She'd almost fallen asleep in the truck, but determined to stay awake so Andre wasn't alone and exhausted—and driving.

Zander stood in the hallway just inside the doors, arms folded across his chest and a look on his face that said he wasn't super impressed they'd been kidnapped.

"Did you secure the"—Andre glanced around—"thing we found?"

Zander nodded. "The Pentagon sent a team to take it off my hands."

She let out a breath she hadn't realized she'd been holding. They'd gotten her back from those dirty agents and now the nuke was back in official hands. Andre had been captured. Now they were both free.

Zander said, "Nora's going to be up all night doing paperwork and fielding phone calls."

"At least it's secure now." Lucia was glad about that. The last thing they needed was for a dangerous weapon to be loose, probably in the wrong hands. The fact her entire task force team had been involved made her want to curl up and cry. But now it was done. Most of them were dead, and she would write a full report to ensure justice was done. If anyone was still out there, they would be rounded up sooner or later.

Zander and Andre were probably more worried about Isaac and his team, whoever they were. Lucia still needed to identify the woman she'd seen.

She blew out a breath. "I don't really need to get checked out. We should get back to work."

Andre said, "She's right. Burgess was headed back to Vegas. He's probably here right now."

Zander stared them both down. "The FBI is on-site, and the rest of the team is lending a hand. He's not going to get a bomb into the hotel."

Someone gasped behind them—the young orderly holding onto the handles of her wheelchair.

The nurse lady said, "This is all fascinating, but these two need to be checked out."

Zander nodded. "Good idea."

Andre started to object, but she figured he didn't have much leeway considering there was a bullet hole in the side of his leg and a stab wound. Plus all the other injuries he'd sustained. She was bruised and exhausted. Her wrist hurt. She shuddered in the wheelchair seat.

Maybe she wasn't okay.

"Let's go." The nurse led the way to the elevator.

Andre shot her look, but she wasn't about to tell him she was only remembering the sensation of all her nerve endings being hit by lightning. She didn't want to talk about it. Kind of the way she didn't want to talk about her team, or the time she spent alone with Burgess.

The idea of going after him again now might be her doing her duty, but for the first time she wanted to leave the job to someone else.

And what kind of person did that make her? What kind of agent?

Lucia figured she was probably entirely too tired to be having this kind of thought process. She'd probably end up making some drastic decision when she was overtired.

She closed her eyes and pushed all thoughts from her head. She became aware of how dirty she was, how gritty her skin felt, and how her limbs felt like lead. Andre touched her hand. She didn't open her eyes, just turned her hand face up, and he laced his fingers through hers.

She heard the elevator doors slide open, and his hand disconnected from hers.

He was pushed in front of her, down the hall, and they were wheeled into separate bays.

That was the last she saw of him before the nurse helped her get cleaned up and assessed. Then the doctor came in, and a couple of her cuts were stitched. She wound up with seven stitches in total.

Her swollen wrist was x-rayed and declared fractured. The doctor rewrapped it with a clean bandage, and she was given an injection. Soon she would need a cast.

Lucia felt her eyelids grow heavy. It was tempting to simply fall into the sensation, to allow the drug to help her rest and regain her strength. But the last thing she wanted to do was dream when she figured that would only bring Burgess and any number of his men back into her mind. Or one of her teammates.

She doubted the dream would be the good kind, where she got to spend more time with Andre.

When she blinked next and opened her eyes, a suited older man sat in the chair beside her bed. He looked up from his phone, concern in his expression. Gray hair, bushy gray eyebrows.

"Assistant Director Alton."

He lifted a cup from the side table and angled the straw to her mouth. Lucia took a sip.

"Thank you."

He frowned and retook his seat. "It's not you who should be thanking me." He paused a second. "The entire task force?"

Lucia made a face. "I didn't even realize, but it looks that way. Except the two men who were killed with me. Simon and Bill." Though, she didn't know.

"And you feel you should have seen it coming? Assistant Director Campbell and everyone under his command—with the exception of you—followed his lead. It's unimaginable that the poison would have spread that far without anyone knowing. They were extremely skilled at hiding their true colors."

Lucia didn't think that absolved her from the fact it had taken her so long to figure out the entire task force was dirty.

"I don't want to see you in the office for two weeks."

"I'm being suspended?"

He shifted and pulled two items from a backpack beside the chair. He laid her holstered gun and her badge where she could see it. Where she could reach for it, if she wanted to. "You need two weeks of vacation, and you have more than enough accrued. Find a beach somewhere, or a deserted mountain lake. Don't come back to the office until you've read at least three novels."

Lucia wanted to smile, but her lips didn't move. "As soon as Burgess is behind bars, then I'll take a vacation."

"Or"—he stood—"you can leave that to me. I'll coordinate with the FBI at the hotel. Anything else you need taken care of?"

She nearly choked.

"Special Agent DeSoto?"

Anything else, like the fact one of the FBI's Most Wanted was on Andre's team? She figured her boss would find that interesting. She needed to ask Zander and Andre about the one they called Eas.

But what she didn't do was tell her boss about him.

Everything inside her was twisted around, messed up even. She figured that was a good reason to hand her badge back and walk away. Otherwise, she was in danger of becoming the very thing she had strived all these years to root out of an organization that should be full of good-willed, honorable men and women who only wanted to see justice done.

Assistant Director Alton nodded. "Like I said, take some time. Think about what you want."

"Thank you, sir."

She was at a serious disadvantage laid up in a hospital bed. Now wasn't the time to make a snap decision. She hadn't become a different person in the last few days. Maybe it was more that she had become someone she liked a whole lot better than who she was. Andre didn't think she should keep apologizing for the hurt she had dished out, but the truth was she would always feel it.

The way she would always feel the need to do the right thing and ensure the people around her were doing everything they could. Making a real difference in the world. Not just skirting the line in getting the job done.

What would Andre think about her leaving the DEA?

"THIS WAS DONE WELL." The doctor felt around the wound on Andre's thigh. Some of the stitches had been torn out, and he'd repaired additional damage. But overall it seemed like his gunshot wound was doing okay.

"Of course," Andre said. "We have the best doctor."

The doctor lifted his gaze and raised his eyebrows. "Okay, then. But you don't leave this bed until I'm satisfied you're not going to pass out. I'm a little worried about your reactions."

"Being shot up with a lethal chemical that makes you feel like there's lightning in your nerve endings will do that to you." Andre wanted to shrug again, but was honestly exhausted. "Even if it was only a little bit."

"And you don't know what the substance was?"

"If we can disarm the bomb that's probably right now in a hotel on the strip, we can bring some of the substance here. You could test it."

"Hmm." The doctor didn't seem to know what to make of that.

Across the room, Zander scratched his jaw to hide a smile. His boss hadn't left, despite Andre wanting an update on Lucia. Instead, he'd had the nurse go find out if she was doing okay. The nurse had come back and reported that she was talking with her boss. Andre figured that was a good thing, and he didn't want to disturb her.

There was hopefully plenty of time for them to talk through

what would happen next. But they still needed to take care of the bomb. And Burgess, along with his men.

"Any word from——"

Zander cut Andre off. "I told you I'd tell you when they——" His phone rang.

Andre resisted the urge to smirk as Zander shot him a look and pulled it out.

"I'll leave you two to save the world."

Andre grinned at the doctor. "Thanks."

The doctor frowned but pulled the curtain behind him.

Andre had no intention of being admitted to the hospital. As soon as the doctor breathed one word of that, he would sign himself out against medical advice. Didn't matter. They had a doctor anyway, so it wasn't exactly as though he would be walking away from necessary medical care. As long as Lucia came with him.

"Copy that." Zander shifted the backpack from his shoulder and pulled out his laptop, the phone still against his ear. He handed it to Andre, then dug in the pack again and pulled out the little case where they kept earpieces. He shifted the phone away from his face. "Put this in."

Andre stuck the earpiece in. "Breaker, breaker. How copy?"

"As much as I'd love it if we had time for that," Judah said, "we're hunting for a bomb in a hotel the manager refuses to evacuate because everyone is in bed."

Andre glanced at the clock and realized it was barely five in the morning.

Only an hour or so until sunrise.

"Burgess probably wanted maximum carnage. There's less chance people are out of the hotel, partying somewhere else, when they're in bed."

"Then he should have set it off at nine in the morning," Badger said. "No one gets up before then here anyway."

The guy was right. Andre had seen firsthand how dead

Vegas was before a normal workday, when most cities would bustle with the morning rush hour.

"So you didn't find the bomb yet?" Andre flipped open the lid of the laptop and waited for it to boot up. He used his fingerprint to log in. On screen was a video program that displayed the body cam Badger wore. Two other windows loaded: Judah and Eas.

"Working on it." Eas never sounded irritated, and Andre wanted to ask him how that was even possible. His teammate worked out aggression and frustration by pounding a heavy bag. And running. And swimming. And he got on the rowing machine.

Maybe that was the trick. When he was out of the hospital, he would give all of those a try.

Then again, he and Lucia had always been about the fire that burned between them. Whether that was the passion they shared, which he could tell was still there, or the sparks that flew when they butted heads. Either way, he wanted to see how it would work with them as adults.

He might be busy.

"How's the wife?" Judah's question startled him.

"Getting checked out now."

"Is she joining the team?"

"I don't know." Andre glanced at Zander, just to get a feel for how his boss would take that issue.

Zander stared at him with a measured expression, not giving anything away. He knew exactly what he was doing, and it was on purpose. Zander was going to make Andre ask for what he wanted. Not as a test, but to ensure he had fully thought through all the consequences of her being in their lives.

"She's a DEA agent." Andre knew he didn't want to lose her again. "I'm not sure what's going to happen. But when I do know, I'll definitely inform you first."

Judah chuckled.

Badger said, "Just send out a company newsletter. Much easier."

"I do not read those."

Zander cracked a smile at Eas's comment.

"Just talk to me about the bomb, okay?" Andre needed to get this going.

Badger said, "Tell me you at least put some kind of failsafe in it, so when he goes to arm the thing, it just malfunctions. Or preferably blows up in his face."

"The schematics allow it to be armed by either typing in the code…or dialing a phone number."

"So he may not be anywhere near here," Judah said. "He could dial the number and set off the bomb."

"How do we disable that?" Eas asked.

"Short of setting off an EMP in the hotel, there aren't a lot of options." Andre thought about it for a second. "He'll need to set it off close to an air duct, preferably in the HVAC closet. That way he'll get maximum dispersion as quickly as possible."

"That's where I'm headed now." Badger's camera view shifted with each footstep, going blurry for a second every time.

Judah's was the same. "Me, too."

Eas said, "The feds are in the security office looking at feeds, running facial recognition to try and find Burgess or any of his known associates."

Given Eas was wearing a disguise, Andre figured he didn't think it was likely they would find the man responsible for all this. Things had been busy there, according to Zander, after the head of security had disappeared—taking Lucia with him.

"I'd love to know where he went." Andre blew out a breath. "We're also assuming he already set the bomb."

"And if he did that," Badger said, "then why hasn't it just exploded and killed us all yet?"

Everyone agreed, though no one said that aloud. He'd worked with these men long enough to know they felt the same way he did.

On Badger's camera feed, Andre saw him open a door and enter a room full of air-conditioning units. Heaters, though those likely weren't used much even in the winter.

"Bingo." Badger crouched.

"Angle your camera down a little farther."

Badger did as he'd asked. "This is what you built?"

"I'm more interested in the timer. Once those two chemicals mix, there's no point in even running."

"You know I'm going to try, though. Right?"

Andre figured he was correct. "Because you have healthy survival instincts. Now pull out a screwdriver."

Everyone was quiet.

"You see that panel in the middle? Unscrew three corners and rotate the whole thing out of the way so you can see underneath."

"Please tell me I just need to cut the green wire…or something."

Andre wished it was true, but sometimes things just worked out in different ways. "Something like that."

"Okay, I'm in." Badger sounded nervous. Or simply sober where he normally would be nonchalant or even cracking jokes.

Zander came over and looked at the screen over his shoulder. "Show me."

Badger angled the camera down. "Where's the green wire?"

"It's too late for that." Everything inside Andre stilled, then flipped upside down as though he had reached the top of a roller coaster and suddenly plummeted over the rise to careen down. "Take the right-hand vial, twist it like you're unscrewing the whole thing, and remove it. Now."

Judah's feed bumped up and down as he ran toward Badger.

On the other screen, Eas came up against a dark figure in the hallway and drew his weapon. The man yelled something at him. Eas squeezed off a shot, and the man fell to the ground.

Badger's fingers blurred on the screen. "Oh, crap—"

"What—?" Zander put his hand on Andre's shoulder and squeezed. Andre stopped what he'd been about to say.

Badger pulled the vial back.

And coughed.

"Judah," Andre said. "Grab that vial before he drops it."

"Got it." Badger came into view on Judah's camera. A second later, he began to convulse.

"Both of you get out of there." The order came from Zander.

Andre couldn't tear his gaze away from his teammate.

The one whose death certificate he had just signed.

29

———————

The curtain slid back. Lucia expected Andre. It would have been much better had it been him. But instead, Special Agent Brinton stepped inside.

"I thought you were dead." Lucia stared.

He hadn't still been at that abandoned office building when the team came?

This wasn't going to be good. The man was dirty as the rest of the team, and he'd kidnapped her along with Gage. She'd honestly thought he was dead, and now here he was. He had to have gotten away in the confusion.

"What do you want?" She should scream the whole floor down. Likely he'd be expecting that, and whatever he planned to do here would snap into action the next second.

Like pulling a gun and shooting her.

Did he know Assistant Director Alton had given her gun back to her? She doubted that.

She also doubted he could spot where she had put it.

For just such an occasion as this.

He started to approach her, and Lucia held up a hand. "That's close enough."

He narrowed his eyes.

"What am I supposed to think about why you're here? I suggest you talk, before I scream this whole hospital down."

"We lost everything because of you." His face contorted, rage suffusing his gaze with fire.

"And I'm supposed to be sorry about that?" She stared him down, wondering if she should've looked threatened by him and his appearance here. Maybe he should believe she wasn't in possession of a weapon. "I should apologize, when you're the ones who broke your oath?"

"It's all gone." He glared down at her. "Because of you."

"And because of you guys, I was kidnapped and taken to Burgess's compound. Then I was kidnapped again after you guys took me. Stuck with a needle." She'd been threatened with death so many times she hardly knew where to start listing each of them. Probably he didn't care, but it would make her feel better about lying here in a hospital bed if he understood what trouble he'd caused.

Yeah, he definitely didn't care. Someone who betrayed their oath wasn't worried about the people who would have to deal with the fallout.

Brinton shifted, reaching into his jacket to pull out a needle.

"I don't think so." Lucia lifted her chin. "That's not happening again."

He moved.

She pulled her free hand from under the blankets and pointed her gun at him. "That's quite enough."

He screamed with rage, lifting the needle high above his head as though he was going to swing it down and stab her with it.

She waited until there was no question as to his intentions.

A split second, and his hand swung down to her.

Lucia squeezed off a shot. The needle slammed into the skin of her upper arm, and Brinton jerked.

He slumped against the bed.

The curtain swung open again. Andre stood there, grief and anger on his face.

Behind him, Zander said, "What happened?" He barked the question, a demand from a superior.

Lucia held the gun on Brinton as he blinked at her. He lost his grip on the needle, and nothing had gone into her. But it still stuck out of her arm. "I need a little help."

Andre grabbed Brinton with both hands and threw him into the hall, bleeding everywhere. She'd shot him in the shoulder, and he wasn't dead.

Lucia let out the breath she'd been holding, set the gun down beside her leg, and pulled the needle from her arm. She wanted to throw it across the room, but it needed to be bagged as evidence.

Commotion erupted in the hallway. Zander stepped out, pulling the curtain closed. Doctors and nurses, hospital staff, and who knew how many other people started to yell to each other instructions. Orders and requests for assistance.

They would try to save Brinton's life. That was what hospital staff did, regardless of who the person was that they were taking care of. All they knew was that someone was injured.

In a way, they were better than Lucia. Doing whatever they could to treat an injured or ill person, regardless of whether the person deserved it or not. She didn't like seeing people in pain, even those who had betrayed their oath. But Lucia didn't think that if she was a doctor, she'd have tried all that hard to save him, so she was glad it wasn't up to her.

Andre slumped against the side of the bed and touched her shoulders. Her cheeks. He stroked a hand from her hair down to the side of her neck, where he rubbed his thumb against the underside of her jaw. He opened his mouth a number of times, but didn't say anything.

"What is it?" Lucia knew this reaction wasn't about her. "What happened?"

Zander appeared by the curtain.

Andre still didn't say anything, his eyes red rimmed.

"Badger." Zander paused. "He inhaled a drop of the chemical, but he's being brought in. Judah too, considering he was in the room."

She looked at Andre. "The same one we were dosed with?"

"Airborne." He shook his head. "It'll tear up his lungs."

Zander disappeared again, back out into the hallway where she heard him tell someone to give them a minute.

Andre's face blurred. She was so glad to see him, but hadn't wanted it to be like this when she had just shot a man. She pressed a kiss on one cheek, then the other. "Everything will be okay. And if it's not, then you guys will take care of him, right?"

There was no way they would allow their friend to suffer on his own.

"Of course we will," Zander called from behind the curtain. "Now I need to go down and meet them when they come in."

Andre dipped his head so his forehead touched her shoulder.

"We probably only have a minute before a security guard or cop comes in," she said. Someone needed to explain why there was a man with a gunshot now being carried from the hallway to the emergency room. Everyone had come running, something she was exceedingly grateful for.

"If Badger dies, it'll be because I killed him." Andre's voice was muffled against the hospital gown she wore. "I'm the one who built the bomb. He was trying to disarm it and a drop escaped."

"So because Burgess kidnapped you, forced you to make a device, and then planted it in a hotel, somehow it's your fault that when Badger tried to save everyone's lives, he was exposed to the tiniest bit? That doesn't seem to me like you'd be the one responsible. You were acting under extreme duress." She wasn't even sure if Badger would actually die as a result.

Maybe he would be permanently injured.

She had to ask, "Do you know for sure that he's going to lose his life?"

Andre lifted his face to hers. He cared deeply about his friend and could only shake his head.

She touched his cheeks this time. "Then we should pray for him. Because he could make it, and in the right hands he could live a long life driving you crazy. Irritating you like a little brother you never wanted, but who you couldn't imagine not having in your life."

He pressed his lips together in a thin line. Considering her words.

"And if he does pass away? It won't be your fault."

She had to pause then, absorbing her own words and what they meant. She might have felt the guilt for her father's death all these years. But the truth was, she wasn't the one responsible for his life. Things happened for which there was never a good explanation.

Her only hope was that one day she would see that some good had come of it. Or, that her father had been at peace since. Lucia was still trying to figure out what possible outcomes there might be. Maybe Nora had a few ideas, and they could have girl talk about it.

"Feels like my fault."

"I know." She leaned forward and touched her lips to his. "Part of you would always feel responsible. But that's because you care about your friend, and you'd rather have him with you."

Andre nodded. His gaze hardened. "Burgess is still out there."

"No one found him yet?" Her boss had gone to the hotel. Surely he and the other feds had some leads.

"I'm going to go take him down." He started to pull away from her. "Badger deserves it, no matter what happens to him."

"Andre—"

He leaned down and pressed a kiss to her forehead. "I love you. I always have, and I always will. No matter what happens."

"I know you do." Her heart soared at hearing the words. "Because I feel the same way. But it's okay to let the feds find Burgess and take him down. You don't have to go after him. Not when you're injured like this."

"He forced me to make that bomb. I'm going to find him."

ANDRE BUCKLED HIS SEATBELT. Though, only because if he didn't then Zander wasn't going to pull out of the hospital parking lot.

As soon as Zander hit the street and headed toward the hotel, and the Las Vegas strip, he said, "So you're just going to leave your girl there, go off, and get revenge?"

He and Zander had been friends a long time. Andre was willing to give him a serious amount of leeway. But in this case? Surely Zander knew why Andre was doing this.

Andre decided to ask a question of his own instead. "Did Badger get to the hospital?"

"He and Judah were both brought in by ambulance a couple of minutes ago." Zander looked at his watch. "Ted has full power of attorney with them, the way he has with all of us. And Windemere, the same thing. Between the two of them, we'll know the second there's any change. But when they wake up, I want to be back at the hospital, ready to be there."

"Understood." Andre figured that was a decent proposition. In the meantime, they just had to take Burgess down.

The fear still eclipsed everything else. Especially after realizing the worst might've happened to Badger, then on top of it seeing that special agent try to kill Lucia. She'd shot the guy from her hospital bed. Realistically, Andre didn't figure he needed to worry all too much about her.

But did that change how he felt?

The hospital staff wasn't going to like that she'd had a gun in her room. But the fact remained, the woman was a federal agent. Now that she had faced down an attempt on her life, they would be all about protecting her. Posting a guard or local cop on the door to make sure it didn't happen again.

Andre couldn't believe he hadn't even considered that as an option.

Yet another thing to kick himself over.

"There are things that happen, and they are beyond our control," Zander said. "What good does it do to fuss and scream when it changes nothing? Lucia needs you to support her."

Andre wanted to retort back about Zander now being the world's biggest relationship expert, all because he had been married for a couple of weeks. In reality, Andre had been married for nearly two decades now. But the fact he and Lucia had been estranged so long counted against them.

The truth was, he didn't know how to straighten things out. They'd done their best, but at the end of the day they were still at odds over this. She probably would've rather he stayed with her. Andre couldn't relax and pretend everything was fine when it wasn't.

And he had a serious score to settle with Burgess.

Andre said, "I intend to support her. Just as soon as Burgess is taken out."

Zander glanced over. Andre didn't bother looking at the expression on his face. He figured he wasn't going to like it, whatever it was.

"She already knows I'm stubborn and hardheaded. Because she's the same way."

Lucia had pushed him away because of her guilt. In her own way, she had isolated herself and worked for years to set the record straight again. To even the scales.

That was what he was doing right now. Go off on his own to make sure she would never be scared of Burgess again, the way she'd been.

Andre still didn't know what Burgess had done to her when they were alone. Maybe he didn't ever want to know, unless she wanted to tell him.

He would've said that he understood how she felt about her father's death, but now that he had to work with the fact he might have killed Badger because of his compliance, he could say honestly that he hadn't understood.

He hadn't understood at all.

Andre scrubbed his hands down his face. He could feel the hot burn of tears behind his eyes, but it wasn't like he was actually going to cry. He'd only done that once, alone in his car right after Lucia screamed at him and told him to get out of her life.

Now she was back.

Badger's life was on the line. Maybe even Judah, as well. He'd been in the room seconds after. Their British friend and teammate might have also inhaled some of the compound.

Andre blew out a long breath.

"We do this fast. Then you're taking a break." Zander always knew when each of them hit their breaking point. He said he tried to pull them off active duty before that happened, but life didn't always work out perfectly.

Andre should've been there, in the hotel when Badger had been disarming the bomb. He built the device. He should've taken it apart again, doing a better job of safeguarding it. But he'd had to create a functional device, or they would've been killed for sure.

Zander's phone rang. He put the call on speaker and set the phone in the cup holder with the speaker facing up. "What is it?"

"It's me." Ted didn't sound happy at all. "A plane at the airport just filed a flight plan to South America."

Andre shifted in his seat. "You think it's Burgess?"

"Oh, hey. Are you doing okay?"

As Ted asked the question, Zander changed lanes. Probably

to head for the airport already, even though Ted hadn't explained.

"Just tell us about the plane." Andre didn't need to get sidetracked right now.

"Fine," Ted said. "But they are doing a bronchoscopy on Badger right now so they can assess the damage. Judah is on oxygen, but he's nowhere near as bad as Badger."

"Thanks." Andre managed to swallow.

"As for the plane, it's registered to a holding company I traced back to the task force's dirty money."

Zander said, "You think Burgess commandeered their funds?"

"Someone is using it. And everyone from the task force is either dead…or in jail. Thanks to Lucia and the incident that's all over the police band."

Andre gritted his teeth.

Ted continued, "You have forty-five minutes before the plane is due to take off. But you know those flights, they never leave on time."

Zander turned a corner and hit the gas. "What about the feds who were at the hotel?"

"Most are doing wrap-up. But I let them know about the flight, and they're sending the two FBI agents, along with the team from the local office, to meet you guys there." Ted paused. "At least, I assumed you would be going."

"We are." Andre didn't want to waste any more time. "Can you see if Burgess is there?"

"Security at the airport is good. I could probably get in, but it'll take a while." Ted clicked keys on his computer keyboard. "GPS says you'll get there way faster than I can get in. I'll send the hanger number, and you can rendezvous with the feds."

"Understood." Zander ended the call.

They arrived at the airport minutes later, in time to see uniformed federal agents surround the warehouse.

They geared up and headed over. Andre lagged behind

Zander, more because his friend could move faster but also because he trusted him. He wanted to blow something up, but how was that going to help right now? Regardless of how satisfying it would feel.

Andre frowned. "Why is my default stress reliever causing an explosion?"

Zander glanced over his shoulder, a slight grin on his face. "We all have our ways to cope. I cook, you blow stuff up." He shrugged. "When Badger gets out of the hospital, he'll go back to spamming us all with Bitmojis until we take his phone away."

"We should change his Screen Time settings now. Before he wakes up."

Zander nodded.

Inside the hangar, a couple of gunshots went off, then a third. Seconds later, a man raced out a side door trying to get away.

"Burgess." Anger heated Andre's middle. He wanted to take a potshot at the guy, even from this distance. Just to see if he could hit Burgess. So the man would know how it felt to be hunted.

Zander said, "Let's go get him."

They raced after him. To a vehicle, where Burgess pulled open the driver's seat.

Feds poured out of the warehouse behind them. Andre heard their boots on the asphalt. Then yelling, as they told everyone to lower their weapons.

Zander and Andre trained their guns on Burgess.

"Stand down." Zander's order was clear. "It's over."

Burgess reached into the car, his movements frantic. He drew out a gun. Before he could get off a shot, both of them fired at the same time.

Burgess hit the ground.

Dead.

30

"Hey, there. You're awake." Lucia squeezed Badger's hand. "It's good to see your eyes open."

The younger man had stark blue eyes, so different than Andre's dark brown ones. He blinked at Lucia, and she wasn't sure exactly how much he was understanding given he'd just woken up. But he seemed decently alert. The tube down his throat meant he wouldn't be able to speak, but she could understand his expression well enough.

"You're in the hospital, and your lungs are going to heal." It might take some time. But she wasn't going to lie to him. "I'm sure they'll explain more to you. But you're still here."

A shadow moved over his expression. For a second she wondered if he even wanted to wake up. Was that really true? Could part of Badger have accepted the fact he might not make it through today?

"Another day for your teammates to drive you crazy." She tried to keep it light, hoping he would rest a little. Give up some of that shadow and find a little peace. The way she had.

Andre wasn't back yet. Zander had gone with him, a fact she was glad about. Together they would be all right. She shouldn't worry. Probably she should be angry that he'd made his declaration and then limped through the curtain without further explanation.

Not that he needed to justify himself to her.

She probably would've gone with him, if he'd even bothered asking. But he hadn't.

Badger shifted his hand under hers and squeezed her fingers.

"Sorry," she said. "I was miles away for a second. It's been a long day." Neither of them let go of the other's hand. She was glad for Andre, that he had friends like these. It was entirely possible she had been adopted by them. Whether things settled into a good place with Andre, she wanted to be friends with his teammates.

She didn't have any other family.

"Judah and your other friend are in the hallway."

Eas had been wearing that same disguise, so that Lucia didn't even recognize him when he first walked down the hall. Not until he'd spoken to her, and she'd remembered seeing him in the car. She still couldn't believe he was here with the team.

Whatever his story was as to how that had happened, she was sure it would come out sooner or later. She just hoped the team was prepared for the fallout.

There was no way they could avoid the repercussions of hiding his identity and keeping him a secret. Living and working with them. They had to have known that eventually someone would find out.

But it wasn't going to get out because of her. She knew that much. And while it may be construed as her betraying her oath, Lucia wasn't all that sure she wanted to be a DEA agent anymore. Maybe she needed a change in her life.

"Do you know…is Zander hiring?"

Badger nodded. He squeezed her hand.

"Maybe I'll ask for an application." She smiled. "I'd like to see Andre's face when that happens."

He smiled around the tube in his mouth.

"Andre feels bad about what happened."

Badger made a face she didn't mistake. Even intubated, he could communicate just fine.

"I'm glad you're all right."

"He is?"

Lucia turned to find Andre by the door and winced as pain shot through her injured wrist. She pulled her fingers from Badger's. "Judah said he was awake, so I came to say hi."

"Sounds like they're both going to be fine." Andre stood at the foot of the bed. "I'm sorry about what happened."

Badger lifted his hand and made a swiping motion.

"Yeah, I know. You're going to get me back at the first opportunity. I'll be checking under my pillow for grass snakes for the next few months." Andre winced, his lips curling up into a smile. "I'll make it up to you at Christmas."

Badger seemed satisfied by that.

Lucia said, "What happened with Burgess?"

"We got him." Andre kept his expression blank. "He's dead."

Lucia pushed out a long breath, unaware she'd been holding in that much tension just waiting to find out what happened after he left.

"It took a long time to work through everything with the feds, and there's more to do tomorrow. But they released us to come back here." He glanced at Badger. "You'll be back up to full strength soon enough."

Badger closed his eyes for a second in acknowledgment. When he opened them, he blinked again.

"We should let you rest." She moved the chair back from the bedside. Judah and Eas had been in there when she asked for a minute.

"Zander wants to come in next." Andre squeezed Badger's foot. "Judah went back to go lay down. They want him overnight."

Badger lifted two fingers, letting out a long exhale as his eyes drifted closed.

Andre took her hand as they left the room in intensive care. Neither of them moved well. They should probably still be in beds like Badger, but she'd been given a robe she pulled over her gown and they'd let her visit her friends as long as she promised to take it easy and not be long.

And not shoot anyone.

"I'm supposed to go back upstairs," she said.

Andre nodded, and his friends gathered around.

"Did everything go okay with Burgess?" she asked.

Andre tucked her to his side. "Zander and I took him down."

Lucia dipped her head, and he turned her to face him. She wrapped her arms around him, even if her injured wrist didn't want to be that high on his back. She needed to feel his strength. The way he carried on, even though he'd been shot in the leg. Most people—her included—wouldn't be upright, let alone running through the desert. She'd have thought he would crash. He never did.

Her husband was an amazing man.

"Seems like the two of you need a vacation." There was a hint of something in Zander's tone.

Andre's chest rumbled with a chuckle under her cheek. "Are you giving me vacation days?"

"I'll keep you posted on Badger. Once Windermere gets here, and the kid is stable, we'll get him back to Last Chance, where he can recuperate at home."

She turned her head and looked at Zander.

"How are you doing?" he asked her.

"I'm on vacation too, apparently." She glanced up at Andre. "My boss gave me two weeks off." She winced. "I've never taken that much time off in my life. What am I supposed to do with two weeks?"

"You want me to answer that in front of our friends?"

His answer warmed her, even as she chuckled. Maybe it was just the fact her cheeks heated.

"What?" Andre said. "We're married."

Lucia smiled. She touched his chest with her good hand, looking at the spot where a simple gold band had once been on her ring finger. "Yes, we are."

Always had been, always would be.

"Great." Zander slapped his hands together. "It's set then. Tell Ted where you want to go. He'll make the arrangements. See y'all in two weeks."

She couldn't help the smile, joy rising in her. It was such an unfamiliar feeling Lucia wasn't quite sure what to do with it.

She still had an apartment. And a job. Two weeks sounded like a wonderful break from her life. The chance to recuperate and figure out what she wanted next.

What *they* wanted.

Zander tossed Andre a set of car keys.

Eas squeezed her shoulder.

Judah leaned down and kissed her cheek.

"Watch it, Bub."

Ignoring Andre's comment, Judah said, "Welcome to the family, little sis."

Lucia ducked her head against Andre's shirt again, feeling the material wet from the tears she couldn't help shedding. He was giving her everything she'd never had. How was she supposed to handle the overwhelming feeling that brought with it?

It was far simpler to live a solitary life. Nothing but the mission.

Being with Andre brought with it an overwhelming amount of feeling she didn't even begin to know how to process.

And now she had two weeks to do it.

"Let's get you back to your room."

She nodded and pulled away. "Are you going to leave again?"

He tugged on her hand until she turned back. "I wasn't planning on leaving, ever." He studied her face. "How do you feel about that?"

"So you'd go with me, wherever?" Or was she supposed to follow him, like a lost puppy with nowhere else to go?

"Uh-oh." He winced. "I thought we'd have more than five minutes before you found something we can argue about."

Lucia set her hand on her hip. "Excuse me—"

Andre leaned down and touched his lips to hers, kissing away her argument. Not that she'd even known what she would say. "Let's go on vacation. You can argue with me the entire time, if you want."

He tugged on her hand, and they started walking.

Hand in hand.

Finally.

Two days later Andre pulled into the drive of the house where he and Lucia would be spending the next two weeks. She started in the passenger seat, squinting as she awoke from her doze. Both of them had slept on the plane most of the way here, and he was glad she had rested on the short drive to the house as well.

Now it was time for breakfast, and Andre had requested bacon be stocked in the fridge. The management company had sent someone over with groceries.

"We're here?" Lucia rubbed her eyes.

He leaned over and kissed her, not getting tired of doing that whenever he wanted to. Which right now was frequently. She also didn't seem to mind in the slightest. Maybe in a few weeks it would slack. They would get used to each other again, and things wouldn't seem so new.

There wouldn't be an edge of fear between them.

Wondering if at any moment the other shoe was going to drop and things would upend themselves again.

Eventually something would come up. But he wanted them to have a solid foundation before that happened.

Andre pushed the door open. "Breakfast time. There's bacon."

She chuckled, and he rounded the front of the car, only limping slightly.

He opened her door for her and held out his hand. "Mrs. Martinez?"

Her eyebrows rose, and she put her hand in his. "Yes, Mr. Martinez?" She lifted out of the car and kissed him that time.

Andre got their suitcases from the trunk of the rental. After she was released from the hospital, they'd packed up her things and then headed to Last Chance, where they'd done the same with his. Enough clothes to last them a few days at least. If they needed more, they could just hit the shack along the beach and buy another pair of swim shorts for him. Another bathing suit for her. A couple more clean towels, until they felt like doing laundry.

There was a jewelry vendor he'd seen last time that he hoped was still there. Andre was going to buy her a ring.

Lucia glanced toward the house, looking up at the blue sky of the sunrise. "Is that the ocean?"

He grinned. "Come on, I'll show you."

The airplane had headed back to the mainland, where the pilot would transport Doctor Windermere and Badger back to Last Chance County. They'd taken his friend off intubation a day ago, and he was doing well. He still couldn't talk and had trouble breathing deeply. But the damage to his lungs would heal with time.

"You've been here before?"

He nodded. "Only once, and it was a while ago." The management company seemed to have kept up repairs, and the house had been painted recently. Completely square, it would be snug with only the two of them. But it was just about perfect for spending a couple of relaxing weeks with their own private section of beach and a long lawn between the house and the waves.

He found the hidden key and let them both in, entering the code to disable the security system.

When he turned around, Lucia was already over by the dining table, looking out the doors at the ocean beyond. As he approached her, she didn't turn around. "It's beautiful. Whose house is this?"

"Technically it belongs to Badger, but I don't think he's been here in a long time." Not since the last time, years ago, when Andre was here as well. As far as he knew.

Smiling, she glanced over her shoulder, the expression on her face completely at peace. He had never seen that look on her. Not even when they'd been teens and hardly comprehended everything the world would throw at them. All that they would see, and experience, in life.

Even with all that, Andre had managed to eclipse it just by being here with her. Because they were together again. "Move in with me."

He'd seen her apartment. Barely big enough for one person, and it had been obvious she didn't spend much time there. She was a workaholic like he was, except that he lived and worked with his team. The brotherhood. The camaraderie. Now Nora was part of it, and Andre was looking to expand the group further with the inclusion of his wife.

Lucia lifted one eyebrow. "So forward, Mr. Martinez. We've only known each other five days."

"Really? Seems like much longer." He slid his arms around her waist. "Mrs. Martinez."

"I figured we would talk about it at some point, but I think I want to quit my job. I'm ready for something new."

He planted a kiss on her cheek, feeling the scratch of his mustache. In a way, he did suppose they were little more than strangers to each other. But in reality their connection went back further than most relationships—a deeper connection than most people would ever dream of having.

She chuckled, swaying with him as they danced to a silent tune and the sound of the waves hitting the shore outside.

"What do you say?" She still hadn't answered his question.

"The big house in Last Chance?"

Andre winced. He shared a bedroom with Badger, so that wouldn't work anymore. "We could build a new one, behind the house."

Her eyes lit. "A townhome." She practically bounced with excitement in his arms. "One of those three-story ones where the bedroom is on the top level. With a balcony, so we can admire the view but also make sure everyone knows we're lording it over them." She grinned.

"The boys are going to love that. Especially the part where they have to haul all our furniture to the top floor." He gave her a squeeze. "It's the best idea I've ever heard."

She giggled, and he kissed her again.

Things were getting interesting as he kissed her neck.

She patted him on the shoulder. "Didn't you say something about bacon earlier?"

He lifted his head. "I've forgotten what that is. I'm not sure I remember." He ducked his head and went back to kissing her neck.

"Breakfast," she reminded him.

"Hmm."

"Or dinner," she said. "Depending on how you feel about it. I like putting bacon with my pasta."

"Mmm. Keep going."

"It's also really good if you crumble it up and put it in pancake batter."

"Now you're talking." He smiled against the skin of her neck, and she shifted, indicating he'd found a ticklish spot.

Despite his intentions, he could tell she wanted him to slow things down.

As far as Andre was concerned, they had the rest of their lives for the good stuff. If she didn't want to jump back into married life in the first hour of their vacation, that was fine by him.

"Pancakes sound good." He lifted his head.

"Yeah?"

He nodded. "And coffee."

She studied him, and he could tell she was wondering if he was okay with the direction their morning was heading. "Sure?"

"Do you know how to make pancakes?"

She frowned. "Well…no, not really."

"Me either. But we can watch a video and learn how."

Lucia pulled out her phone and started tapping the screen. Andre followed her to the kitchen, where he made coffee because he knew how to do that at least. He figured between him and Lucia, they could do anything.

As long as they were together.

The story continues in book 3:
Last One Still Standing
Releasing Oct 28, 2021

Turn the page to find out more!

THE FIGHT never let them go.

PLUCKED from a life on the streets and trained as a covert agent, Karina chose loyalty until the secret organization she worked for pushed her too far. Falling for the target on a mission was never the plan. When he turned out not to be the good man she loved, Karina faked her death and built a safe life for their child.

EAS NEVER WANTED to wear a mask, but his life is the tragic tale of a boy born into a family at war. Raised in secret, he's the answer to taking down a powerful company. At the helm is the cousin who murdered his parents, and the sister he needs to rescue from that life.

. . .

Now the secret organization has found Karina, and they won't let her go. His family's company wants him out of the way, but Eas never wanted to take over.

Between them is the child that represents everything they meant to each other.

Which one of them will be the Last One still Standing?

Find out more at:

https://lastchancecounty.com/chevalier-series

I sincerely hope you enjoyed this story. Please take a moment to leave a review to help provide insight to others, it really does make a difference!

Also, I love to engage with readers. You can contact me through my website:
https://authorlisaphillips.com/about-the-author

ABOUT THE AUTHOR

Find out more about Lisa Phillips, and other books she has written, by visiting her website: https://authorlisaphillips.com

Would you also share about the book on Social Media, leave a review on Lisa's page and share about your experience? Your review will help others find great clean fiction and decide what to read next!

Visit https://authorlisaphillips.com/subscribe where you can sign up for my NEWSLETTER and get free books!

ALSO BY LISA PHILLIPS

The Series Continues in Book 3

Book 3: Last One Still Standing – Oct 2021

Book 4: Last Man To Survive – Nov 2021

Book 5: Last Line of Defense – Dec 2021

Find the whole series here:

www.lastchancecounty.com/chevalier-series

Find out about Lisa's other books at her website:

authorlisaphillips.com

Other series:

Last Chance County

Northwest Counter-Terrorism Taskforce

Double Down

WITSEC Town (Sanctuary)

Love Inspired Suspense titles